SWEET HAVEN

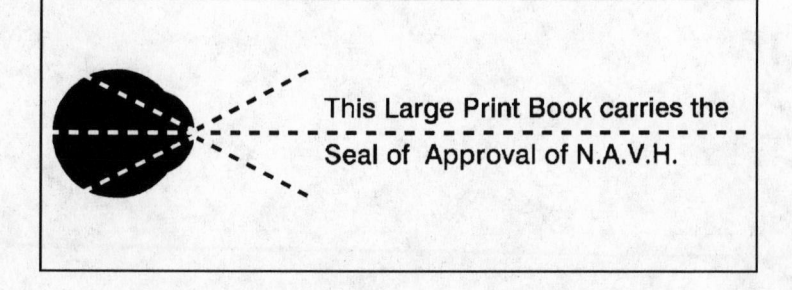

This Large Print Book carries the
Seal of Approval of N.A.V.H.

SWEET HAVEN

SHIRLEE MCCOY

THORNDIKE PRESS
A part of Gale, Cengage Learning

Farmington Hills, Mich • San Francisco • New York • Waterville, Maine
Meriden, Conn • Mason, Ohio • Chicago

GALE
CENGAGE Learning®

LIBRARY OF CONGRESS CATALOGING-IN-PUBLICATION DATA

Names: McCoy, Shirlee.
Title: Sweet haven / by Shirlee McCoy.
Description: Large print edition. | Waterville, Maine : Thorndike Press, 2016. | ©
   2016 | Series: A Home Sweet Home Novel #1 | Series: Thorndike Press large
   print clean reads
Identifiers: LCCN 2016003255| ISBN 9781410488343 (hardcover) | ISBN 1410488349
   (hardcover)
Subjects: LCSH: Large type books.
Classification: LCC PS3613.C38574 S94 2016 | DDC 813/.6—dc23
LC record available at http://lccn.loc.gov/2016003255

Published in 2016 by arrangement with Zebra Books, an imprint of
Kensington Publishing Corp.

Printed in Mexico
1 2 3 4 5 6 7 20 19 18 17 16

SWEET HAVEN

CHAPTER ONE

The dress wouldn't zip.

Seeing as how the wedding was ten days away, that was going to be a problem. Adeline Lamont expelled all the air from her lungs and tried again. The zipper inched up her side, every slow, excruciating millimeter reminding her that she had bigger problems than a butt-ugly, too-small, tangerine-colored bridesmaid's dress. The fudge, for one. The chocolate shop, for another. Neither of which was being dealt with while she was trying to shimmy into the most hideous dress she had ever seen.

"Addie!" May Reynolds called from the other side of the bathroom door. "How's it going in there?"

"Peachy," Adeline called back, the zipper finally finding its way home.

Thank God!

The last thing she wanted to do was spend twenty minutes explaining her inability to fit into the dress to May. Too much to do. Too little time.

And now . . .

This.

She glanced in the mirror above the sink. Orange. Lots of it. Skin too. Shoulders. Arms. Chest. All of it pasty and white from too many days in Chocolate Haven's kitchen. She needed to get outside, get a little fresh air and a little sun. She'd add that to her list. The one she'd been adding items to all day.

"Addie!" May knocked frantically. Probably with both her wrinkled fists. "Please tell me it fits! I don't have time to alter it. I barely had time to make it!"

"I wish you hadn't," Addie muttered, tugging at the huge ruffle that drooped over her chest and fluttered to a stop somewhere in the region of her stomach.

"What's that, dear?" May yelled, her voice edged with panic. The poor woman would have heart failure if Addie didn't open the blasted door.

Then again . . .

Addie eyed the white flesh burgeoning out of the bodice of the dress.

. . . she might have heart failure when she got a look at Addie squeezed into the dress.

A lose-lose situation any way Addie cut it,

so she opened the door and stepped into the narrow hall that led from the front of the shop to the kitchen.

It smelled like chocolate. Vanilla. Maybe a hint of the blood, sweat, and tears she'd been pouring into the place since Granddad had broken his hip and femur. She gagged, but managed to keep down the sixteen pounds of fudge she'd consumed while taste-testing batch after batch of Lamont family fudge.

God! If she ever ate another piece of fudge again, it would be way, *way* too soon!

"Dear God in heaven!" May breathed. She stood just a few feet away, hands clasped together, her blue-white hair a little wild. "You have breasts!"

Addie would have laughed if the dress hadn't squeezed all the air from her lungs.

"Most women do," she managed to say, her head swimming from lack of oxygen or, maybe, too much sugar and too little real food. When was the last time she'd eaten a meal? Two days ago? Three?

"Not Alice," May huffed. "Your grandmother was reed slim. She wore clothes beautifully. Didn't matter what, she looked good in it."

"I am not my grandmother," Addie pointed out. *And even* she *wouldn't look*

9

good in this dress, she nearly added.

"You're standing in for her at my wedding, dear," May responded, tugging at the bodice of the dress, trying desperately to get it to cover a little more of Addie's flesh.

Wasn't going to happen, but Adeline let her try. Just like she'd let her insist that Adeline be maid of honor at her wedding since Alice had passed away five years before the big day. Sure, Adeline would be the only under-thirty member of the wedding party, but she loved May. She'd loved Alice. For them, she'd stand at the front of Benevolence Baptist Church wearing a skintight tangerine dress. She just hoped to God that Randal Custard didn't decide to do a human interest story on the event. Sure, it was cool that May had found true love at seventy-six years old. Sure, it was wonderful that she was finally getting married after so many decades of longing for marital bliss.

What would *not* be cool or wonderful would be a picture of Addie plastered across the front page of the *Benevolence Times,* her fudge-stuffed body encased in tangerine satin! Since she'd turned down Randal's dinner invitations seven times in the past month, it might just happen.

"May," she finally said, the thought of Randal and his camera and that picture

10

souring her mood more than the last mediocre-tasting batch of family fudge had. "The dress isn't going to cover any more than it's already covering."

"But I measured you," May responded, giving the bodice one last tug. "And I never measure wrong."

"I may have gained a pound or two since I took over the shop for Granddad." Or ten, but who was counting? "I'll lose it before the wedding."

"Promise?" May asked, her lined face caked with powder, her drawn-on eyebrows giving her a perpetual look of surprise. She'd always been a little high-strung, a little nervous. The exact opposite of Adeline's grandmother, who'd been calm in the face of crisis, reasonable in the face of difficulty.

"Of course," Adeline assured her.

What else could she do?

"All right. I guess we'll just make it work," May said, probably channeling someone she'd seen on some sewing or fashion show. She'd been a home economics teacher at Benevolence High for nearly thirty years, had owned a fabric shop right next to Chocolate Haven up until a month ago. For as long as Adeline could remember, May had been obsessed with fashion.

Too bad that obsession had never translated into a good sense of style.

Unique was more the word for it.

Or *atrocious, horrible, dated.*

Adeline could think of a dozen other words, but it was late, she was tired, and the kitchen needed a thorough scrubbing before she left for the day.

"Of course we'll make it work." She cupped May's elbow and urged her toward the front of the shop. "The wedding is going to be beautiful. Every last detail of it."

"How could it not be?" May raised her chin a half inch. "I've planned every last detail. Every flower, every bow, every song."

Every word that Jim and I shall speak during our vows. Every strain of music that shall play during the reception, Adeline added, mentally repeating the spiel she'd heard dozens and dozens of times.

Scrooge, her better-self whispered.

She was a scrooge. She could admit that.

But . . . doggone it! She was an accountant. Not a chocolatier. Not a shopkeeper. Not a master creator of the coveted Lamont fudge. After nearly three weeks of trying and failing to be those things, she was getting grumpy.

The too-tight tangerine dress wasn't helping things.

12

Poor May wasn't either. She meant well. Addie knew she did, but May had a habit of making mountains out of mole hills and creating drama everywhere she went.

"I know you have," Addie soothed as she bypassed the glass display cases that had been in the shop since the doors opened in 1911. She'd already stocked them for the following day — chocolate bonbons in beautiful foil wrappers, milk chocolate truffles with cocoa powder dusted over them, chocolate mint bars, chocolate mallow cups. Chocolate, chocolate, and more chocolate.

It's what the Lamonts did.

Only it didn't seem to be what Adeline could do.

Sure, the chocolate was there, but the fudge was missing, and that was the thing that had put Chocolate Haven on the map.

May must have noticed the full display cases. She paused next to them, leaning in to study the goods, her left eye twitching. She was going to ask about the wedding favors, because that was how May was.

Please don't ask, Adeline willed, but May's mouth opened and out it came.

"How are the wedding favors coming along?"

"Great," Adeline lied. Truth? She'd made

twenty of the five hundred chocolate hearts May had ordered. She'd had to toss every last one of them, because what should have been a beautiful high-sheen chocolate exterior had been rough, dull, and bumpy.

"Oh! Wonderful!" May's surprised eyebrows lifted a notch. "I'd love to see them. How about —"

"I've got so much work to do, May, and I know you're busy with wedding preparations," Adeline said, cutting her off. "How about we wait until I have a few more to show you? I've only done the milk chocolate, and you wanted dark chocolate and white chocolate as well. I'll put together a little sampler for you one day this week."

"Well, I . . ." May glanced toward the kitchen. "Are you sure they're turning out okay?"

"Absolutely certain," Adeline said with so much emphasis, her chest nearly popped from the dress.

"Good, because I can't have anything go wrong." May reached out, yanked at the tangerine ruffle. The dress didn't move. "Not one thing."

"The favors will be perfect," Adeline assured her. "And I'll jog every night from now until the wedding."

"You may need to run," May murmured,

14

releasing her hold on the dress. "Or sprint. That might work."

"Sure. Sprint. Sounds good." Adeline wasn't even sure she could manage a jog. It had been a while since she'd had any kind of fitness routine. A while meaning years. She'd try, though. Because there was no way on God's green earth she was standing in front of five hundred of May and Jim's closest friends, looking like an overstuffed orange sausage!

"Okay. Good." May offered a wan smile. "Now, I really have to get going. Doris Linder is creating a special updo for me and the wedding party. I'm going to have her do a trial style on me tonight."

"Doris?" Addie hoped she'd heard wrong. Doris had been doing hair in Benevolence, Washington, for longer than Addie had been alive. Maybe longer than *May* had been alive.

"Who else would I have chosen?" May patted her hair. "She does a wonderful beehive."

"Your hair is too short for a beehive."

"Have you never heard of extensions?" May stepped outside, cold February wind ruffling her short locks. "The other ladies and I will have them. Your hair is plenty long enough to do without."

15

Thank God for that, Addie wanted to say.

She kept her scrooge-mouth shut.

May hiked her purse a little higher onto her shoulder and picked her way across the sidewalk that separated the shop from the street. She'd parked at the curb, her gold Cadillac gleaming beneath the streetlight.

"I'll call you tomorrow," she said as she climbed into the car. "To see how the weight loss is going and set up a time to see the favors."

"You do that," Addie said as she let the door swing closed, locked it, and flicked off the light.

There.

Now maybe she'd be left alone. To get out of the dress. To clean the kitchen. To close out the register so that she could finally go home to the puppy she'd adopted four months ago.

Poor Tiny.

He was probably miserable penned up in Nehemiah Shoemaker's back room. It had been sweet of her neighbor to offer to take care of the puppy while Addie helped her grandfather, but Nehemiah was nearly ninety and Tiny was too big for him to handle. The two of them spent most of their time in Nehemiah's family room, watching reruns of *Hogan's Heroes* and *I Love Lucy.*

Nehemiah seemed to enjoy Tiny's company, but the puppy needed some time to play outside. If Adeline had known that Grand-dad was going to break his hip and femur . . .

But she hadn't, so she'd adopted a puppy because she'd been just a little lonely in her 1920s bungalow.

"It will be okay," she told herself. "Just get out of the stupid dress and get back to checking things off the list. Go through it one item at a time until you finish. And you *will* finish. Eventually."

She tugged halfheartedly at the zipper. It didn't move. She tugged a little harder. Nothing. She scowled, sucking in her gut and yanking the zipper with all her might as she walked into the kitchen.

Snap!

Something gave. She yanked the dress around so the zipper was in the front, eyeing the damage. The top part of the zipper held fast, but the middle section had opened to reveal an inch of pasty white skin.

Holy heck, she'd busted the thing!

And now she was stuck. An overstuffed sausage in synthetic orange casing. She'd have to cut herself out and replace the zipper. Good thing she'd taken two years of May's home economics class. She knew how to take out a zipper and how to replace one. What she didn't know was how to get out of the mess she'd gotten herself into when she'd agreed to take over Chocolate Haven for her grandfather.

She stalked to the whiteboard that hung near the back door, snagged a dry-erase marker from a drawer, and scrawled *Fix zipper* across the bottom of a list she'd been working on all day.

She probably should have written *Go for a jog* beneath that, but she didn't have the heart to.

The thing was, she'd left her house before dawn, had been shut inside Chocolate Haven all day, smelling chocolate, *eating* chocolate, serving customers chocolate, and trying her best to recreate some facsimile of her family's fudge. The last thing she wanted to do was jog off ten pounds of extra weight so that she could fit into May's god-awful choice of a bridesmaid's dress. As a matter of fact, right at that moment, all she wanted to do was go home.

She grabbed her faded blue jeans and soft gray T-shirt from the bathroom and searched for scissors. There were none in her grandfather's tiny office. None in the front of the shop. Which left the kitchen. Several batches of discarded fudge sat on the counter there. The last and final batch lay in the sink, the scissors she'd used to try to hack it from the pan sticking out of the rock-solid mess.

She didn't dare get within a foot of it. If she got chocolate on the dress, May would never forgive her.

She bypassed the sink and walked out the back door. The stairs to Granddad's apartment were there, pressed up against the side of the brick building. An empty parking lot lay in front of her, separating the row of brownstones from a public green. Addie and her sisters had spent hours playing there when they were kids.

That had been before everything else.

Before Dad died.

Before Willow had gone quiet and secretive.

Before Brenna had decided Benevolence was the worst place in the world to grow up.

Before their family that had once been close and loving and wonderful had turned into four people going four separate ways.

She jogged up the stairs, metal clanging under her feet. She fished the spare key out from under the potted plant on the landing, had barely touched the knob, when the door creaked open.

Surprised, she peered into the apartment, eyeing the shadowy furniture and the oversized TV they'd bought Granddad for Christmas. That would probably be the first thing a thief would go for. Not that there were many thieves in Benevolence.

She stepped into the silent apartment and flicked on the light. Granddad should be there, sitting on his plaid sofa, eating chips and salsa and watching *The Price Is Right*. Instead, he was lying in a hospital bed, waiting for the doctors to decide if he was going to need a third surgery on his leg. The thought left a hollow ache in the region of her heart.

From her position, she could see down the narrow hall that led to two bedrooms, a bathroom, and small office. Despite the unlocked door, the apartment looked untouched, the empty feel of it reassuring.

"There's no one here," she said aloud.

A door slammed, the sound so jarring, she screamed — probably loud enough to wake the dead — and took off, her jeans and T-shirt falling from her arms as she ran.

Sinclair Jefferson had seen a lot of things in his thirty-four years of living, but he'd never seen anything quite like the woman who was barreling toward him. Body encased in a

20

skintight orange *thing* that could have been a dress or a costume, she sprinted down exterior metal steps as if all the demons of hell were chasing her.

If she saw him, she didn't let on.

As a matter of fact, if she kept coming at the pace she was, she'd crash into him. He stepped to the side, pulling his real estate agent, Janelle Lamont, with him.

"Watch it," he cautioned.

"How can I not? It's like a train wreck. I can't look away," Janelle murmured, her attention focused on the orange-encased lunatic who skidded to a stop in front of them.

"Mom!" the lunatic yelled. "There's someone in Granddad's apartment."

Mom?

This had to be one of the Lamont sisters, then.

Not Willow. He'd gone to school with her. She'd been as polished as a brand-new penny, every bit of her perfect. Hair. Makeup. Clothes.

This Lamont wasn't polished or perfect.

As a matter of fact, it looked like she'd split the zipper of the ugly outfit she was wearing. He caught a glimpse of taut pale skin as she crossed her arms over her stomach and hid the gap in the fabric.

Janelle sighed. "What are you talking about, Adeline?"

Adeline.

The middle sister.

He had a few vague memories of a quirky-looking kid with wild red hair, but none of them quite matched the woman in front of him. Wide, almond-shaped eyes; a curvy, compact body; long braid of hair falling over her shoulder; she was almost pretty and almost not. *Interesting* was probably the word he was looking for.

"What I'm talking about," Adeline responded, enunciating every word, "is someone being in Granddad's apartment. I walked into the living room and heard a door slam."

"A vacuum effect from you opening the front door. There's no one in there." Janelle's gaze slid to Sinclair and she offered an apologetic smile. "This is a very safe town, Sinclair. Just like it was when you were a child."

"I'm sure it is," he responded, because, as far as he could tell, nothing much had changed in Benevolence since he'd left sixteen years ago. The streets were still clean, the houses and properties neat and tidy. Except for his brother Gavin's property. The one they'd both inherited from

22

their grandfather. *It* was still a mess — old cars and trucks rotting on acres of riverfront property, weathered farmhouse filled to the brim with decades of junk, piles of trash scattered across what should have been a beautiful lawn.

Sinclair had come to town to take care of that. To turn the place into a home that his sister-in-law would be proud of. Gavin was supposed to be helping. Maybe if he could stop whining about missing his wife long enough, he'd be able to.

"It's why so many people prefer Benevolence to the big city," Janelle said with a beatific smile. "Come on. Let's see if Byron's place will work for you. If not, I've got another in mind. On the opposite side of town from your brother's place, but it's quiet. Just like you want."

She started up the exterior staircase, metal clanking under her feet as she hurried up to the apartment she was hoping Sinclair would rent. She'd spent the past twenty minutes singing the praises of the place, describing in detail all the benefits of living in an apartment over a chocolate shop. Sinclair wasn't all that concerned about the benefits. As long as it was cleaner than the last place they'd seen, quieter than the second, and didn't smell like wet dog and cigarette smoke like the first, he'd take it. He had too much work to do to waste time looking for an apartment. Unfortunately, the closest hotel was thirty miles away. He could have continued staying with his brother, but Gavin had spent the last five days whining and moaning about the fact that his pregnant wife had walked out of their single-wide trailer and gone to live with her family.

Seeing as how the single-wide trailer was packed to the gills with stuff, Sinclair couldn't blame Lauren for walking out. He'd have done the same. He *was* doing the same. No way did he plan to spend another night in that hellhole. He'd sleep in his truck first.

"Here we are," Janelle called cheerfully as she stepped over what looked like jeans and a T-shirt and walked into the apartment. "Built in 1887 for railroad magnate Lincoln Bernard. His family lived here for nearly twenty years before they built that beautiful home on River Bluff. Grandview Manor."

He nodded because he knew the place and because he thought that Janelle expected a response.

"My senior prom was there," he offered, stepping over the clothes and walking into the apartment behind her.

24

"My daughter Willow's, too. You graduated together," she reminded him. As if he could have forgotten. There'd been thirty-five kids in his graduating class. He'd known every one of them by name. They'd known him too.

That was the way things had been in Benevolence. Unless he missed his guess, it was the way things still were.

"I really don't think we should be in here," Adeline interrupted from the doorway.

"Of course we should." Janelle flicked on a light in a small galley kitchen and motioned to the dinette set that sat in an alcove created by a window dormer. "What do you think, Sinclair? Perfect for a bachelor, yes?"

"Sure." He moved past the kitchen, peered down a dark hall. There was a window at the far end, moonlight filtering in through the glass and speckling the floor with gold. The place looked homey, clean, and comfortable.

Good enough.

And, that was all Sinclair needed.

"I'd like to look at the bedroom," he said, but Adeline grabbed his arm before he could walk down the hall.

"I'm telling you, someone is in here." She gestured into the dark hall, the jeans and T-shirt Sinclair had stepped over clutched to her chest. "He's probably hiding in one of the rooms, waiting for his chance."

"His chance at what?" Janelle asked, her smile brittle. "Stealing a five-year-old computer? Or maybe you think he's after the television we bought Byron for Christmas?"

"Maybe he's after some*one,* Mom," Adeline replied, a sliver of her taut abdomen flashing every time she moved. "He could be biding his time, waiting for one of us to come in here alone."

"You've been watching too many horror movies," Janelle said with an exaggerated sigh.

"I hate horror movies," Adeline replied.

"I hate standing around when I could be getting something done," Sinclair murmured, running his hand along the wall until he found a light switch. He flicked it on. Wide-planked pine flooring stretched along the length of the hall, the scuffed and nicked wood adding a layer of charm to what might otherwise have been a boring interior. Two doors flanked each wall and a small cushioned bench sat under the window. The ceiling was high, the paint fresh. Nothing special, but he didn't need special. He needed a place to sleep. Far away from his brother's whining.

He opened the closest door, glanced into

a tiny office. No one there, but the room was clean and didn't smell like dog.

He opened the next door and the next, Adeline right on his heels. A bathroom. A nice-sized bedroom. No one in either. The last door opened into the largest room. The master bedroom, he'd guess, the furniture heavy nineteenth century. There were two doors on the far wall. One opened into a small closet filled with suits, dress shirts, and polished shoes. The other door was locked. He turned the knob twice. Just to be sure.

"That goes into the building next door," Janelle said as she swiped her hand over the antique dresser and frowned at the layer of dust on her palm. "May Reynolds had a fabric store there up until a month ago. I'm sure you remember it from when you were a child."

Maybe. He'd been too busy trying to keep the farmhouse from falling down around his ears to pay much attention to what anyone else was doing, but he thought he remembered May — a tiny little woman with a lot of nervous ticks. He also thought he remembered sweeping the sidewalk in front of her shop for a little cash or a couple of home baked cookies.

"She was a nice lady," he said, mostly

because he thought Janelle expected it.

"Nice?" Adeline plucked at the shiny orange fabric of her . . .

What was it? A dress?

"That's debatable," she continued with a scowl.

"Adeline!" Janelle snapped. "You know that May is one of the kindest human beings on the face of the earth. She wouldn't hurt a fly."

"No. She'd just dress one like a giant pumpkin and make them stand in front of the entire population of Benevolence while she married the love of her life," Adeline muttered.

Sinclair's lips twitched, a bubble of something that felt a lot like laughter settling right in the middle of his chest.

"Is May getting married?" he asked, meeting Adeline's eyes.

Despite the orange outfit, she didn't look like a pumpkin.

She looked more like a peach. The kind he used to pluck from the neighbor's tree. Round and ripe and delicious.

"May *is* getting married," Janelle said, moving between Sinclair and her daughter. "But, that's not what we're here to discuss. What do you think of the apartment?"

"Is the door locked from the other side?"

He wriggled the knob again.

"Of course! It would take a tank to get through it."

Sinclair thought a well-placed foot might do the trick, but he didn't say that. He'd done two tours in Iraq and one in Afghanistan. He'd slept in dugouts and under the stars. This place, locked door or not, was way safer than those had been.

"Byron had a new metal door installed," Janelle continued, obviously hell-bent on convincing him to rent the place. "If you'd like to go next door and take a look at the door from the other side, I'd be happy to take you."

"*I'd* like to take a look. If it's not locked, maybe that's the door I heard slamming," Adeline said. She smelled like chocolate and berries, and something that reminded Sinclair of home.

Or what he'd always imagined home should be like.

Home growing up had been a house filled with junk, a grandfather who drank himself into a stupor every night, and cold soup served in chipped white mugs. Home now was his high-rise apartment overlooking Puget Sound. Clean lines. Modern. Dinner out most nights because he didn't like to cook.

"Adeline, really." Janelle sighed. "Let it go. No one is in the apartment. No one *was* in the apartment. The door on this side and the other both need keys. Byron and May are the only people who have them."

"I know that, and I also know what I heard." Adeline's hands settled on her hips, the clothes she'd picked up hanging limply, the gap in her dress revealing that sliver of creamy flesh. His gaze dropped to the spot. How could it not? The woman had curves. Nice ones. And the kind of smooth, silky skin that begged to be touched.

"For God's sake, Adeline! Put your shirt on," Janelle snapped. That got Adeline moving.

She pulled the clothes back over her stomach, her entire face the color of over-ripe tomatoes.

She had freckles.

He hadn't noticed that before.

And eyes that might be violet.

She left the room too quickly for him to see.

"I'm sorry about that, Sinclair. Adeline has always been very imaginative." Janelle ran a hand over her perfectly styled, perfectly highlighted hair. She had to be in her fifties. She looked a couple of decades younger.

He knew how much time and money it took to achieve that.

Kendra had been thirty and determined to never look older than twenty-one. He'd put up with her obsession because she'd been smart and driven. They'd been a good match. Until they weren't.

Then they'd both walked away without a second glance.

Just the way he'd wanted it.

No months of back and forth sparring. No breaking up and getting back together. None of the overly emotional stuff Gavin was going through with his wife. Just *this isn't working out anymore. It's time to move on.*

"How do you know Adeline was imagining things?" he asked, running his hand over the doorframe. Old wood. Probably original to the house. Too many layers of paint, but that could be removed if the owner cared to do it. "It's possible she heard a door closing."

"Whatever she heard, it wasn't someone lying in wait to commit some horrible crime. This is Benevolence, Washington. The crime rate is so low we barely need a sheriff's department."

That wasn't quite true, and they both knew it. There'd been a murder when Sin-

31

clair was a kid. Quite a few petty crimes. Vandalism. Drug use. Domestic violence. Those things existed in every town. Even ones that seemed as perfect as Benevolence.

He didn't bother correcting her. The apartment was as good a fit as any would be. He had an overnight bag in his truck, a six-pack of Pepsi, and enough paperwork to catch up on to keep him busy until dawn. He wanted to sign the lease and get on with things. "I'm not concerned with the crime rate or lack thereof. I'm concerned with having a place to sleep. I think this will work."

"Wonderful!" she exclaimed. "I had a feeling it would."

"You're sure your father-in-law is willing to give it up for a couple of weeks?"

"The lease is for a month," she reminded him, as if they hadn't spent the better part of the afternoon hashing out the terms of his rental agreement. He'd pay for a full month, but he had no intention of being there that long.

"With the option of extending for a second month," she continued. "You never know. You might decide Benevolence is the place for you. You won't believe how many people come here for a visit and end up staying."

He'd believe it.

The place had plenty of small-town charm, lots of interesting architecture, and enough appeal to attract people from all over the country.

What it didn't have was enough appeal to keep him there for any longer than necessary. He'd seen the beauty of Benevolence when he was a kid. He'd seen the ugliness too. The gossip, the whispers. The pointed fingers. His family had always been on the wrong side of those fingers. He and his brother had been the topic of one too many whispered conversations, the focus of one too many sad shakes of the head.

They'd grown up in the shadow of the tragedy that had taken their parents. Sinclair had no intention of living here again.

He followed Janelle into the living room.

Adeline was there, a gray T-shirt pulled over the orange outfit, her long braid tucked into its collar. She eyed him as if he were a snake in the garden, her pale-pink lips pursed together.

Janelle must have noticed.

She hurried across the room and grabbed her daughter's arm. "I'm going to get the rental agreement. Why don't you come with me, Adeline?"

"Rental agreement, huh?" Adeline said, pulling away from her mother. "If you're leasing the place, I'd better look around, make sure there's nothing here that Granddad might need."

"I already packed up most of Byron's things." Janelle frowned.

"Did you clean out the guest room? I bet there are a couple boxes' worth of stuff in there."

"No need to move everything out," Sinclair cut in. "I just need a place to sleep. If Byron needs anything, you're welcome to come in and get it when I'm not here."

"A place to sleep?" Adeline pulled the braid out of her collar and flicked it over her shoulder. "Good luck with that. I'm running the chocolate shop for my grandfather while he recovers, and I work pretty late. I also make a lot of noise."

"Adeline!" Janelle nearly shouted. "Please, will you just leave well enough alone! Byron agreed that a short-term rental while he was recuperating was a good idea."

"He's on morphine, Mom. He'd agree to anything."

"For God's sake! The man knows his own mind. No matter how much morphine he's been given. I'm getting the lease!" Janelle stalked from the apartment, her high-heeled boots clicking against the metal stairs.

"That went well," Adeline said, dropping

onto the couch, shiny orange fabric shimmying up her pale thighs.

Sinclair thought of those peaches again.

The ones hanging from the neighbor's tree.

The ones he'd never quite been able to resist.

"What went well? Pissing your mother off?" he asked, and she smiled.

"Getting her out of the apartment so I could cut myself out of this . . . thing." She stood, silky orange fabric sliding down over her thighs again.

"You're stuck in it?"

"*Stuck* is such a subjective word, Sinclair," she responded. "I prefer to say that I am temporarily constrained by a broken zipper."

"And you don't want your mother to know it?"

"I don't want May to know." She strode down the hall, and he followed, the scent of chocolate seeming to fill the air. "And my mother is just the kind of person who would tell her."

"Doesn't sound like you think very highly of her," he remarked, watching from the hallway as she rummaged through the medicine cabinet in the bathroom.

"Of my mother? She's great. Perfect, as a

matter of fact. She would never ever get herself temporarily constrained by a broken zipper." She pulled scissors out of the cabinet, held them up triumphantly. "Success! Excuse me while I extract myself from the sausage casing."

She closed the door with a quiet *snap,* and Sinclair realized he was smiling.

He didn't want to be amused by her.

He didn't want to be amused by anything in Benevolence.

He'd spent most of his childhood planning his escape from it. He'd wanted to put it all behind him — every moment of living in *that* house on *that* property in a town where perfection was the chosen sport and people competed for the honor of having the best garden, the best Christmas decorations, the best-kept yard.

The only thing his family had ever competed for was the title of laziest homeowner.

They'd won, hands down, every day of every year for as long as there'd been Jeffersons in Benevolence. That had been nearly as long as the town had been a town. Not that that mattered to Sinclair. Not the way it had when he'd been the kid that teachers pitied, the one who received hand-me-down clothes from well-meaning church ladies every Christmas.

They hadn't understood the truth.

He hadn't wanted slightly used mittens, boots, coats. Hadn't really needed faded jeans and cotton T-shirts. Grandpa was pretty adept at picking those things out of trash cans and Dumpsters.

What he'd wanted, what he'd longed for, what he'd needed about as desperately as he'd needed air to breathe and water to drink, was a home. The kind that friends could visit. The kind that smelled like good food and furniture polish. The kind his friends lived in.

No church lady could have brought him that.

So, he hadn't really wanted anything at all.

Except to escape. Which he had. Thank you, Uncle Sam and the good old Marine Corps! Seven years. Three tours. A bum knee and an honorable discharge, and he'd taken the money he'd saved and put it into restoring a row of painted ladies in San Francisco. He'd turned those around for a profit and continued on, building the kind of business his grandfather had always talked about having — using reclaimed materials from condemned buildings to bring at-risk properties back from the brink.

That was the difference between Sinclair

and most of the men in his family. He didn't just dream. He did.

Maybe he could teach Gavin to do the same before he left Benevolence.

He doubted it, but he'd give it as good a try as he'd given his relationship with Kendra. He'd put his all in it. If it didn't work out, he'd walk away with a clear conscience and no regrets, go back to his life and his business and his clean, quiet apartment.

The empty one.

Which hadn't ever bothered him before.

The last couple of days, he'd been thinking about all those old childhood dreams. The ones where he'd come home and smell cookies in the oven or fresh-baked bread cooling on the counter. Where there was someone waiting for him with a smile and a *How was your day?*

Maybe it was coming back to Benevolence that had made him think about those youthful fantasies. Probably it was.

All the more reason to get out of Dodge as soon as humanly possible.

"Sinclair?!" Janelle called, her high heels tapping on the wood floor. "I've got the agreement."

Good. He was ready to sign it.

He might have to be in a town he hated, but he didn't have to spend his nights in a cluttered and dirty single-wide trailer listening to his brother complain.

That was the beauty of working hard.

It paid off. Gave a man the ability to do what he wanted when he wanted. Gave him the freedom to make decisions about where he wanted to be and when.

It couldn't warm his bed at night, couldn't fill a house and make it a home, but Sinclair would be happy for what he had.

That was part of his life plan. Contentment. Something his father hadn't had, his grandfather had never found, his brother longed for.

Elusive as mist on the water, but Sinclair had been managing to grasp it. It was that or drown his disappointments in a bottle the way three generations before him had.

The way *he* almost had.

One drink away. That's all he was, and there was no way in hell Sinclair was ever going to forget it.

CHAPTER TWO

The scissors had done the trick. Ten seconds and Adeline was out of the dress. Ten more and she was back in her jeans. She could have tucked the scissors into the medicine cabinet and left the bathroom, but facing her mother was out of the question. Not only did Adeline not want to hear another lecture on her overactive imagination, but she didn't want to be asked the question that she'd been asked every day since May announced her engagement: *Do you have a date to the wedding, dear?*

Just thinking about it made her break out in a cold sweat, because . . . No! She did not have a date.

Furthermore, she was not going to have a date.

Not unless some handsome stranger who happened to like chubby redheads suddenly moved to town.

She knew this for a fact, because she'd

called every unattached guy she'd ever had any contact with. They were all either busy or newly attached. That was the problem with being everyone's good friend and no one's lover. When you really needed an escort to some major event, you couldn't count on having one.

Not that it mattered to Adeline.

She'd tried the love thing. She'd headed down that happy path of commitment and promises, her heart doing a joyful little dance the entire way. She'd had a ring on her finger and every intention in the world of saying *I do.* Right up until the moment that Adam had said he didn't, Adeline had been committed to *them* and had been absolutely sure that they had the real thing.

Why wouldn't they? They'd grown up together. Attended school together. Went off to college together. They'd fit like pieces of a puzzle, and there hadn't been a person in Benevolence who'd doubted that they'd last forever.

She snorted.

Forever?

That had lasted until Adam got a job offer he couldn't refuse. Good money. No. *Great* money. Adeline had wanted to get married before he left to join the law firm in Houston, but he'd had a dozen reasons why they shouldn't. He'd said good-bye with tears in his eyes and promises on his lips — *I'll send you a plane ticket as soon as I get settled. I won't sleep a wink until you're by my side again. It won't seem like home until you're with me.*

Bull crap. All of it.

A month later, Adeline had gotten an e-mailed Dear John letter. Adam had said that he thought they should take a break, see other people. Oh. And by the way? He'd like the ring back.

She'd tossed it in the Spokane River, and she'd gone on with her life as if her heart hadn't been broken in a million pieces.

Fickle things, hearts.

So easily swayed, so easily fooled, so easily broken.

Not hers. Not anymore.

She liked her life just the way it was, but dang if she didn't wish she had someone to go to the wedding with, because Janelle? She wanted nothing more than to see her three daughters married. To her, it was a source of never-ending disappointment that there hadn't been a wedding yet. Three daughters, and not one of them had walked down the aisle. At least she could say that Willow and Brenna were in committed relationships. Willow was even engaged.

Both of Addie's sisters had exciting lives in exciting cities. A fact Janelle pulled out at every church function, every community event, every situation where bragging about children was considered a social norm.

But Adeline?

She was still living in town, working as an accountant with no man in sight. There wasn't a whole heck of a lot that her mother could say about that. *My daughter crunches numbers all day and spends most of her evenings alone?* Not exactly bragging material.

Not that Addie usually cared.

Janelle was Janelle. She'd met Addie's father in high school, fell in love with Brett Lamont and never once looked back. Their relationship had been one for the record books — true love that only seemed to grow as the years passed. If cancer hadn't taken her father, Addie was quite sure her parents would still be together and still be madly in love.

Was it any wonder that Janelle wanted that for her daughters?

Too bad she didn't realize that some of her daughters . . . *one* of her daughters . . . didn't want the same thing. Whether or not Addie was happy with her choice to remain

43

single didn't play into Janelle's thought processes.

Which was a shame, because Addie *was* happy.

Very happy.

Or had been until Granddad fell and ended up in the hospital. Now her nice routine life had turned to chaos.

She was under too much stress. That's why the dang Lamont fudge wasn't turning out and why every heart she made seemed to be weeping chocolate. The last thing she needed was her mother hounding her about having a date to the wedding.

She also didn't need to be hiding in a bathroom in her grandfather's apartment. An apartment that was being rented by a guy who looked like he'd stepped off a magazine cover.

Sinclair Jefferson had been handsome when he was a kid.

Now . . .

Wow!

Women were going to be falling all over themselves trying to get his attention.

Not Addie.

All she wanted to do was get back to work and get home.

"Screw this," she muttered. "I am not going to hide. If Mom asks me about my date for the wedding, I'll just tell her I'm taking Tiny."

She stalked into the hall.

The apartment was silent.

No sound of high heels clicking on wood. No murmured voices. Not even the soft sigh of fabric.

She hurried into the living room, the ugly orange dress under her arm. Empty. No one in the kitchen. Maybe they'd gone down to the parking lot, and maybe . . . just maybe . . . she could get into Chocolate Haven, get the kitchen cleaned up, and get home without hearing one word about wedding dates.

"Leaving so soon?" Sinclair asked as she reached the door.

She didn't know where he'd come from.

The office maybe? Or Granddad's bedroom? Didn't matter. She wasn't going to be able to sneak out. She turned to face him, hoping to heaven her mother wasn't there too.

She wasn't.

Thank God.

"Soon? I figured I'd already outworn my welcome," she replied, her hands itching to smooth her hair and to tug at the end of her T-shirt to make sure it was covering the rip in the thigh of her jeans.

45

She didn't do any of those things, because Sinclair was just a guy who was renting her grandfather's place, and it really didn't matter what she looked like or what he thought of her.

His gaze dropped to her thigh. Obviously, her shirt wasn't covering the tear.

"If I'd been in a hurry for you to leave, I'd have let you know," he said, his gaze traveling from her thigh to the splotch of chocolate in the middle of her shirt. "Since you make the place smell like chocolate, I figured it would be okay for you to stay for a while."

That made her laugh, all the tension she'd been feeling sliding away. "You have a thing for chocolate?"

"Doesn't everyone?"

"Not me." Not anymore.

"Too many days in the shop?"

"Something like that." She kept her voice light. No need to announce to an almost complete stranger just how desperate she was to be done working at Chocolate Haven.

"We could switch off. You can help my brother. I'll work at your grandfather's store," he suggested.

It was a joke.

She knew it was, but she'd have happily switched places with him for a day or two.

46

Or a thousand.

"I wouldn't want to ruin your fun," she said.

"Fun?"

"I heard you and Gavin were cleaning out your grandfather's house, trying to get it ready for the baby." She'd also heard that Gavin's wife had moved out. Seven months pregnant, Lauren had insisted that Gavin make the house he'd inherited habitable for her and their child before she returned to him. According to the blue haired ladies at the diner, he hadn't been making much progress toward the goal.

"I guess not much has changed since I left town," he said, all the humor gone from his face and eyes. "Gossip still travels faster than the speed of light."

"Gavin is the one pushing the gossip along," she replied, suddenly defensive and not sure why. She loved Benevolence, but not everyone did. Sinclair had every right to his opinion about the town.

"What's he been saying?"

"He's told everyone who cares to listen that Lauren walked out on him."

"He needs to shut up. No one in town needs to know his business or Lauren's."

"Maybe you should tell *him* that." She stepped outside, cold air bathing her hot

47

cheeks. Perfect. That's what this was. The perfectly horrible end to a perfectly horrible day.

"I will." He'd moved to the door and stood in the threshold, backlit by the living room light.

"Then I guess there's nothing more to say but good night." She flounced down the stairs. At least, she hoped that's what it looked like she was doing — a nice energetic retreat from a guy who she hoped wasn't going to prove to be another complication in her already too complicated life.

She tripped on the last step, nearly landed on her face, but managed to right herself before she hit the pavement.

"Careful," he called.

She offered a quick wave, doing everything in her power not to look at him again. No sense staring into those eyes, taking in those long lean muscles, those very broad shoulders. Let the other women in Benevolence drool and dream. She had work to do.

She stepped into Chocolate Haven, grabbed Granddad's apron from the hook, hung the dress in its place. Chocolate permeated the air, the scent of it so heavy and thick she was sure she could stick out her tongue and taste it.

"I see you finally made it down here,"

someone said, the words so startling Adeline nearly jumped out of her skin.

She whirled to face the speaker, spotted Janelle in the hallway that led to the front of the shop, a broom and dustpan in her hand.

"You nearly scared the life out of me, Mom," she said, wishing to God she'd cleaned the kitchen right after the shop closed for the day. There were pots on the stove, chocolate dripping from a bowl on the counter, splotches of chocolate on the floor.

And then there was the fudge, sitting in a pan in the sink, the scissors poking out of it.

Janelle noticed. Of course, she did. The woman could spot imperfection a mile away, and there wasn't one bit of perfection in Chocolate Haven. Not now. Not in all the time Adeline had been running the place.

"Sorry. I wanted to talk to you about the new renter and decided to sweep while I was waiting." She set the broom and dustpan against the wall.

"What about him?"

"Sinclair is a very successful man, Addie."

"And?"

"He's paying a lot of money to rent Byron's place."

"Okay."

Janelle sighed. "Don't be obtuse, Adeline. You know what I'm getting at."

"If you're getting at me not causing your new renter any trouble, don't worry. I've got enough on my plate without adding that." She grabbed dirty pots from the stove, set them in the sink, and ran hot water over them. Chocolate melted and mixed into the swirling liquid, the scent of it drifting up from the steamy sink.

God! If she had to smell chocolate for one more minute, she was going to puke.

"It's not that, Addie." Janelle nudged her out of the way, plunging her hands into the chocolate- and soap-filled water and scrubbing the first pot.

"Then what is it?"

"I just don't want you to be loud while he's upstairs. He's a busy man —"

"I'm a busy woman." She cut her mother off, because sometimes she thought Janelle forgot that Adeline had a life, that she had a thriving accounting business and dozens of clients and plenty of friends to spend time with. Just because she hadn't moved out of town like her sisters, Willow and Brenna, didn't mean she didn't have more than enough to keep her occupied.

"Busy in a different way." Janelle finished

50

scrubbing the pot and handed it to Adeline to dry.

"What's that supposed to mean?"

"Just that this is small-town America. We're here doing small-town things. Sinclair is like your sisters. He's living at that frantic city pace. He —"

"Mom, is there some point to this? I have a lot to do." She gestured at the messy counters, the chocolate-dotted floor.

Janelle handed her another clean pot. "Look," she said with a sigh, "I didn't come in here to upset you. I came because I don't want Byron stressed more than he already is."

"Neither do I."

"And I don't want you to be more stressed than you already are."

"I'm not stressed," she lied, drying the pot and setting it in a cupboard.

Janelle raised one perfectly shaped eyebrow, gestured toward the scissors that were still stuck in fudge. "No?"

"Minor setback in the fudge-making department," she explained.

Janelle nodded, scrubbing another pot, sadness flitting across her face — there and gone so quickly Adeline wasn't 100 percent sure she'd seen it. "It's just difficult for me to watch you spend so much time here,

51

Adeline. You're young. You have so many things you could be doing, but you're devoting every minute of every day to this."

"Just until Granddad recuperates."

"What if he doesn't?"

An odd question, and one that filled Adeline with cold dread. "Is there something you know that I don't, Mom? Is Granddad sick? If he is, just tell me."

"No!" Janelle said hurriedly. "Aside from the broken bones, he's healthy as a horse. But he's not a young man, Addie."

"I know." She did. Byron had turned seventy-five a few months ago. They'd had a big party to mark three-quarters of a century. But Byron seemed younger than that. He walked every day, ran Chocolate Haven, volunteered at church and at the community center.

"Then you must know that there's a possibility he won't be able to go back to what he was doing before the accident. He wants to. We all want him to, but he might not be able to, and if he can't, I don't want you wasting your life here."

"First," Adeline responded, "I have an accounting business to run. There's no way I could take over this place permanently. Second, if I did decide to do that, it would be because I wanted to, and that wouldn't be a waste."

"That's what your father said. Look what happened to him."

There it was. The crux of the issue. Finally out in the open. "Dad loved this place."

"That's my point. He loved it to his dying day, and it gave him nothing in return. If he hadn't spent most of his twenties and thirties learning the business from Byron, maybe he wouldn't have . . ." She shook her head. "Look, I don't want to open old wounds. I just don't want to see you consumed by this the way your father was and your grandfather is."

"You mean the way you've been consumed by real estate?" she asked and regretted it immediately.

"Someone had to support you girls, Addie. Your father didn't have life insurance. He didn't have savings. Everything he had was tied up in this place." She smoothed her hair, took a deep shaky breath. "But, like I said, I'm not trying to open old wounds. I just worry about you."

"You'd be better off worrying about Willow and Brenna. They're the ones who are out in the great wide world," Adeline said, hoping that she didn't sound as snide and petty as she felt. Her sisters had run from Benevolence as soon as they'd had the opportunity, and Janelle had applauded them every step of the way. Adeline had stayed, and her mother just wouldn't let that go.

"They're not like you."

"That's pretty obvious, Mom," Adeline said, yanking the scissors from the fudge and tossing them onto the counter. "They were smart enough to say no when Grandad asked them to help out around here."

"That's not what I'm saying."

I know what you're saying, Adeline almost responded. *You're saying they have fantastic careers and exciting lives and men, and I've got a tiny little house in a tiny little town with nothing but a huge puppy to keep me company.*

She pressed her lips together to keep the words from escaping. No sense in stirring *that* pot.

"I just want you to be happy," Janelle continued, the harsh overhead light emphasizing the tiny crow's feet that fanned out from the corners of her eyes, the shallow commas that bracketed her mouth. Her mascara had smudged a little and it looked like she'd chewed off most of her lipstick. She'd always looked young. She still did, but the years were beginning to show.

Something about that, about those fine

lines and that smudged mascara, made all Adeline's frustration seep away. "I am happy."

Sort of. If she didn't look at the mess, the discarded fudge, the list hanging next to the back door.

"I hope so. Lily Jamison at the hair salon said you haven't been in for a trim since last February. That's over a year, Adeline."

"And?"

"They say that when women are depressed and have given up on life and love, they stop taking care of themselves."

"Who says that?"

"I read it in *Cosmo* just the other day, and in *Woman's World* the day before that. And don't get me started on what I saw on the Internet." She shook her head. "Article after article about depression and —"

"The Internet is a dangerous place. You really need to be careful what you do on it." Adeline cut in because her mother could go on and on for hours about a pet subject, and Adeline didn't have hours to spend listening.

"Don't try to change the subject. I've been noticing things. Your clothes, for one."

"What about them?" Adeline plucked at her favorite T-shirt. Not pretty, but it was sure comfortable to work in.

"You've got no style."

"I've never had style."

"You never wear makeup."

"I do when I'm going out."

Janelle's eyes lit at the words.

Adeline wished she could yank them back. She'd opened the door, and there was no way Janelle wasn't going to step through it.

"You *don't* go out." There it was. The biggest bone of contention between them. "When was the last time you went on a date?"

"Mom . . . Seriously, I have a million things to do. I don't have time to discuss my dating status."

"Just because Adam was a loser," Janelle continued as if Adeline hadn't spoken, "doesn't mean all men are. Look at your father. Sure, he loved this shop, but he loved me too. We had a great life together, and —"

"Not everyone is going to have what you two did, and some of us don't even want it."

"That's a ridiculous thing to say, Adeline. Of course you want it. You just need to find the right man. Look at your sisters —"

She'd rather not. According to Janelle, her other daughters had it all — wonderful careers, wonderful homes, wonderful men.

56

"I hate to cut the conversation short, but I need to finish cleaning the kitchen, and then I've got to get home. Tiny has been cooped up all day."

"That dog." Janelle shook her head and stepped outside, buttoning her wool coat as she went. "Not a good idea, Adeline. I told you that before you got him."

"You did. Thanks for the advice. I'll see you tomorrow, Mom. Love you." She closed the door. Locked it.

Went back to the sink.

Clean the shop.

Get Tiny.

Go for a jog.

She ran through the list because she needed to wipe out all the memories that had been stirred up. Memories of her father. Of Adam.

Adam.

The guy she'd pinned a million childish dreams on, wasted nine years of her life on. Maybe not wasted. She'd learned some valuable lessons from Adam. Like how a heart could be broken and still keep on beating.

High school sweethearts. College lovers. Couple most likely to make it forever.

Only Adam had wanted bigger and better than Benevolence, Washington. Apparently he'd also wanted better than Adeline.

She glanced at the dress, hanging limply from the hook, the silky fabric bright enough to sear her corneas. She'd been planning a wedding once upon a time. Big, fluffy princess gown. Pretty lilac bridesmaid dresses. She'd had an entire folder filled with all the details of the wedding she and Adam had been discussing for years.

Only it hadn't happened.

She didn't know what she'd done with the folder. Probably tossed it in the trash when she'd moved out of her mother's house and into the bungalow.

Speaking of trash . . .

She glanced at the overflowing garbage can, the ugly chocolate hearts scattered on top of the burgeoning mess.

She seriously had to get the shop cleaned.

She ran steaming water into the fudge pan, hoping to heaven that would loosen the cement-like goo.

A soft thud sounded from somewhere above, followed by the rhythmic strumming of a guitar.

Sinclair?

If so, he knew how to play, the melody light and soothing and familiar. She couldn't put a name to it, but she hummed along as she ran more water into the pan and kept on cleaning.

Sometimes music soothed the savage beast.

Sometimes it didn't.

This was one of those nights when all the guitar strumming in the world couldn't chase away the memories of gunfire and blood and explosions, couldn't make the pain and sorrow and loss disappear. Not even for a minute.

It was a shame.

Sinclair had paperwork to catch up on, a proposal bid to write up, but he was on edge, every creak of the old building, every rumble of pipes making his heart jump.

He set the guitar aside. Two hours, and he still hadn't quieted the beast. He grabbed a Pepsi from the bag of stuff he'd carried into the apartment and took a sip of the lukewarm soda. For about a half a second he wished it was an ice-cold beer. He'd given those up three years ago. Right around the time he and Kendra had split and he'd realized that he was enjoying his beer a little too much. A few beers a week had become a few beers a night, then a couple of beers an hour. He'd looked in the mirror one night and seen his father looking back at him — bleary eyed, slack jawed, a little puffy from too much alcohol and not enough nourishment.

No way in hell was he ever going to turn into his dad, so he'd emptied the fridge of beer, dumped it all down the sink. He hadn't had more than a couple of sips of wine since then.

He might not like what he felt, but feeling was better than the alternative — numb apathy. His father had perfected that. He hadn't cared about anything or anyone. Not his kids. Not his wife. Not his jobs — one after another lost because he'd been sleeping off a binge.

Yeah. There was no way Sinclair planned to become that, so he sipped more soda, changed into running gear, strapped a brace on his knee.

When music couldn't quiet the beasts, running could.

He tucked the key to the apartment into his vest pocket, zipped his cell phone in with it, and headed outside.

Main Street was quiet at 10:00 P.M. No cars. No people. Lights glowed outside a few businesses, but there was no sign of life. He'd forgotten this part of small-town life — the way night came and peace with it. Aside from a few dogs barking, it was silent, a breeze whipping a few stray leaves across the pavement.

He jogged along Main Street until he hit his stride, felt that sweet spot that came when pain and effort became freedom. When he hit it, he turned off the main drag, headed away from the business district and into the residential area. Even after all these years, he knew the place. It helped that nothing had changed. The Daily Grind was still sitting at the corner of Main and Boone, the drive-through coffee shop closed up for the night. The elementary school still stood at the end of Anderson, the dead-end road opening out into a well-lit school yard and an empty playground. He sprinted up the hill behind the school, memories of Iraq and Afghanistan chasing him. He'd lost a lot of friends there but had kept a lot too. Every year, he got a boatload of Christmas cards from people he'd served with — most of them photos of happy families standing in front of Christmas trees or young children sitting in Santa's lap. The bonds that grew in the worst of times seemed to last the longest. Even now, nearly six years after he left the marines, he got texts and e-mails from people he'd served with.

That was something to remember on nights when the demons were breathing down his neck.

He crested the rise of the hill, still sprint-

61

ing, some of his tension easing away. It was hard to hold on to when the body was working so hard. He'd learned that during the months he'd spent in rehab.

He ran along Fitzgerald Lane, turned onto Madison. The houses were smaller here, the 1920s bungalows and four-squares much simpler than the Victorian mansions that lined the streets closer to Main. He passed a FOR SALE sign, forced himself not to stop to take a closer look at the neglected property.

He wasn't going to buy and restore a house in Benevolence. Not because he didn't think he could do it and not because he didn't think it would sell. There were always people charmed by the town, always someone desperate to buy property there.

He could restore a house there. He could sell it. He could make money off of it. That's what he'd been doing in Seattle, Portland, San Francisco, and just about every other city and town he'd visited.

The problem was, restoring a property the right way — finding period materials, reclaiming windows and fireplace mantels, and even old floorboards and tiles — that took a lot of time. Time he wasn't willing to spend in Benevolence.

He rounded a curve in the road, slowed

his run to a jog. He felt better, calmer. He could go back to the apartment, do a little work and get a little sleep before he had to face Gavin and their grandfather's house again. He'd feel better for it, and hopefully his mood would be better too. Gavin drove him crazy, but Sinclair loved his brother. The last thing he wanted to do was spend the next couple of weeks arguing with him.

Up ahead, something darted across the road.

A deer? Wolf? A young black bear?

Whatever it was, it was big and it was running hard, dashing across a yard, circling back around, nosing a trash can at the corner of someone's house.

"Tiny!" someone yelled, the feminine voice breaking the silence. "Get back here. Right now!"

Tiny?

Was she yelling for the giant beast that had its head in the trash can?

He moved closer to the animal, got a better look at dark scruffy fur and a wagging tail.

Yep. A dog.

"Tiny! Seriously! If you're in the Langfords' trash can again, I'm going to disown you!"

The voice was familiar, and Sinclair

scanned the area, finally spotted someone jogging around the corner. Small. Curvy. Familiar. Just like the voice.

Adeline.

He probably should have been surprised, but he wasn't. If anyone in Benevolence was going to be chasing after an overgrown mutt at ten in the evening, it would be someone like her. Just a little quirky, a little different. Not nearly as perfect as the rest of the town pretended to be.

She must have seen him. She slowed, stopped.

"You're out late," he said, and she cocked her head to the side, her face a pale oval in the streetlight.

"Sinclair?"

"That's right."

"I'm not the only one who's out late."

"Guess we both needed some fresh air."

"What I need," she said, moving a little closer, "is to get my puppy before Morris Langford hears him and comes out with his shotgun."

"That's a puppy?" he asked as she dashed toward the dog and the trash can.

He didn't think she heard him.

She was too busy diving toward the dog.

She missed by a hair, her fingers skimming Tiny's collar.

Tiny seemed to think that was an open invitation to play tag. He darted away, dragging a leash with him.

"Dear God in heaven, why?! Why did I have to pick the biggest, most stubborn puppy in the pound?" Adeline moaned, taking off after the mutt.

Sinclair followed, because . . .

Why not?

Adeline and her oversized mutt were the most interesting thing that had happened all day. They'd covered about a mile when Adeline started panting, her breath gasping out in wheezing heaves that made Sinclair wonder if she needed an inhaler.

He snagged the back of her shirt. "You know you're never going to catch him, right?"

"Thanks, Pollyanna, for that overwhelming vote of confidence," she gasped.

He laughed. "Just being honest. He wants to play, and you're his favorite game."

"I suppose you have some suggestion for ending the game?"

"Just wait." He released her shirt. "Once he realizes you're not playing, he'll come back."

"I don't have time to wait." She tugged the ends of her shirt down over hips encased in black spandex. Firm round hips. Muscular thighs. That oddly pretty face.

Yeah. She and her dog were definitely the most interesting thing that had happened that day.

"You don't have time to wait, but you do have time to chase the dog all over creation?"

She offered a half smile. "You have a point, Sinclair."

"I usually do."

She shook her head, her smile broadening. "Pessimistic *and* arrogant? Nice."

"It's served me well, and it looks like it's working for you too." He gestured to the end of the street. Tiny had stopped. Seconds later, he loped back in their direction. He made it about halfway and stopped to sniff a trash can sitting near the curb.

"Ti—"

"You call him, and he's going to go running again," Sinclair warned. "Just hang back for a few more minutes, and he'll come right to you."

"For the love of Pete," Adeline muttered. "I need this like I need a hole drilled through my head."

"Bad day?"

"How'd you guess? Was it the fact that I had to cut myself out of a dress I'm supposed to wear in ten days? The fact that the dress was butt ugly? Or the fact that I'm out chasing my dog when I should be home, eating a nice bowl of beef stew and listening to Bing Crosby croon?"

"Bing Crosby?"

"He's an icon, Sinclair," she responded, every word dripping with disgust. "One that most people in our generation can't appreciate."

"You being the exception?"

"I cut my teeth on Bing Crosby records. Literally. I actually gnawed on one when I was teething. My grandmother cried for a week after that. Or so the story goes."

"She liked Bing, huh?"

"Liked him? She loved the guy. If she'd had a choice between Bing and Granddad, she might have chosen Bing."

"She knew him?"

"Only in her dreams."

He laughed, and she smiled in response. "You got the reference."

"I did. Wasn't Bing a little before your grandmother's time?"

"Bing," she huffed, "is timeless. My grandmother's mother listened to him, my grandmother listened to him, I listen to him."

"And your daughter will listen to him one day?"

"If I had a daughter she would. Look" —

she grabbed his wrist and pointed at her giant mutt — "he's coming." She whispered the last part as if Tiny might hear her and change his mind about returning.

The dog *was* coming, ears flopping, tail wagging, huge paws slapping the ground. One second, he was a couple of yards away, the next, he was leaping up, nearly knocking Adeline off her feet as he licked her face.

"Down, Tiny!" she commanded.

Tiny didn't seem all that keen to listen.

Sinclair grabbed his collar and pulled him away.

The dog's tail thumped rhythmically, his tongue lolled from his mouth, and Sinclair could swear he was smiling.

"Interesting dog," he said, taking the end of the leash before the mutt could run off again.

"That's putting it mildly." She took the leash from his hand. "Thanks for the help, Sinclair. If you hadn't come along, I'd have probably been chasing him all night."

"You would have figured things out eventually." He followed her as she walked across the street, turned right, and headed toward a small bungalow that sat on a mature lot — large oak tree, towering pine, a few shrubs that would probably flower in the spring.

"Yes, but I don't have time for eventually. I have a million things left to do today."

"And just a couple of hours to get them done. Maybe you should do a few of the million tomorrow," he suggested, and she scowled.

"There you go again, Pollyanna." She dug in her jacket pocket and pulled out keys. "Ever the optimist."

She marched up the porch stairs, Tiny prancing along beside her.

He could have said good night and headed home. He probably should have.

"Cute place," he said instead, running his hand over the porch railing.

"I think so. Janelle thinks it's too small."

It *was* small — shotgun style with a steeply angled roof and dormers that hinted at finished attic space. "Depends on how many people are living in it."

"Just me. And Tiny. He thinks he's a person, so I guess that counts." She unlocked the door, opened it. "Of course, Janelle lives in as close to a mansion as Benevolence has ever seen, so I guess she's used to grander things."

He knew Janelle's house. Everyone who'd grown up in Benevolence did. A huge Victorian that sat on double lots in the heart of town, the place had turret rooms, wraparound porches, and gingerbread trim. Built by the first Lamont to settle in Benevolence, it had been passed down from one generation to the next. According to the rumors Sinclair had heard growing up, it had been gifted to Janelle and her husband after their first daughter was born. He hadn't cared much about the rumors, but he'd been fascinated by the house. "I always thought it was the coolest place in town," he said.

She shrugged. "That's probably because you didn't live in it."

He'd lived in a hell of a lot worse, but he didn't say that. She knew it. Everyone in town did. "You didn't like living there?"

"I wouldn't say that exactly." She stepped inside, motioning for him to follow.

"What *would* you say, then?" he asked as Adeline unhooked Tiny's leash.

"I'd say that it was like living in a museum. Lots of pretty things that could be looked at and not touched."

"Tough life," he said, just a hint of sarcasm in his voice.

She must have heard it. Either that, or she suddenly remembered who she was talking to — a man who'd grown up in a place so filled with junk, it had been almost impossible to walk through the rooms.

Her cheeks went pink, and she frowned.

"You know it wasn't, Sinclair. I had a great life. I also had an entire list of things that I wanted to do. None of them could be done in the Lamont family home."

"What kinds of things?"

"Sliding down the railing. Having sleepovers with friends. Dinner in the living room. Tag in the family room."

"Big dreams," he said. All *he'd* wanted was to sleep in a bed that wasn't covered with crap in a room that wasn't filled to the brim with his grandfather's junkyard finds.

"Yes. I've replaced them with bigger ones."

"Like?"

"Dinner. I'm starving."

He figured that was a hint for him to leave, and he reached for the door handle. "Guess I'll leave you to it, then."

She hesitated, and he knew she thought she owed him, that she was trying to figure out the proper way to repay the debt.

He could have told her it wasn't necessary.

He didn't do things he didn't want to, and he didn't help people with the expectation that he'd be helped in return.

"I'll give you a ride back to Byron's," she finally offered.

He wasn't surprised. Good manners were bred into people like Adeline. They had a

71

family image to uphold and social expectations to meet. One of the few benefits of being born into his family was that there had been no expectations. Teachers, preachers, counselors, they'd all made allowances for the Jefferson boys.

Poor things don't know what good manners are.

He'd heard that whispered more times than he could count, so he'd worked doubly hard on having good manners and a good work ethic. It hadn't mattered. Name was everything in Benevolence. The Jefferson name had been mud for longer than Sinclair had been alive.

"No need for a ride," he said, shaking off the frustration that he always felt when he thought of his family. "I've still got to finish my run."

"Do you always run this late at night?" she asked.

Only when the demons were chasing him. He wasn't going to tell her that, though.

"Depends on how busy my day is and how late it is when I finish my work. How about you?"

"I only run when I'm chasing Tiny, or when I've got a god-awful orange dress to wear for a wedding and I'm too big for it."

"You're not too big, Adeline," he said,

opening the door and stepping out onto the porch. "The dress is too small."

"Same difference."

"Not when one means you have the problem and the other means the dress does."

"The dress has many problems." She laughed. "My size is not one of them."

"Your size," he responded, "is perfect."

"That's nice of you to say, Sinclair, but I don't think May and my mother would agree."

"You know what I think?"

"What?" She stood in the doorway, her deep red hair shimmering in the interior light.

"That a woman like you, someone who's put her life on hold to take care of her grandfather's shop while he recovers, shouldn't be worried about what other people think. See you around." He offered a quick wave and jogged across the yard.

When he looked back, she'd gone inside. Probably to eat dinner with her pigheaded dog.

He needed to eat too.

Now that he'd run off his anxiety, he thought he probably could. Not that he had much in the apartment to eat. Just a few things he'd picked up after he'd finished work for the day. Tomorrow he'd buy groceries.

He'd also get Gavin working. Real work. Not the *picking up one piece of garbage for every hundred that Sinclair bagged* kind of work he'd been doing for the past few days. Gavin wouldn't be happy with the turn of events, but Sinclair was finished taking up his slack. He'd agreed to help, not do the entire project.

Two weeks.

The house would be done or it wouldn't, but by the end of that time, Sinclair would be heading home to his apartment that overlooked Puget Sound. He'd be catching up on all the work that he'd put on hold to help his brother. He'd be sleeping in his own bed, listening to the quiet rush of traffic below his window.

He'd be alone again, running from the demons and the nightmares.

Most of the time, that was exactly how he liked it.

CHAPTER THREE

Adeline dreamed of chocolate.

Gobs of it. Dripping off the counter, spilling onto the floor, bubbling over pots and pans. Tiny running through the mess, the tangerine dress clutched in his mouth.

She woke with his scruffy muzzle in her face, his dark eyes staring into hers.

"Go away." She moaned, flipping onto her stomach and pulling the pillow over her head. Before Tiny, she'd always set her alarm for seven. After Tiny, the alarm clock had been destroyed, chewed up while Adeline was in the shower one morning. She'd have bought a new one, but Tiny had taken its place, waking her at the edge of dawn every morning, his hot puppy breath fanning her face.

He whined, shoving his ninety-pound body closer and pawing at the pillow.

"You're a menace. You realize that, right?" she muttered, shoving the covers aside and getting out of bed.

She yanked on yoga pants and a sweat-shirt, grabbed Tiny's leash, and wrestled the puppy into it. Her cell phone rang as she layered the sweatshirt with a lightweight coat. She glanced at the caller ID. Grand-dad.

She answered as she walked outside. "Good morning, Granddad!"

"It would be a better one if we were both still asleep," he responded, his gruffness making her smile.

"You're always up at the crack of dawn," she pointed out, Tiny scrabbling at the sidewalk, trying his best to get her to move faster.

Wasn't going to happen while she was on the phone. She couldn't run and talk at the same time.

"Only when I have something to do be-sides lying in bed staring at the ceiling and hoping someone will come visit me."

"Better watch it, you're starting to sound like a bitter old man."

He chuckled. "Leave it to you to not give me a lick of sympathy. Your sisters? *They* were very quick to reassure me that I am loved and appreciated and that they'll be here in just a few short days to spend some time with me."

"That's because they feel guilty." She had it straight from Willow and Brenna's mouths. They both felt bad for not being at the hospital during Byron's surgeries and recuperation, but neither felt guilty enough to come home sooner than May's wedding.

"They *should* feel guilty. I'm an old man, on limited time. It isn't such a hard thing to understand that I want to spend as much time as possible with my family before I go."

"Granddad, really, you're wasting all this on me. Save it for Willow. She's the one with the softest heart."

He laughed. Just like she'd known he would. "How's the shop-keeping coming, kid? That's what I really called about."

"About as well as can be expected."

"What's that supposed to mean?"

"I'm no chocolatier. You know that."

"You could be. If you'd put a little of your heart into it."

"I'm putting blood, sweat, and tears into it. Isn't that enough?"

"Not when it comes to chocolate. That requires a little something extra."

"Speaking of extra," she interrupted, anxious to change the direction of the conversation. Byron was like a dog with a bone. When he got his mind on something, he didn't let it go. Lately, his mind was on

77

her taking over the shop permanently once he retired. "I've been using the recipes you keep locked up in the office. Are all the ingredients for Lamont fudge on the recipe card?"

"Why wouldn't they be?"

"I just . . ." What could she say? That the fudge tasted okay at best and horrible at worst? "Wanted to be sure before I make it for May's wedding."

"Haven't you been making it for daily sales? People love that stuff, Addie. They come from all over the world to get it." An exaggeration. People didn't come from all over the world. They did *order* it from all over the world. She'd gotten orders from places as far away as Japan and Australia. Filling those orders would be impossible if she didn't figure out how to make the stuff.

God! Why had she ever suggested that Granddad expand to Internet sales? That had been five years ago, and in the time since he'd done it, Chocolate Haven's profit margin had tripled. She knew. She did Granddad's taxes every year. She also knew that without those sales, Chocolate Haven would be just another family owned chocolate shop struggling to survive. Her throat tightened on the thought, and she took a deep calming breath.

She would not drive the business into the ground.

She wouldn't.

"No worries, Grandad," she said, trying to keep panic out of her voice. "I'm making the fudge." It wasn't edible. At least not compared to what Chocolate Haven usually sold, but she was making batch after batch of it.

"Well, that's a relief. I can't hand the shop over to someone who isn't capable of running it."

"You're not handing the shop over to anyone," she said, his words sending ice through her veins. She didn't want to take over the business. Not today, tomorrow. *Ever.* "You'll be back to work in a few weeks —"

He snorted.

"You will!"

"Addie, I love you like a flower loves the sun, but you're delusional if you think I'll be back in a few weeks. Once I get out of this joint, I've got therapy to do. Lots of it. Sometime after that, I'll be able to work in the shop part-time. Only God knows if full-time work will ever happen for me again. The hip is bad. The leg is worse, and I'm just about ancient."

"You're not ancient," she protested.

"You say that because you love me, and you don't want to see the truth."

She also didn't want to have this conversation. "Granddad, you're the youngest seventy-five-year-old I know. You'll be back full-time, feeling better than ever."

"Maybe. In the meantime, you're running that place for me, and I appreciate it."

Running it into the ground.

The words echoed through her head as Tiny tugged her along the sidewalk. She didn't have the energy or the heart to try to pull him back. She felt hollow and a little sad and more overwhelmed than she'd been the very first day she'd walked into Chocolate Haven knowing she was going to have to make all the chocolate, fill all the orders, keep the Lamont family legacy alive.

"You still there, doll?" Granddad asked.

"Just trying to walk the dog and talk at the same time," she responded, her words thick with tears she wasn't going to shed.

"How is that Tiny dog of yours?"

"Great," she lied. "He's learning all kinds of neat tricks." Like how to drive the neighbors crazy, how to dig holes big enough to swallow cars. How to eat alarm clocks and wake her at the crack of dawn every morning.

"That's not what your mother told me."

"Mom doesn't like Tiny."

"She doesn't like dogs. Me? I'm glad you got one. They're good bodyguards, and a single girl like you might find herself in need of that."

"Granddad, the only thing a person needs to protect herself against in this town is gossip."

"Humph!" he replied. "There's danger there, Addie. Danger that I keep warning everyone about, but no one is listening."

"I'm listening." And *had* listened, a dozen times since the accident.

"You may be listening, but you're not believing," he growled. "Of course, that's better than what your mother is doing. By a long shot, it's better."

Uh-oh. This wasn't going to be good. Granddad and Janelle got along great. Until they didn't. "What's Mom doing?"

"Telling everyone that I've lost my marbles."

"She isn't telling people that, and you know it," she protested. She wasn't certain, though. Janelle had strong opinions about things. Currently, she was convinced that Byron had hit his head when he fell and that hitting his head had caused him some memory loss and confusion.

"She is. She told the doctor she thought I

have dementia."

"Where did you hear that?"

"From the doctor. Guy was asking me a few too many questions about presidents and birthdays and moon landings, and I wanted to know why. Your *mother*" — he nearly spit the word — "told him that she thought I might be having problems with my memory."

"She's just worried about you, Granddad."

"Because there was someone in my apartment and I had the nerve to say it?" he demanded. He was getting riled up, heading back to the story that he'd been telling since he'd fallen down his apartment stairs — someone standing in the hallway of his apartment when he'd returned home, his quick dash outside to call for help, the tumble down the stairs.

"You know that James McDermott saw you fall," she said, her grip on Tiny's leash a little tighter than it had been. Not because of the dog. Because of Granddad. They'd been down this path before. Several times, actually. It had yet to end well.

"And?" he snapped. "What's that got to do with anything?"

"You told him that there was someone in your apartment, and he ran up and tried to catch the guy. No one was there." James had been sheriff of Benevolence before he retired. Addie had no reason to doubt his word.

Then again, she had no reason to doubt Byron. Her grandfather had always been honest to a fault. Integrity flowed through the blood of the Lamonts the same way chocolate was supposed to.

Only with her, the chocolate gene had obviously been skipped.

The hot, tight feeling she'd been carrying in her chest since she'd made the first batch of Lamont family fudge threatened to suffocate her.

"I don't care what he found or didn't find. I know what I saw," Byron retorted.

"It was dark in the apartment. Maybe —"

"Maybe nothing. Someone was there. You and your mom can go tell anyone you want that I'm losing it, you can convince them that I need to be moved into a home —"

"No one is going to move you into a home!"

"Your mother brought me the paperwork today. Said it's a convalescent center and just until I'm able to walk upstairs, but I know the truth."

"She brought you paperwork?" They'd been discussing Byron staying with Janelle while he attended physical therapy. There hadn't been any mention of a convalescent center. "I thought you were staying at her place."

"*Her* place? I gave that house to her and your dad because I thought it would always be the Lamont family home. Guess I was wrong about that."

"Granddad —"

"I know I'm getting old, but that doesn't mean I'm getting stupid. Your mom already rented my apartment. She's moving me toward living in one of those old folks' homes, and I've got news for you. I'm not going."

"Of course, you aren't," she said, tightening her hold on Tiny's leash as a pickup truck passed.

Byron snorted. "Your optimism isn't going to change anything. Once I'm in the convalescent center, it's all downhill from there."

"I'll talk to Mom," she promised. Not that she thought it would do any good. Janelle was great at hearing things, but she wasn't always great at listening. When she thought she had the right idea, there wasn't a whole lot anyone could do to change her mind. "I'm sure we can come up with a better plan."

"Why would the two of you come up with a plan? Am I a child? Do I need others to make decisions for me? Because if that's what you think . . ." He continued on, but Addie only half listened. She'd heard the speech so many times, she could have recited it. Plus, it was hard to listen to anything with Tiny lunging at the truck that had pulled up to the curb. It wasn't a vehicle she recognized.

That was surprising.

She knew almost everyone in Benevolence. She served as accountant for most of them. If she didn't know them from her business, she knew them from church or from Chocolate Haven.

"Did you hear me, Adeline?" Byron asked.

"Of course I did," she replied, her gaze fixed on the idling truck. What was the driver doing? Texting? Calling someone? Watching her watch him?

She took a step back, trying to drag Tiny with her.

He wouldn't budge.

"Then, what do you think? It's a good solution, right?" Granddad demanded.

She wasn't sure since she hadn't heard, but Byron was right. He could make his own decisions about treatment. He could decide where he wanted to stay and how he wanted to handle rehab. If he wanted to stay at her mother's place — the Lamont place — he should be allowed to do it.

"It's a perfect solution," she responded, nearly falling to her knees as Tiny dragged at the leash.

"I knew you'd agree, doll! I'll tell the doctor I'm moving in with you. Hopefully, he'll let me out of here a little sooner."

"Me!? I only have one spare room, and it's —" She started to protest, but he'd already hung up.

"Not ready for a guest," she muttered, tucking the phone into her pocket and using two hands to drag Tiny away from the curb.

The truck engine died, the taillights going dark.

Tiny whined frantically. No vicious barking from him. No protective stance. He dropped to the ground, rolled onto his back, his tail wagging frantically, as a man got out of the truck.

"Everything okay, Adeline?" the guy called, his face illuminated by the streetlight, his nearly black hair gleaming.

Sinclair Jefferson looked good in the morning.

But then, he probably looked good all the time.

He bent to scratch Tiny's belly and offered Addie a smile that would have melted a lesser woman's heart. Her heart didn't even warm up. She'd been down that path before — the one where sweet smiles led to tentative kisses, where tentative kisses led to whispered promises and shared dreams.

She wasn't going down it again.

"Fine," she managed to say, her muscles trembling as she tried to tug the puppy to his feet. Unlike her, Tiny seemed determined to get as close as possible to the man.

"Good. I saw you standing there, and worried that maybe you were having trouble getting your dog back home."

"I was talking to my grandfather," she responded, brushing a few pieces of dog hair off her yoga pants. "I couldn't talk and walk the dog at the same time."

"How is Byron doing?" He took the leash from her hand and pressed his palm to her lower spine.

Suddenly they were walking, heading back toward her house, Tiny trotting along beside Sinclair as if he loved the leash and never ever tried to escape it.

"He's . . . fine."

"I'm hearing that as, 'he's miserable.' "

"He doesn't want to go to a convalescent

center to do his rehab. He wants to stay with Mom."

"And Janelle doesn't want him there?"

"There are a lot of stairs in that old house. Stairs up to the porch. Stairs up to the bedrooms. He could reinjure himself."

"Right," he said, and she heard a world of censorship in that one word.

Which, of course, made her want to jump to her mother's defense. "My mother is constantly on the road, traveling to show properties. She wouldn't be home enough to help Granddad, and he's really going to need it for a while."

"Right," he repeated, and she flushed.

"It's not like we're going to make him do something he doesn't want to do."

"I don't remember Byron as being the kind of person who would let someone make him do anything."

True. He wasn't.

"But," he continued, "your mother isn't that kind of person either."

They'd reached her street. She could see her little house — the porch light gleaming, the windows dark. What she wouldn't give to be able to hide out there for one day. Just one day to sit alone and try to get her thoughts together. "Fortunately, we've found a solution that will satisfy both of them."

"Let me guess," he said, his long strides shortened to match hers, his work boots crunching on the frozen grass as they crossed her yard. "He's going to stay with you."

"Good guess," she responded, digging the key out from her pocket and sliding it into the lock.

"I didn't know anyone around here did that," he said, Tiny sitting right next to him, calm as could be.

"Had their grandfather live with them?" She stepped into the vestibule and reached for Tiny's leash. She'd have to keep it on him. The clock was ticking, and she needed to get him to Nehemiah's and get to the shop. She had about twenty hours of work that needed doing before it opened.

"No." He chuckled, the sound as warm and rich as a cup of hot chocolate. "Locked their doors. Your mom has been reminding me for days that this is a nice, safe town."

"She's probably trying to undo the damage she thinks my grandfather is doing," she said without thinking.

"What damage is that?" He stood on the threshold. He might have been waiting for an invitation to come in, but she didn't have time for niceties. She didn't have time for conversations, either, but . . . there she was, conversing, and looking into eyes so green she was wondering if the man wore contacts.

"It's a long story, and —"

He cut in before she could say what she was thinking. "We both have busy schedules, so maybe you can tell me later?"

"Sure," she found herself saying. Even though she had no intention of talking to Sinclair again. Not if she could help it. The last thing she needed was more trouble, and Sinclair? He looked like a boatload of it.

He nodded, stepped back. "See you around, Addie."

Seconds later, he was crossing the yard, his stride a little hitched, as if one of his legs was bothering him.

Not her business if it was. Like she kept reminding herself, she didn't need more trouble or problems or any other crap that came with relationships. Mother-daughter, grandfather-granddaughter. Sister-sister.

She scowled. That might just be the stickiest relationship of all. Especially lately, when both Willow and Brenna called once or twice a week to check on Granddad's progress. They both had a hundred excuses as to why they couldn't visit.

At the heart of the excuses was the truth

— they hated Benevolence. They didn't want to be part of the town they'd grown up in.

As far as Addie could tell, they didn't want to be part of the family they'd grown up in either.

She shrugged off the frustration of that. Life was filled with opportunities and choices. Her sisters had made theirs. Whether she liked the results or not, she had to try to be supportive.

Even if there *were* moments when she wanted to shake some sense into both of their heads.

Relationships with family should be easy, right?

You were born into a group of people. You grew up surrounded by personalities, steeped in whatever drama or trauma existed within your familial unit. You learned each other the way dawn learned daylight — intimately with no separation of one from the other. That being the case, it stood to reason that a guy who'd grown up with a brother should have absolutely no problem understanding his sibling's choices.

Sinclair was having plenty of problems.

He was *trying* to understand why Gavin did the things he did.

God knew he was.

But he couldn't wrap his head around his brother's lazy approach to winning his wife back.

They were brothers. They'd been raised together, spent every moment of their early childhood together. They shared genetics and parentage. Shouldn't Sinclair at least have some basic understanding of the way that Gavin operated? Barring that, shouldn't he feel at least a smidge of sympathy for a guy whose pregnant wife had walked out on him?

Sinclair didn't.

All he felt was pissed.

He lifted a stack of newspapers dating from the 1960s and tossed them into a garbage bag with about ten other stacks. He cinched the bag, threw it into a pile near the pocket doors.

Or what should have been the pocket doors.

Now there was just a wide opening that looked out into the foyer. That, at least, was finally clear. No more furniture shoved into the corners. No church pews lining the wall. The space had opened up nicely, the intricately patterned wood floor finally visible.

Sinclair hadn't realized how much craftsmanship had gone into the house. He'd known it was large, that it dated from the end of the nineteenth century, that a railroad magnate had built it as a wedding present to his daughter.

His daughter who'd had the misfortune of marrying a Jefferson.

Yeah. Sinclair had known all that. But he hadn't realized what a masterpiece the place really was. If he had, he'd like to think that he'd have come back a few years ago to clean it out and restore it.

He'd like to think that, but the truth was he'd probably still have avoided the place like the plague. All his memories of the house were of wanting and needing, of struggling, of trying to keep the place warm in the winter, dry in the spring, cool in the summer. Of fixing leaking pipes to keep wood from rotting, and fixing wiring to keep the house from burning down.

That was the beginning of what had become a lucrative career, but the memories weren't fond ones, and he'd always hated the house. Or, more precisely, what it represented.

It was a beautiful old place, though.

Or would be when Sinclair finished with it.

He'd already procured pocket doors from a place in Massachusetts. They should arrive in the next couple of days. By the time they did, he'd have the lower level of the house cleaned out.

He could refinish the floors, repair plaster ceilings, replace the peeling Victorian wallpaper with something that matched pretty closely. He could re-side the house with period clapboard, whitewash the wraparound porch, and replace the rotting steps.

He could make the house into a home that Lauren would be proud to live in.

What he couldn't do was fix his brother.

"Gavin!" he shouted, his breath visible in the frigid air. He'd turned off the boiler their first day of work, and was keeping it off until he got some of the newspapers cleared away from the radiators. The last thing they needed was a fire. Once it started, there'd be enough fuel to keep it burning for a week.

"Gavin!" he yelled again. "You'd better get in here, or I'm quitting for the day!"

"Hold your horses, Sinclair!" Gavin responded. "I just threw twelve bags into the Dumpster. I needed a drink."

"Your 'drink' better be water," Sinclair said as his brother pushed a wheelbarrow into the room. He'd actually dressed for the job — jeans, a flannel shirt, work boots. Maybe . . . just maybe . . . Sinclair was making some progress with him.

"I didn't grab a beer, if that's what you're implying." Gavin held up a soda can. "But it's not water either. I need caffeine. Being pulled out of bed at the crack of dawn doesn't agree with me."

"It better start agreeing with you, because Lauren isn't coming back until this place is finished." Personally, if he were Lauren, he'd have packed up and moved out for good.

But that was him.

He didn't waste time on things that weren't going to work out. Some old houses were ripe for restoration. Some had foundations that were crumbling, walls that were falling in on themselves, and so much wrong that no amount of fixing could ever make them right. Relationships were the same. Some could be salvaged. Some couldn't.

Based on what he'd seen his brother doing — or not doing — the last few days, he'd say Lauren would be better off cutting her losses and moving on.

He could be wrong. That had happened a time or two with a building project that someone with more money than sense wanted to salvage. He'd always been willing to give it a shot as long as the client's commitment was as deep as his pockets. It took money *and* determination to bring a property back from the brink. Sinclair had managed it enough times that he knew it could be done. Often, though, it came at a higher price than the owner really wanted to pay.

Resentment could build when that happened. Sinclair had seen the way passion for a project could become ambivalence. He'd watched as beautiful restorations — buildings that had every detail and color chosen by hopeful owners — were put on the market before the family that had planned to live there ever moved in.

He hoped that Gavin and Lauren's marriage wasn't going to be like that, nothing more than a pretty monument to what could have been.

He lifted another stack of newspapers and chucked them into the bag with a lot more force than necessary. He'd been working since dawn. Nonstop. No break for soda, coffee, or food. He was hungry, thirsty, and pissed that his brother kept finding excuses to disappear.

He was also sorry that, as a whole, the Jefferson men weren't the kind who could be counted on. They were lazy bastards. That was the truth. Lazy *alcoholic* bastards was even more the truth. The women who married them inevitably ended up working themselves to death to try to keep roofs over their heads and food in their pantries.

Except for Sinclair's mother.

She'd been a party girl too. Not the best choice for a guy like his father. They'd been decent enough parents when they were sober. That wasn't often. By the time Sinclair was six, he was making sure Gavin had breakfast, lunch, and dinner. By the time he was eight, he was getting both of them dressed and ready for school. His mother worked as a preschool teacher in Spokane, and he'd learned to wake her up from her alcohol-induced stupor so that she could make it to her job.

Not a pretty childhood, but it was better than what he and Gavin had had after his parents died.

That's when his grandfather had taken them in.

Their only family because his mother had cut off all ties with her straitlaced parents. Sinclair had a vague memory of them showing up for the funeral, but they'd had no desire to take in two wild little boys. At least, that's the way he'd always figured it. He didn't know. They'd moved away from Spokane while he was in the military and hadn't bothered to leave an address.

"How about I get the rest of these bags

out, and we go get some dinner?" Gavin suggested, apparently oblivious to Sinclair's mood.

"How about you get the rest of the bags out, and we don't?" Sinclair responded. He didn't snap like he wanted to. Keeping calm in stressful situations was a requirement in his line of work.

Gavin was pushing him to the edge, though.

And Sinclair thought he knew it.

"You haven't taken a break since you got here this morning," Gavin pointed out. "You've got to eat sometime."

"I've got to get this project done more than I need to eat." He finished filling the bag, cinched it, and tossed it in Gavin's direction.

To his credit, Gavin managed to snag it. He'd always been a good athlete. Maybe if he'd pursued sports, he'd have gotten a scholarship to college, obtained a degree, and had more job opportunities.

"Working yourself to the bone isn't smart, Sinclair." Gavin took a last sip of soda and placed it on the fireplace mantel. "You're not getting any younger. A guy your age —"

Sinclair cut him off. "Get the bags out, and let's get on to the next room."

"The next room? I thought we were finishing this one and calling it a day." Gavin scowled. "I have plans."

"With who?"

"Does it matter?"

"Yeah. It does. I came here to help save your marriage. You go off with some lady you met an hour ago, and that's not going to happen." He surveyed the room. Aside from dozens of bags of trash, a few pieces of Victorian furniture, and about two inches of dust, it was empty.

"I would never cheat on Lauren," Gavin said, his eyes flashing as he chucked trash bags into the wheelbarrow. "I'm not that kind of guy."

"Yeah? Then what's so important that you need to leave a job you're doing for Lauren?"

"Not your business."

"But somehow, cleaning this place up for you and your wife is?"

Gavin's jaw tightened. "Are you going to keep throwing this in my face? Am I going to be hearing about how you ran to the rescue for the rest of my life?"

"Not if you tell me what I want to know."

"Fine," Gavin snapped. "You want to know what my plans are? I'm going to counseling. Alone. To work on my problems. Because," he continued as he wheeled the trash through the doorway, "despite what you think, I know I have them, and I love Lauren enough to try to fix them."

That was it.

Just those few words, and he was gone, leaving Sinclair standing right where he was, the nearly empty room still layered in dust, the late afternoon sunlight streaming in through the dirty windows and a tiny bit of hope fluttering somewhere in the region of his heart.

CHAPTER FOUR

Sinclair worked until the sun went down and the house grew so cold that his fingers hurt. He didn't mind the quiet that had settled over the place after Gavin left. He didn't mind being alone. What he minded was the frigid temperature. If not for that, he'd have stayed later. As it was, he was chilled to the bone, his bad knee aching as he got in the truck.

He felt good, though. The parlor, sitting and dining rooms were cleared. The kitchen was getting there. Tomorrow he'd finish that and move upstairs.

To an even bigger mess.

He wasn't sure how his grandfather had managed it, but somehow Elijah Jefferson had carted more stuff up to the second floor than he'd stored in the lower level. Sinclair and Gavin would have to haul it all down. He estimated seven hours to finish the job. Everything after that required skill and intensive labor. It would be interesting to see how Gavin handled that.

Or frustrating.

Either way, Sinclair would deal with it.

He pulled away from the house, heading down a dirt driveway that had once been paved. Bits and pieces of asphalt peeked out from between tangled weeds and piles of dry earth. Other people might have called it ugly. Not Sinclair. Decay had its own kind of beauty. *If* a person was willing to look for it. Sinclair could see it in the crumbled driveway and the wrought-iron fence that had once surrounded the front yard but now listed inward, nearly touching long yellow blades of grass. Even covered with junked cars and pieces of old trucks, the place had appeal. As a matter of fact, it wasn't bringing back nearly as many bad memories as he'd thought it would.

That was the positive side to working hard and keeping busy. He was too distracted by what *was* to think much about what *had been.*

The negative? He was damn tired. For him that meant deep sleep, which meant nightmares, the kind that woke him up drenched in sweat, sure he was back in Iraq, the medical caravan he'd been escorting under attack.

He knew the drill, could almost hear his therapist at the VA hospital telling him to take a long walk, relax, put himself in the right frame of mind for nightmare-free sleep. Maybe call a friend, spend some time talking and listening and doing all the things normal people did. People without boatloads of baggage and a million bad dreams chasing after them.

He frowned, pulling onto the road that led into town. A two-way country lane, it meandered across three miles of fallow farmland. No lights illuminated the road. No houses huddled in the middle of fields. There was nothing between Jefferson land and the town limits. That was the way Elijah had liked it. He'd been a hermit, enjoying his solitude almost as much as he'd enjoyed his whiskey.

Good thing he'd married well. His wife had been the only child of a Seattle banker. She'd just happened to be driving through Benevolence on her way to somewhere else. She'd stopped in the diner, backed out of her parking spot and right into Elijah's old Ford pickup. The rest . . . well, it was a story Sinclair was sure was still being told at the local hair salon.

Personally, he'd never met his grandmother, but he'd heard stories. She'd worked several jobs in Spokane, making the long commute daily so that her husband could stay on Jefferson land. She'd inherited money, and she'd put some of that aside for their only child, hiding it away so that her son would never struggle the way she had to.

Sinclair's father hadn't been any better with money than Elijah had been. He hadn't been any better at holding down a job either.

Sinclair had broken the Jefferson mold on that one, and he was pretty damn proud of it. He doubted his grandfather and father would have felt the same about his accomplishments. From what he could remember of his father, Randy Jefferson had been pretty damn proud that he'd married a woman who could support him. Elijah had been proud that he could drink most men under the table.

Water under the bridge, and not something Sinclair spent a lot of time thinking about.

He'd made a good life for himself.

He had everything he needed and almost everything he wanted. He'd lived with Kendra for a few years, tried the happy-couple thing, found that it wasn't quite the fit he wanted.

Now he was content to build his business,

restoring homes all over the country, returning to his home base in Seattle when the jobs were done.

Seattle?

Yeah. That was more his speed. Just big enough for a guy who'd come from a place like Benevolence, population 1,521 (including animals). At least, that's what the sign said. He didn't plan to be in town long enough to take a head count. Or to be added to the number.

Something darted in front of his truck, and he slammed on the brakes, barely avoiding what looked like a gray hairy deer.

It took him about five seconds to realize what he was seeing.

Not a deer.

A dog.

And not just any dog. Adeline's dog.

He pulled over and jumped out of the truck. Tiny had disappeared in a small copse of trees. Sinclair wasn't in the mood to go after him, but an image of Adeline flitted through his mind: wild red hair, violet eyes just a little too big in her freckled face. She'd be heartbroken if the dog got run over.

It wasn't his problem and shouldn't be his concern, but he headed toward the trees anyway, pulling out his pocket Maglight and shining it toward the spot where the dog had disappeared.

Addie held the cell phone to her ear as she carefully released milk chocolate hearts from their molds. Twelve glossy, beautiful hearts. They were perfect. Her day had been nearly perfect too. Good sales. Happy customers. Even newlyweds who'd driven from Spokane to buy a pound of chocolates for their road trip to Glacier National Park.

Yes. Things had been going wonderfully since she'd arrived at the shop. Until now.

"I can't believe I let this happen!" Nehemiah's voice rang through the phone, his tone just short of panic. "You entrusted the dog to me, and I've failed you!"

"You haven't failed me," she assured him, trying to ignore the sick feeling in the pit of her stomach. Nehemiah was a good guy, but he wasn't as young as he used to be. He'd been known to misplace his glasses, his cane, his shoes. Maybe he'd just misplaced her giant puppy. "Are you sure he's not just hiding somewhere?" she asked as she flipped another mold, watched the beautiful hearts release onto the marble board.

"Addie, you're a smart girl, so what would make you ask such a stupid question?" Nehemiah responded. "He's huge. Where could he possibly hide?"

"Under the coffee table?"

"Three months ago, he could have gotten under there. Not anymore. I think he slipped outside when I went to get the paper. The storm door wasn't closed when I got back from the mailbox."

An open door? That was an invitation for Tiny to run.

The sick feeling morphed to full-out dread. "How long do you think he's been gone?"

"Let's see . . . I went out to get the paper before the sun set. So . . ." He mumbled something. Maybe a calculation of the time the sun went down and the current time — six thirty.

"Two hours?" he finally said.

She didn't curse. She thought about it, though. God, did she think about it!

"Two hours?" she repeated, hoping to heaven that she'd misheard. That maybe he'd said two minutes. Or twenty. Or anything but two hours.

One hundred and twenty minutes for Tiny to find trouble.

"I'd say about that. Seems to me I was thinking about starting my roasted chicken when I got in. That would have been about

107

four thirty."

"And you didn't see him in the house after you got the paper?" she pressed, hoping against hope that somehow he was mistaken and Tiny really wasn't gone.

"I wasn't really looking for him. He was sleeping right near the fireplace when I went for the paper, relaxing on that old throw rug I brought down from the attic. Same as every day. I went into the kitchen, had me some coffee and a couple of those short-bread cookies I like so much. The ones from Ella's Bakery Emporium? You been there, right?"

"Right," she managed to say through gritted teeth.

She'd been there. She'd eaten a scone. She'd enjoyed every bite of it, but she didn't want to discuss it. Not while Tiny was missing and presumed to be causing trouble.

"Great baked goods, that girl. She knows how to do things right. Reminds me of my Mary Sue's baked goods. Mary Sue? She could —"

"Nehemiah," she interrupted as gently as she could, as kindly. Mary Sue had died the previous spring. They'd been married for nearly seventy years. "I need to go look for Tiny. I'll call you as soon as I find him."

"I really hope you do find him, Addie. I

really do. I feel responsible for that dog, and I've grown to like him. Problem is, I'm too slow and old and he's too young and fast. Maybe it's just not a good match, me dog-sitting him."

Maybe not. *Probably* not, but she didn't have another option. Janelle wasn't going to take the dog. All Addie's friends had pets or kids or a combination, and she didn't feel like she could burden them with a high-energy, trouble-finding giant.

That sick feeling, that hard-hitting dread that was building in her stomach seemed to fill her chest, and she could barely breathe. "It's okay, Nehemiah. I'll find Tiny, and then we'll discuss ways of keeping him from escaping again."

She said good-bye and grabbed her coat from the hook near the back door, the beautiful chocolates left on the marble slab on the counter. She'd managed to mold all three flavors. Milk chocolate, white chocolate, dark chocolate. She'd purchased cute orange and white polka-dot cupcake wrappers to set the chocolates in. Hopefully May would be pleased.

If not, she'd have to start from scratch, come up with another presentation for the chocolate wedding favors May had ordered.

May, who had called three times to ask

about the diet, the exercise program, and the dress. The one that still didn't have a working zipper. Addie walked to the whiteboard list, put a red check near *Fix dress,* scribbled *Find Tiny* at the very top, wrote *Figure out what to do about Tiny* at the bottom.

She wanted to believe Nehemiah could continue to take care of the puppy, but she didn't want to stress out her elderly neighbor. She also didn't want to put a strain on their friendship. She'd been there nearly every day when Mary Sue was dying. She'd cooked meals, swept floors, dusted. Mostly she'd just listened to her neighbors share stories of the life they'd had together. As Mary Sue's illness grew worse, she'd lost the ability to speak, the cancer settling into her brain and stealing her ability to communicate. That's when Nehemiah had started to talk about what he was losing and about how much he'd loved what he'd had with his wife.

Only he hadn't been talking to Addie. He'd been speaking to Mary Sue, saying the words over and over again as he held the hand of his dying wife. *I loved you the day we met. I loved you the day we married. Every day after I have loved you, and I will love you through eternity.*

Thinking about it made goose bumps rise on Addie's arms and tears burn at the back of her eyes. What Nehemiah and Mary Sue had? *That* was love, and when she'd seen it, she'd known that what she'd had with Adam had been a poor facsimile. She'd also known that Nehemiah would be lost without that love to guide him, that half of his whole would be gone and that he'd need someone to fill just a tiny bit of the space Mary Sue had left.

She'd tried to do that, making him meals and visiting him every afternoon. It had been harder to do that since Granddad's accident, but Nehemiah had seemed happy enough with Tiny keeping him company. Until now.

No. She couldn't add stress to Nehemiah's life, and she couldn't hurt their friendship over a dog.

She'd come up with another plan for Tiny's day care, and she'd bring Nehemiah to the local animal shelter, help him choose an elderly companion dog. One that would spend all day lying by the fireplace and thumping its tail every time Nehemiah spoke.

She locked the shop's back door, jogged to her car. Thank goodness she'd closed up for the evening. Without an assistant to man

111

the shop, she'd have had no choice but to close down during business hours. That wasn't something Byron would ever have done. Chocolate Haven was his first priority. Always.

Unfortunately, she had other things that needed her attention. Like her accounting business, her dog, her life.

She climbed into the car, pulled around the side of the building and onto Main. A light in Granddad's apartment was on, the soft glow of it spilling out onto the awning that covered the entrance to Chocolate Haven. Sinclair must have returned, but she hadn't seen him or his truck.

Not that she'd been looking.

She'd been too busy to pay attention to the comings and goings of her grandfather's tenant.

Sure you were, a little voice whispered.

She ignored it.

She scanned the road as she drove down Main Street. No sign of Tiny. Two hours was a long time for a dog to be wandering around. He could be miles away, trotting down the highway heading for Spokane or Seattle or Idaho.

God, she hoped not. He was a pain in the butt, but she didn't want anything to happen to him.

She passed Nehemiah's saltbox-style house and pulled up in front of her bungalow. She hadn't left any lights on, and the place was dark and a little lonely looking. She'd have to remember that she didn't want to come home to that, because . . . well, she didn't.

She jumped out of the car, ran across the yard. Tiny wasn't waiting on the front porch the way she'd hoped he would be. She called him, but he didn't peek out from behind a bush or run around the side of the house to tease her into thinking he was actually responding.

Across the street, Mendelssohn Reynold's trash can was sitting at the curb, several bags of garbage overflowing the bin. Tiny hadn't been there. If he had, there'd be trash strewn from one end of the street to the other.

"Tiny!" she called, knowing that he wouldn't answer. He was gone. Really and truly gone. "Tiny!?"

If she were a dog, where would she go?

Somewhere with food?

Or . . . other dogs?

She hopped back in the car, did a quick U-turn and headed back toward Main Street.

A vehicle moved toward her, headlights

splashing on black asphalt. She barely noticed.

She was too worried about Tiny. He might
be a giant, but he was gentle and sweet,
troublesome but completely harmless. If
he'd been injured, hit by a car, kidnapped
by someone who would neglect or abuse
him . . .

She couldn't bear thinking about it.

She passed the approaching vehicle, had a
quick impression of a truck with a huge dog
sitting so close to the driver it might have
been in his lap.

It took a second for that to register — the
huge dog, the male driver, the pickup truck
that she'd seen earlier that day.

Sinclair? He'd been at the apartment,
hadn't he?

She glanced in the rearview mirror. The
truck was slowing as it neared her bungalow.
It was Sinclair! And the huge dog had to be
Tiny!

She did another quick U-turn, nearly
jumping the curb in her haste. By the time
she pulled into the driveway, Sinclair was
out of the truck, Tiny on a leash beside him.

"You found him!" she cried.

"I think he wanted to be found," he
replied, the leash wrapped around his left
hand. "He ran out in front of my truck."

She took the leash from his hand, realized it was a rope. "What'd you do? Lasso him?"

"If only it had been that easy." He smiled, a charming smile that made her pulse jump.

She had to look away, because she didn't want to be looking into his eyes and into his face, seeing that smile and having her heart respond.

"He wanted to be found," he continued, "but he didn't want to be caught."

"He gave you a run for your money, huh?" She couldn't avoid his eyes forever, but she could dang well try. She dug in her pocket, pulled out a set of keys, plucked a twig from Tiny's coat, did everything she could not to look at Sinclair.

"Run? I was at a full-out sprint, and I still only managed to get him because I had a pack of crackers on me. For future reference, Tiny loves peanut butter crackers."

"Tiny loves anything edible." She tugged the puppy with her as she headed toward the house. "He also loves things that aren't edible."

"Like?"

"Alarm clocks. Pillows. Couch cushions. The vet says he'll grow out of the chewing stage soon, but I'm not sure that's going to happen." She unlocked the door, hesitated on the threshold.

How long had it been since she'd invited a guy who was younger than seventy into her house? A couple of months? A year? Longer?

Was it sad that she couldn't remember?

"That explains it," Sinclair murmured, eyeing Tiny as if he were a puzzle that needed to be figured out.

"Explains what?"

"Why he didn't wait for me to take the crackers out of the package. I ripped it open, and he scarfed the crackers down so fast, I'm not even sure he chewed."

"Wrapper and all?" she asked, moving into the living room and reaching to untie the rope from Tiny's collar.

"Wrapper and all," he agreed, brushing her hand aside, his skin warm and a little rough. "Let me. I made it extra secure because I didn't want to have to sprint through the woods again."

"I really appreciate you going after him."

"What else was I supposed to do?" He looked up from the knot. For a moment she was caught, just kind of staring into his eyes.

"Some people would have just let him go."

"I hate to tell you this, Adeline, but he's a menace. I figured if I didn't catch him and bring him home, he'd start digging through people's garbage looking for food scraps."

"Then I guess I should thank you on behalf of the entire Benevolence community."

He laughed, finally freeing the knot and releasing Tiny. True to form, Tiny trotted into the kitchen to search for food. "I wasn't worried about Benevolence, I was worried that someone would see him scrounging through the trash, think he was a wolf, and shoot him."

"I was worried about that too," she admitted. "Tiny doesn't have a mean bone in his body, but anyone looking at him wouldn't know it."

"It might be best to keep him locked up when you're not home," he suggested, reaching down to rub his left knee. He had fine lines at the corners of his eyes and a small scar above one eyebrow. He also had a couple days' growth of stubble on his chin, dark hair that was just a little long, and eyes that . . .

Well, they were the greenest eyes she'd ever seen. Probably the most intense too. As if he had a boatload of energy and it was all just shining out of him.

Maybe that was Janelle's reason for wanting him in Granddad's apartment. With the wedding approaching, and all three of her girls attending, she probably had big plans for hooking one of them up with Sinclair. Sure, Willow was engaged, but Brenna still hadn't gotten a proposal from her boyfriend. In Janelle's mind, that meant a possibility of things not working out. If they didn't, she'd want to have a backup plan.

"Adeline?" Sinclair prodded, and she realized she'd been staring too long and thinking too deeply about something that didn't matter.

"Tiny is locked up while I'm gone. My neighbor keeps him for me."

"The guy in the saltbox house?"

"Yes."

"I saw him looking out the window when I drove up. Looks like he's closing in on ninety."

"He's a few years older than that. And I know he's elderly, but he's done a good job with Tiny." Up until now.

"It was just a comment," he said, touching the fireplace mantel, running his hand down the carved wood. "I'm not judging you."

"That's nice, because the rest of the town probably is."

"Do you care?" He turned his attention back to her.

"Not really," she responded honestly. Benevolence was filled with people who had

118

all sorts of opinions about all kinds of things. She tried hard to never let that bother her. She wasn't always successful, but Sinclair didn't need to know that.

"Meaning sometimes?"

"Something like that." She walked into the kitchen to check on Tiny. The dog had devoured every bit of kibble and was sitting mournfully at his bowl. "Next time," she muttered as she grabbed the kibble bag from a cupboard, "chew."

Tiny's tail thumped, and Sinclair chuckled, and for just a moment, it felt like they'd all done this a thousand times before: the conversation after a long day of work, the dog devouring his food, Sinclair's quiet laughter.

Adeline poured more kibble into the bowl, her cheeks hot with something she absolutely refused to acknowledge. "How did the work at your brother's go?" she asked, because she felt the desperate need to break the silence.

"About as well as I could have expected."

"Will you finish before the baby comes?"

"That or die trying," he muttered, and it was her turn to laugh, the expression on his face saying way more than his words did.

"Gavin isn't easy to work with?" she guessed, and he shook his head.

"He isn't easy to get working. The guy takes more breaks than any five people would need."

"He's not used to that much manual labor, Sinclair. He's a writer."

He snorted, his eyes blazing with frustration. "He could write and have a job that helps pay his bills. Instead, he's relying on his wife's teaching job to see them through."

"He works. He designs websites for twenty businesses. Most of them are in Seattle or Spokane."

"He didn't tell me that." Sinclair frowned, the tiny lines near his eyes crinkling, the scar a pale slash against his tan skin.

"I don't think he tells many people. I only know because I do Gavin and Lauren's taxes."

"Seems like an odd thing to hide."

"It seems odd that everyone in town assumes he's living off of Lauren and that he doesn't want to support his family, but they do." *It seems odd that* you *assume the same.* She kept the thought to herself. She didn't want to get between brothers. She had enough trouble dealing with her own family.

"It's not like there haven't been a long line of Jeffersons who have done the same. It's a valid assumption," he pointed out.

She shrugged, turning on the coffeepot and taking two mugs from the cupboard. She hadn't intended to offer him a cup of coffee. Then again, she hadn't intended to have him in her kitchen. "I prefer to not assume things. I prefer to have the facts before I judge."

She had cookies in one of the higher cupboards, hidden away until after the wedding. She thought Sinclair might like one, so she levered up on her toes, reaching for the tin.

"Let me," he murmured, his breath ruffling the hair at her nape.

God, he was close!

Did the man know nothing about personal space?

She eased out from between him and the counter, her cheeks so hot she wanted to splash ice water on them. "Thanks. That top cupboard is a little hard to reach."

"You could store them somewhere else." He set the tin of shortbread on the counter, muscles rippling beneath his coat. At least she assumed they were rippling. She couldn't actually see them through the thick down.

"That would have made them too easy to access. I've got that dress —"

"I thought we agreed that the dress was

the one with the problem." He cut her off, opening the tin and holding it out to her. Beautiful golden shortbread cookies lay inside, some of them dotted with dark chocolate chips.

Her stomach growled, and he smiled. "Don't bother telling me you're not hungry."

"I wasn't going to."

"And don't tell me that you have to lose weight. You're perfect the way you are."

"No need for compliments, Sinclair," she said, her cheeks blazing even hotter. "I was planning to share the cookies. So sit down and be quiet, or I might change my mind and keep them for myself."

To her surprise, he did what she asked, dropping into one of the dinette chairs, his long legs stretched out beneath the table.

"Aside from my drive here," he said as she put a cup of coffee in front of him, "this is the first time I've sat all day."

"Were you heading back to your brother's place when you saw Tiny?" she asked, placing a few of the shortbread cookies on a plate and setting it in front of him.

She had leftover roast in the fridge, and she actually considered taking it out and heating it up for him.

Not a good move if she planned to keep

him from complicating her life. Which she did.

"I haven't been back to the apartment since this morning." He sipped coffee, rubbed his knee, and winced. "I was heading there when I found Tiny."

"That's funny," she said, an image of that light shining down onto the awning filling her head.

"What?"

"One of the lights was on there. I saw it when I was leaving the shop. I thought you were back."

"I was in the woods. Chasing your dog." He stood, grabbed a couple of cookies, and headed for the door. "Guess I better go check things out."

"It might be a better idea to call the police."

"Because there's a light on in the apartment?"

"Because there could be someone in there."

"I think we've had this conversation before," he responded. "And, if I remember correctly, you had a smudge of chocolate on your face then, too." He ran a finger across her cheek, touched the corner of her mouth, stared into her eyes for about six seconds longer than was probably necessary.

Then he was gone, walking across the yard and climbing in his truck. She stood in the doorway, Tiny trying desperately to squeeze between her and the door.

"Sorry, you've got to stay here," she said, closing the door and rubbing at her cheek, trying to wipe away the warmth of Sinclair's fingers.

It didn't work. The warmth remained as she coerced Tiny into the mud room, gave him a dozen chew toys to play with, and headed back to the shop to make a few dozen more chocolate hearts.

CHAPTER FIVE

The apartment was empty. Just like Sinclair had known it would be. The light in the office was on, though, and that bothered him. He hadn't been in the office. Not the previous night and not that morning. He'd moved his stuff in, dragged his suitcase into the bedroom, and left the rest of the apartment alone.

He flicked the switch on the office wall, plunging the room into darkness, and waited for something to happen.

Nothing did, but the demons that were always clawing at the back of his mind insisted he was in danger.

He searched the apartment again, checking under the bed and in the closets, his heart pounding frantically.

"Idiot," he hissed, frustrated with himself and his weakness.

He knew he was fine, damn it!

But his body sure as hell didn't.

125

He walked into the living room, grabbed his cell phone, and called Janelle. Maybe she'd been in the apartment earlier, picking something up for her father-in-law. If so, that would explain the light that had been off suddenly being on.

"Sinclair!" Janelle answered on the first ring. "What a pleasant surprise! How are things working out at the apartment?"

"They'd be better if someone hadn't been in here while I was gone today," he responded, his voice raspier and rougher than he'd intended.

"Someone was in the apartment?" she asked, her surprise obvious.

"The light in the office was on when I got back. I thought maybe you'd stopped by to pick something up for your father-in-law."

"I've already removed Byron's things. Even if I hadn't, I wouldn't have entered the apartment without your permission," she responded, indignation dripping from every word. "The place is yours for the duration of the rental agreement, and according to that, I have to give you twenty-four-hour notice before entering the property."

He knew that, he'd read it in the contract.

He ran a hand over his hair and rubbed the tense muscles in his neck. "I'm not accusing you of breach of contract, Janelle. Just asking if you were here."

"I wasn't." She was quiet for a moment, the silence filled with the soft creaks and groans of the old building. "But it's possible Adeline was. She and Byron are very close. I'll give her a call, let her know that she can't just barge into your personal space."

"I don't think it was Adeline."

"I'll talk to her anyway. I want you to be comfortable in the apartment, Sinclair. Your happiness is of the utmost concern to me."

"Janelle, that really isn't —"

She hung up, was probably already pressing speed-dial to contact her daughter.

"Shit," he said quietly.

He'd have to fix this.

He headed down the exterior stairs, the cold wind spearing through his T-shirt and jeans and burrowing into his bones. It wasn't just his knee that was aching now. His whole leg hurt. He gritted his teeth, every step sending what felt like jagged glass up through his kneecap and into his thigh.

His mood went from bad to worse, and he thought about turning around, going back up to his apartment, grabbing his keys, and finding the closest dive bar.

That would be the easy answer to his problems, and he'd stopped taking the easy road three years ago.

He knocked on the shop door, the sound jarring in the evening quiet. He knocked again, rapping so hard his knuckles hurt. It didn't make him feel any better.

The door opened a crack, and Adeline peered out. "I figured it was you," she said.

"And I figured your mother was probably already on the phone with you."

"You figured right." She opened the door the rest of the way, gestured for him to enter.

The place was a mess, bowls piled in the large sink, chocolate plastered to the sides of them, drips of chocolate on the floor and splattered on the backsplash. A cell phone lay on the counter, a clear bowl turned upside down on top of it. He could swear he could hear Janelle's voice through the glass.

"It didn't look like this when the shop was open. Everything was nice and sterile and tidy. Just the way Granddad likes it," Adeline said, her gaze skirting over the mess in the sink and on the counter. "Things get a little crazy when I'm working on my fudge-making skills."

She also looked like she was working on not crying, her eyes a little glassy, her cheeks pale. She gnawed on her lower lip as if that might actually solve whatever problem she was having.

"I won't keep you from it," he responded. "I just came down to apologize."

"For my mother?" She laughed, the sound shaky. "There's no need."

"For myself. I shouldn't have called her." He walked to the sink, turned on the water, and ran it until it was so hot steam drifted into the air.

"You had every right to call her with your concerns."

"Is that a direct quote?" he asked, looking up from the dish soap he was pouring under the stream of hot water.

"Good guess, Sinclair. That is exactly what she said to me. Word for word. She's probably still saying it, reiterating the same point over and over again as she attempts to make me feel guilty for something I didn't do."

"You sound bitter."

"I'm overwhelmed. Tiny is home, locked in my mudroom until I can get back to him. May wants her wedding favors yesterday. That stupid dress is still broken and it still doesn't fit. I could go on" — she jabbed at a whiteboard that had the list from hell scrawled on it, twenty items or more scribbled in different areas and different colors — "but I won't."

"What's the list for?"

"It's everything I need to get done. There's not one thing checked off, Sinclair. Not one." She rubbed her forehead, must have suddenly realized that he was washing dishes.

She frowned, reaching past him and turning off the water. "Don't do that."

"Why not?"

"Because you don't work here, and if Janelle —"

"How about we get one thing off your list?" He wiped his hands on a dishcloth and grabbed the phone from under the bowl, Janelle's voice ringing out into the room.

"What are you doing!? That's not on my list!" Adeline whispered, trying to grab the phone from his hand.

"Janelle?" He interrupted Janelle's diatribe, catching her midword. "This is Sinclair. Adeline is busy. She has a lot of fudge to make. She'll call you when she finishes. Bye."

He hung up.

Adeline stared at him for about three seconds, and then shook her head. "Wow," she said.

"What?"

"Just . . . wow. I don't think Janelle has ever had anyone hang up on her."

"I didn't hang up on her. I ended the conversation."

He went to the sink, turned the water back on, and started scrubbing one of the bowls. It was vintage. A giant yellow Pyrex bowl that looked like it had been used a few thousand times.

He liked that. Liked the little scratches in the exterior color. It whispered of things that lasted.

"Really, Sinclair." Adeline pressed in beside him, took the bowl from his hand, and dried it with a clean dish towel. "I can't ask you to help me with these."

"You didn't," he pointed out, grabbing another bowl. Pink with stripes. It fit the candy theme, and he wondered if Adeline's grandmother had picked it. He remembered Alice. She'd had a loud laugh and a soft smile. She'd also been quick to hand out samples of the candies she and her husband made.

Not just candy, either. There'd been times when she'd handed him a paper bag with sandwiches or a Tupperware bowl filled with stew. "We had leftovers," she'd always say. "It's just sitting there rotting in the fridge. You think you and your brother can keep it from going to waste?"

They always had, because Elijah's idea of

cooking had been opening a can of soup and sticking a spoon in it.

He frowned, placing the bowl in the drainer, his arm brushing Adeline's taut abdomen. He felt the silkiness of her T-shirt, the hint of warm flesh beneath, and everything he'd been thinking — all the memories that had been clawing at his mind — faded away.

"I really don't feel comfortable with this," Adeline murmured, and he wasn't sure if she meant him washing dishes or them standing so close that he could feel every breath, smell the hint of chocolate and berries on her skin.

"I can leave if you want me to." He set the pink bowl in the drainer and turned to face her. "But sometimes people don't do things because they're asked. Sometimes they do them because if they don't keep busy, all the things they're running from will catch up to them."

Her eyes went soft, and he wanted to tell her not to pity him. He didn't want or need that from anyone.

"Okay," she finally said. "Wash the dishes. I need to make another batch of fudge."

That was it.

No questions, no digging, no probing at all the old wounds the way Kendra had always done when he'd woken bathed in sweat and fighting an unseen enemy. He'd tried to extend a little grace, allow her to try the best way she could to understand what he was going through. He'd given her what he could, but that had never seemed to be enough.

In the end their relationship had faded out like a sunset over the ocean. Brilliant to black, the process gradual, then quick. He hadn't even realized it was happening until they'd sat across the table from each other one night, looked into each other's eyes, and mutually agreed they felt nothing but affection for one another and that affection wasn't enough.

He finished the last bowl, snagged a handful of spoons from the water, scrubbed and rinsed them, Adeline's off-tune humming making him smile.

"I was playing that on my guitar last night," he said as she butchered "Bridge Over Troubled Water."

"I heard you." She stirred a pot on the gas stove, a thermometer stuck over the edge of it. He liked the apron she'd tied around her waist, the tilt of her head as she looked into the pot. Or maybe he just liked not being alone in that apartment with anxiety pounding through his blood.

"I'll try to keep it down next time," he said, and she met his eyes, shook her head.

"Why would you do that? It was like listening to a live concert while I was cleaning the kitchen. I liked it."

"Then I'll play louder when you're in the shop."

She laughed. "Will I have to pay a concert fee if you do?"

"I take payment in shortbread cookies," he responded, enjoying the banter and the company.

"Not chocolate?" She lifted the spoon, let the silky chocolate slide into the pot. "Because I have plenty of that."

"I don't think your grandfather will be happy if you start giving away his product."

"Trust me, he'll be more than happy for me to give this away." She lifted the pot and poured the chocolate into a square pan lined with some sort of paper.

"Why's that?" He moved closer, wanted to touch that little smudge of chocolate at the corner of her mouth again. Just to see how she'd react.

"It tastes like . . . regular old fudge. Nothing special. Nothing that people are going to travel hundreds of miles to buy." She dipped a finger into the empty pot, tasted the chocolate, and scowled. "I just don't

134

know what I'm doing wrong."

"You have a recipe?"

"Of course, and I'm following it exactly. For some reason, though, I can't get it right."

"Want some help?" he asked, as if he knew something about making fudge.

He didn't, so it was just as well that Adeline shook her head. "Granddad would kill me if I let someone who wasn't family in on the secret recipe. Besides," she continued, eyeing the pan of fudge as if she thought scorpions were going to crawl out of it, "I have to figure it out. It's a point of pride, a rite of passage."

"Says Byron?"

"Says me. But I don't think I'm going to figure it out tonight, and I've got a boatload of accounting work to catch up on, and then there's Tiny. He may have chewed through the mudroom door by now." She took off her apron, hung it on a hook near the door, grabbed a dry-erase marker from a drawer, and walked to the whiteboard.

"Fudge attempt number ninety," she said, putting a line through one of the items. "Complete."

"And the kitchen is clean," he added, leaning past her and running his finger through another one of the items.

"Not quite. I still need to . . ." She turned, and they were so close he could see deep blue flecks in her violet eyes, see that little smudge of chocolate at the corner of her mouth and the golden tips to her red lashes.

Whatever she'd been planning to say must have gotten lost in the moment, in the quick zip of heat that seemed to spark between them.

Her cheeks went bright red, and she scurried away, grabbing a broom from a closet.

"You should probably go," she said, and he thought she was right.

He *should* go.

He didn't really *want* to go, though.

He wanted to take the broom and sweep the floor, and listen to Adeline hum another one of the songs he'd played.

Not good, Sinclair, his brain whispered.

Adeline was as deeply connected to Benevolence as anyone could be. Everywhere he'd gone, he'd heard her name. The diner. The hardware store. The Daily Grind. People loved her, and she seemed to love them. Why else would her whiteboard be filled with things she had to do for other people?

Chocolate hearts for May. Balance Jeb Forsythe's books. Make a batch of white chocolate bark for Maeve Henderson. Visit

136

Leticia Miller in the hospital. Call Janelle.

He ran a finger through that one, smudging the marker.

Lose ten pounds.

He ran a finger through that too.

"Hey!" She marched over, her eyes flashing, her cheeks still pink. "You can't just arbitrarily cross things off the list, Sinclair."

"You already spoke to your mother, and you don't need to lose ten pounds."

She scowled. "I do if I want to fit into the bridesmaid dress."

"You'll fit just fine." He let his gaze skim over her curves, because she looked damn good in a T-shirt and jeans.

"Easy for you to say," she murmured, turning away and sweeping the floor as if her life depended on it. "You're not going to be standing in front of Benevolence Baptist Church looking like a giant orange sausage."

"I can think of plenty of things you looked like in that dress, but a sausage isn't one of them."

She stopped sweeping, swung around. "I don't want to hear any of them. Not one."

"Okay," he said, because she was teary-eyed again, and he thought that had a lot more to do with the wedding and the list than it did the dress and the way she looked in it.

"Just okay? No platitudes? No compliments? No sweet words to soothe my ravaged ego?"

"I could give you a hundred compliments, Adeline, but it wouldn't change the way you feel."

"You're right about that." She sighed, leaning over to sweep a few crumbs into the dustpan, her jeans clinging to the curves she seemed so determined to lose.

"You know what the real problem is?" she continued, oblivious to the direction of his thoughts and his gaze.

That made him feel like the lowest kind of heel, so he took a dishrag and started scrubbing chocolate off the stainless steel counter, focusing his energy on something more productive than eyeing her gorgeous curves. "What?"

"I don't know how to say no. If I'd told Granddad I wouldn't run the shop or told May I couldn't be her maid of honor, or told my mother there was no way I was bringing a date to the wedding, I wouldn't be in the mess I'm in."

"You're *not* bringing a date to the wedding?" He glanced at the list. She'd written that in bold red: *Date to the wedding.*

"Nope, because first, I don't want a date to the wedding. Second, I don't have one to bring." She grabbed bowls from the drainer and stood on her toes to place them on a shelf.

And he found himself noticing again the way her jeans clung to slim thighs and rounded hips, the way her T-shirt pulled across full breasts.

"God knows, I've tried to find one. I've asked every friend, called in every favor, but the only person available is Randal Custard."

"Why not go with him then?"

"Obviously, you haven't met the guy. He's a jackass whose head is so big I'm surprised he can fit it through doorways and into his sporty little car." She paused. "He's the kind of guy who has a new girlfriend every few months. He wines and dines them with his family's money and then cuts them off when a younger, prettier model comes along. He's been married three times. And" — she took a deep breath — "he drives a Mazda." She spit that out as if it were poison, and he smiled.

"I take it you don't like Mazdas?"

"I don't like Randal, and I'm disgusted that he's my only option."

"So, don't go with anyone. You did say

that you didn't want a date, right?"

"Janelle wants me to have a date. Both my sisters will have dates, and I'll be her poor old spinster daughter who can't catch a man." There wasn't a hint of self-pity in her words, no real sound of regret or self-deprecation.

Still, he wanted to tell her that she was the farthest thing from a poor old spinster that he'd ever seen.

She snatched the rag from his hand and rinsed it in hot water, her shoulder pressing against his arm, tiny tendrils of hair curling at her nape.

He couldn't resist, or maybe he just didn't want to. He brushed the hairs from her neck, his fingers sliding over cool, smooth flesh.

She met his eyes, and there was something there between them, something so strong, so undeniable that he leaned in, was so close to tasting her lips that his blood burned with the need for it.

The back door flew open, a gust of icy wind racing in. Janelle raced in with it, her hair perfectly in place, her black coat swishing around slack-clad legs. She had gloves, a scarf, a purse hiked over her shoulder.

"Sinclair," she said, her gaze jumping from him to Adeline and back again. "Just the man I was looking for."

He didn't back away from Adeline.

Why would he?

He did straighten, moving himself a little out of range of her soft lips.

"If this is about the light on in the apartment, it's not a big deal."

"That isn't the way I see it." She crossed the room and set her purse on the counter. She opened it, pulling out a hardware bag. "You are my father-in-law's tenant, and I want you to feel secure in your new home."

"I'm plenty secure," he assured her, but she had a bee in her bonnet, and he didn't think she'd hear a word he said.

"I contacted a friend of mine. He's a locksmith. He'll be here first thing in the morning to change the doorknob and lock on your front door." She opened the bag, pulled out a generic doorknob that wasn't going to do the building justice.

"I can take care of it, Janelle," he offered, because there was no way in hell he was letting anyone put a modern doorknob on an antique door.

"Contractually, Byron is to pay for and handle any and all maintenance issues."

"This isn't a maintenance issue," he pointed out.

Janelle frowned. "It is a security issue, and

141

it's worrying me."

"There's no need to worry."

"I beg to differ," she responded, her attention turning to Adeline again. "You're sure you weren't up there today, Adeline?"

Holy cow! I almost kissed the man!

That was all Addie could think, and thinking it filled so much space in her head that she barely heard her mother's question.

"Adeline?!" Janelle snapped, her gaze razor sharp. "Were you in Byron's apartment today?"

"I already told you that I wasn't," she snapped right back.

"No need to get snippy, young lady." Janelle thrust the bag and doorknob in her direction. "You remember Noah Story?"

"Yes." Noah had been the workshop instructor at Benevolence High for most of Adeline's childhood.

"He's in town for May's wedding, and I mentioned the problem at Byron's apartment. He offered to install the new lock."

"He's already in town, and you've already seen him?" she asked, surprised and a little intrigued.

There was a story she'd heard. One that Janelle had refused to refute or confirm because she and Noah were key players in it. Childhood friends who might have become something more if Janelle hadn't fallen so hard for Brett Lamont, Noah and Janelle had remained friends through Janelle's marriage, through her early years of grief. They'd been such good friends that people had been sure they'd marry eventually, that long-term bachelor Noah would finally get a ring and pop the question.

Some people said that he had. Those people said that when Janelle refused to marry him, he'd left town, brokenhearted and finally willing to admit that the only woman he'd ever loved would never return his affection.

"We had coffee at the diner." Janelle studied the nail on her left index finger. "I think I'm going to have to get a new manicure before the wedding. This one just isn't holding up."

"How is Noah?" Adeline asked, getting right back to the thing she was most interested in.

"Spokane doesn't suit him the way he hoped it would. He's thinking about moving back to Benevolence," Janelle said as if it didn't matter.

That made Adeline think that it did matter.

A lot.

"So, you're planning to show him some properties?"

"Yes. I have a few in mind. He wants something small, and something close to town. He made some good investments and was able to retire early, but he's not the kind of guy who likes to be idle. He's planning to apply as a substitute teacher, maybe try to coach football again. The high school is looking for a coach, so it's good timing all the way around."

Janelle had learned a lot during their coffee meeting, but Adeline didn't point it out. Her mother wasn't one to open up about her feelings. She never shared her hopes and dreams, never talked about future plans unless they involved work. For as long as Adeline could remember, Janelle had done what was necessary to make sure her daughters thrived. She'd helped them navigate elementary school, middle school, high school. She'd pointed out their strengths, tried to move them toward reasonable goals. She'd enforced the importance of education, downplayed the importance of tradition, tried to balance out the Lamont legacy with her more practical outlook on life.

What she hadn't done was share her grief and sorrow, her disappointments and defeats. She'd never talked about her insecurities and vulnerabilities. She'd never ever let her daughters see the woman beneath the façade.

"I told him he could pick up the lock here when he is ready to install it," Janelle continued. "Since you're always at work at the crack of dawn, I didn't think you'd mind."

There was a hint of censure in her voice, as if Adeline's early mornings were a direct insult to Janelle's sensibilities.

Adeline ignored it. "I don't."

"I do," Sinclair cut in. "Byron's door is from the late nineteenth century. The lock needs to be the same."

"Does it matter?" Janelle asked. "As long as it fits —"

"A gunnysack would fit on a princess, but that doesn't mean she should wear it." He cut her off, and Adeline smiled.

She couldn't help herself.

Janelle frowned. "You may have a point, Sinclair, but I don't have time to hunt up a period lock to fit that door."

"I can find one, and I can install it."

"I wouldn't want to put you out."

"You'd be putting me out if you insisted on having that" — he gestured to the new lock — "installed. I make my living by ensuring that junk like that isn't put on beautiful old doors like Byron's."

"In that case," Janelle conceded, "I'll call Noah and tell him I won't be needing his help after all. Keep your receipt and bill me for your time, Sinclair. You're a very busy man, and I know that your expertise is of high value."

"I'll take my payment in shortbread cookies," Sinclair said as he crossed the room and opened the door. "See you around, Adeline."

That was it.

He was gone and the door was closed before she even said good-bye.

"What in God's name is going on, Adeline?" Janelle nearly shouted. "I could feel the sexual tension —"

"Mom!"

"What? You think because I'm fifty-three, I don't remember what desire feels like?"

"Can we stop now? Please?" She grabbed the bag and doorknob and thrust it at Janelle. "I have a million things to do before the wedding. I really don't have time for another lecture."

"Another one? When else did I lecture you?" She tucked the doorknob back in her purse. "By the way, May called me today. She's worried about the wedding favors. I told her that you had them under control."

"I do."

"You think you do, but I don't think you realize how much work five hundred wedding favors are going to be."

"Trust me. I realize it."

"You need to hire some help. I mentioned it to Byron this afternoon."

"Mom, I am seriously busy right now. Can we discuss this another time?"

"No time like the present, Adeline. Besides, you will be less busy if you hire someone. Byron always hires extra help for big events."

"Not in recent years, he hasn't."

"He *has.* You've been too busy with your accounting business to pay much attention. Last year, he hired Glenda Sherman to help with the town council's Valentine's Day gala."

"Glenda?" A war veteran who'd lost her legs in Afghanistan, she designed brochures and advertisements for a living, staying mostly to herself in a cute little rancher that had been made handicap accessible.

"He heard she needed a wheelchair for that racing she does. Paralympics? She's not one to take charity."

"She isn't one to take anything." Adeline had offered to do her taxes for free, but Glenda had very firmly said no.

147

"No, but she'll take a job if she's offered one, and Byron just so happened to mention that he needed help when she came in to buy fudge. She was quick to offer to help, and the way Byron tells it, she's one of the best workers he's ever hired."

"He never mentioned it to me." And she felt a little hurt that he hadn't. She and Byron were as close as a grandfather and granddaughter could be.

"Because you were gearing up for tax season, and he didn't want you to feel obligated to help him with the order."

"I wouldn't have felt obligated."

"You would have." Janelle sighed. "Just like you feel obligated to run this place like it's a one-woman show."

"I do not."

"You do. It's as if you think you have to prove something. You don't. You're a great young woman with a good head on your shoulders. You have a successful accounting business. Your worth is not wrapped up in whether or not you can do all this." She gestured around the shop. "On your own."

"I didn't think it was."

"Then prove it by hiring someone."

"Fine," she said, because she didn't have the energy or the time to argue, and because she really could use some help around the shop.

"Great." Janelle beamed. "I'm glad you agreed, because I already called Randal and asked him to run a help wanted ad. I also brought you this." She pulled a paper from her purse, held it up gleefully.

PART-TIME HELP NEEDED was emblazoned across the paper in bright pink letters.

"I'll just stick it to the window in the front door. By this time tomorrow, you should have people lining up, begging to learn how to make Lamont chocolates."

She hurried into the service area.

Adeline stayed right where she was, the sound of a guitar filling the sudden silence, the light strains of "Young at Heart" making her smile even though she sort of felt like she wanted to cry.

CHAPTER SIX

Janelle was right about Adeline needing help at the shop.

She was wrong about a line of people anxiously waiting to learn the fine art of chocolate making. The next day came and went and not one person called about the job. No one walked into the shop dressed to the nines and hoping to gain access to Chocolate Haven's kitchen. By the end of the day, Adeline had served six dozen customers, boxed and shipped three Internet orders, and received May's approval for the wedding favors. What she hadn't done was gotten an assistant.

She wiped down the display case, humming "Young at Heart" as she worked. She hadn't been able to get the song out of her head since she'd heard Sinclair playing it. Sinclair, who'd been on her mind almost as much as the song.

God! What was it about the man? No matter how hard she tried, she couldn't stop thinking about the way he'd looked when he'd told her that sometimes people stayed busy to keep the things they were running from at bay. She couldn't quite get that feeling out of her head either — the one that had zipped across her skin and made her want to throw herself into his arms. Heat and longing and something else. Something she wasn't sure she'd ever felt before and that she couldn't quite put a name to.

Whatever it was, she had to forget it.

Sinclair was in town until the Jefferson house was cleaned out and fixed up. Even if he'd planned to stay, she had no interest in long-term, short-term, or any-term relationships.

Friendship was great. Anything beyond that was a recipe for heartache. The way she saw things, one heartache in a lifetime was plenty.

She turned off the service area light, walked into the kitchen.

It was spotless. Every bowl washed and put away, every pan scrubbed to a high sheen. She'd wiped down the counters, cleaned the sink, mopped the floor.

She was getting the hang of running the shop.

Too bad she hadn't gotten the hang of

making the fudge.

Three pans of it sat on the counters, the tops glossy and smooth, one dotted with pecans, one swirled with rich dark chocolate, one plain. They looked beautiful, but she knew they tasted . . . good.

Not great.

Just . . . good.

And that wasn't going to be good enough.

She'd serve the three pans tomorrow when Anna Ellis brought her second grade class for a tour of the shop. The kids would eat and enjoy it regardless of Adeline's failures.

Speaking of which . . .

She snagged her gym bag from the hook near the back door, pulled her running clothes out. She'd managed to go the entire day without shoving her face full of chocolates and sweets. She'd microwaved her low-calorie, low-fat meal, sipped water dutifully throughout the day, and avoided anything and everything that might keep her from fitting into the dress.

She scowled, hurrying into the bathroom to change.

Tonight she'd actually get some exercise in. Mostly because Tiny was at Sandy Seaton's house, making good use of her large fenced yard. Sandy hadn't been all that keen on taking the puppy for the day, but Addie had called in a favor earned over several years of free tax preparation. Since Sandy's husband, John, was out of town on business, Addie figured she could ask her friend to dog sit.

She had until seven, and then Sandy was going to set the puppy loose on Benevolence. An idle threat, but Addie wasn't going to make Sandy wait. She'd do her half-hour run and then she'd go pick Tiny up, drop him off at home, and return to tackle a few dozen of the wedding favors. Time was ticking away, each day bringing her closer to the inevitable orange dress mess. At least if the favors were beautiful and tasty, people might overlook the garish tangerine sausage-casing.

She ran along Main Street, turned onto Patterson Place, bypassing a few shops that were still open. This was the touristy stretch of town — Jim's Sasquatch Hunting Gear, Lila's Bead Palace, the Doughnut Hole. They did most of their business during the fall and early winter, before the passes closed and the town became a time capsule waiting to be opened by the next round of visitors.

Nothing much ever changed. Not the white façade of the Baptist church or the dark brick of the Catholic parish church. Not the school or the park or even the shops that had been around for more years than Addie. The closest they'd come to true change had been May closing her fabric store and putting the building on the market. It would be a while before it sold, but Janelle was determined to bring someone progressive into the space. She'd showed the property to a few businessmen from Seattle, a guy from San Antonio, and business partners from Orlando. There'd been talk of a wine shop, an organic market, and a pottery, but so far none of it had panned out.

Addie wasn't disappointed in that. Secretly, she wanted May to come back from her honeymoon in Niagara Falls with a changed heart and a changed mind. Secretly, she wanted everything the way it had always been — predictable, easy, and comfortable.

She raced uphill, heading away from Main Street and deeper into the quiet little town. The houses were farther apart here, the old bungalows and stately Victorians built on large lots. For the most part, people kept those lots manicured and pretty. A few properties had seen better days. Those were the ones that Janelle said would be on the market one day. She was biding her time, waiting for the property owners to decide they'd had enough of small-town life. When that happened, she'd have those places sold before the FOR SALE signs went up.

She was hoping that Addie's house would be one of those properties. She mentioned it every time she talked about Willow and Brenna. They'd made their escapes from Benevolence. It was Addie's turn to do the same.

The problem was, Addie didn't want to escape.

She didn't want to go to a big city or a bustling suburb and get lost in the anonymity of too many people filling too much space. The way she saw it, some people spent a lifetime looking for a place to call home. She'd found hers early.

She made it to the top of the hill and stopped there, breath heaving, heart pounding. It didn't feel as bad as she'd thought it would. Except for the sweat that was now freezing on her cheeks, the icy burn of frigid air filling her lungs.

She swiped at the sweat, tried to slow her breathing. She could see Janelle's house from there, the property spread out over a few acres, the house huge compared to most Benevolence homes. She could have jogged

155

there, walked inside, chatted with Janelle for a while.

They didn't really have that kind of relationship, though. Willow and Brenna had always been more like Janelle. Addie? She was like her father or her grandfather or maybe like Alice. Whatever the case, she didn't mesh with her mother's style. She was too plain, too loud, too unpolished.

And she really did need to get her hair done.

She touched the end of her long braid as her watch beeped.

Time to head back to the shop.

Thank God!

Running might not have felt as bad as she'd thought it would, but it hadn't felt good either. She could check it off her list though. That made her happy, gave a little zing to her steps as she headed back down the hill.

Snap! Crack!

Something plunged through thick hedges to her right.

She went left.

She didn't know what was in the bushes, and she wasn't going to stick around to find out. This time of year, coyotes sometimes wandered through town. There'd been an occasional bear too — out early from hibernation and not all that happy about it.

She should have brought her bear spray or her whistle.

Instead she had her feet, which weren't carrying her away nearly fast enough. She sped down the hill for about three seconds before the thing caught her. It crashed into her back and she fell, her palms and knees skimming along the pavement as she slid down the hill.

Protect your neck! her brain shouted.

She brought her forearms up, shielding the back of her neck from attack. A warm, rough tongue rolled across her knuckles. Puppy breath tickled her ear. She opened her eyes, which she hadn't realized were shut, and looked into Tiny's fuzzy face.

"You!" she nearly shouted.

He barked happily, his tongue swiping across her cheek.

"For God's sake, Tiny! Can't you behave?" She stood, her yoga pants ripped at the knees, her palms dotted with dirt and speckled with blood.

Tiny didn't look repentant, but he sure seemed happy to see her. She didn't have a leash, so she just started walking, Tiny trotting along beside her as she headed back to the shop.

■ ■ ■ ■

God! He hated paperwork!

Sinclair eyed his computer screen, his legs stretched out beneath Byron's old dinette table, his laptop taunting him. He had a bid to write up, and he had to make sure it was a good one. Handwritten notes lay beside the laptop, a few photos lying on top of it. Bidding for a contract was his least favorite part of his business. He'd put it off indefinitely if he didn't have a crew who counted on him to keep the jobs coming in.

Not that they didn't have plenty of work to keep them busy. More often than not, jobs found Sinclair. He was the best restoration specialist on the West Coast, and pretty damn close to being the best in the country. At least that's what write-ups in several national magazines claimed.

Sinclair didn't let it go to his head.

He had a fantastic crew working for him. Men and women who made it their mission to restore every building with historic accuracy in mind. With the team he had in place, he could handle almost any job. Currently he was eyeing an early twentieth-century schoolhouse on the outskirts of Portland. The city wanted to restore it and turn it into a community center. Sinclair wanted the job. Not for the money it would bring or any prestige he might gain from it. He wanted the job because two of the companies writing up bids were known for cutting corners and using modern fixtures in historic buildings. He'd seen some of their handiwork. He'd been hired to correct some of it.

No way did he want either company to get the job.

On the other hand, he wanted to make a profit.

He lifted the photos, studied the double-wide front door opening. It had been boarded up years ago, the door removed. He probably had a replacement in his warehouse. He could donate that, donate a couple dozen doorknobs and some replacement tiles for the two bathrooms.

Somewhere outside a dog barked, the sound barely registering as he recalculated his bid, typed in the estimate for labor and materials. He wouldn't be as low as the other two companies, but his reputation might win him the contract.

The dog barked again, the sound of someone or something bounding up the exterior metal stairs bringing Sinclair to his feet.

Tiny?

He opened the door and the dog barged in, skidding across the wood floor and slamming into the couch.

"Enough," Sinclair commanded, and the dog rolled onto his back, his tail wagging frantically.

Adeline raced into the apartment a few seconds later.

"Oh my gosh! I'm so sorry!" she cried as she ran to Tiny and tried to pull him up by the scruff. "This dog has no manners!"

"I'm the one who opened the door," he replied, but she was too busy trying to get the dog to his feet to hear.

"Tiny," she growled. "Get up! I have to take you home, and then I have to work."

At the shop? She didn't look dressed for it. As a matter of fact, she looked like she'd been out for a run, her legs encased in black spandex, her torso covered by a thick vest. She looked . . . rough . . . her hair escaping its tight braid, bloody knees peeking out from holes in her running pants.

"Did he escape the neighbor's again?" he asked, and she shook her head, her violet eyes the only hint of color in her face.

"My friend had him in a fenced yard. Plenty of room to run around, but I guess not enough for him." She wrapped her arms around Tiny's torso. "Up, you naughty boy!"

"I think he passed naughty a while ago." Sinclair snapped his fingers to get Tiny's attention. The dog jumped up, then settled down onto his haunches, tongue lolling.

"And I passed *patient* around the same time. I'm working up to full-out *pissed*," she responded, her gaze on the dog. "This is the last straw, Tiny. Tomorrow you're going to Spokane for obedience training."

"Wouldn't it be easier to find someone around here who could train him?"

"Based on the way things have gone the past few weeks," she said, plucking at the torn fabric of her yoga pants, "I'd say no."

"He tripped you?"

"He *tackled* me. One minute I was jogging along, feeling pretty good about how much I'd accomplished today. The next thing I knew, a giant puppy was jumping on my back."

"You could have really been hurt," he commented as he grabbed a wad of paper towel, ran it under warm water, and dabbed gravel and dirt from her knees.

"I know, and Nehemiah is much more fragile than I am. So is the friend Tiny stayed with today. Much as I hate to do it, I've got to send him somewhere to get some serious training."

"Puppy boot camp?"

161

"More like K-9 boot camp. I have a friend who works for the Spokane County Police K-9 unit. He and Tiny have met."

"And he offered to train the dog?"

"Yes, but first he offered to take Tiny off my hands. He said that with the right training Tiny would be a good fit for K-9 work."

"You're kidding, right?" he asked as the dog circled the kitchen, tried to squeeze under the table, and nearly flipped it and Sinclair's work.

"I'm not, and neither was Josh. He's called two or three times to see if I've changed my mind about keeping Tiny."

"Have you?"

"No. Tiny is a good dog waiting to happen."

"Meaning he's a bad puppy?"

"He's not bad. He's just . . . busy."

"He's crazy, Adeline. Admitting it and asking for help is the first step in recovery."

She laughed, dropping into a chair, her raw knees jutting out from torn fabric. "Thanks."

"For?"

"Making me laugh. I was starting to feel a little sorry for myself."

"Because Tiny is a pain in the butt?"

"Because I was having a pretty great day right up until he tackled me."

"You can still have a great day. Just leave Tiny with me while you finish your work."

"You seriously do not want my dog in your apartment."

"It's your grandfather's apartment. I'm just leasing the space."

"Exactly. You're leasing it. Which means you're spending money to have a nice quiet place to relax when you're not trying to fix up the rotting corpse of your brother's life."

She must have suddenly realized what she'd said, or maybe she just realized how it sounded. Her cheeks went three shades of red.

"God! I am so sorry. That was one of the stupidest things I've said in a long time."

"Then you must not say very many stupid things," he responded. Truth was truth, after all. He was just as quick to dish it out as anyone, and he was always willing to have it tossed at him.

"I say plenty of stupid things. Just ask Janelle. She'll be happy to fill you in on my verbal transgressions. Speaking of which, I'd better get Tiny home and get back to work. Opening my mouth and agreeing to make a bunch of chocolate for May's wedding" — she shook her head, her braid flopping over her shoulder, loose strands of hair floating wildly around her face — "is at the top of the stupid-things-I've-said list."

"You put up a HELP WANTED sign." He'd seen it posted on Chocolate Haven's front door.

"Do you know how many people have applied?"

"None?" he guessed, and she smiled wryly.

"Exactly."

"Maybe Byron has some ideas. People he's hired for seasonal work who'd be interested in coming back for a couple of weeks."

"We already thought of that, but Glenda Sherman, who we offered the job to, couldn't take it." She stood and stretched, the edges of her vest and T-shirt riding up to reveal pale, silky skin, and just that quickly everything changed. The impersonal discussion about business and dogs and brothers faded, and he was looking at a funny, quirky woman with wild hair and smooth skin that was just begging him to touch it.

And, God, he wanted to. He wanted to slide his finger along that little sliver of flesh, feel the warmth of silky skin and the soft curves.

He clenched his fist and turned away.

"I've been in the contracting business for a long time," he said, his voice still gritty with longing for a woman who belonged to a world he wanted no part of: small town, close ties, responsibility for everyone and everything in the community. "I've been in the same situation you're in more times than I can count — too many jobs and not enough hands to do them."

"You must be anxious to get back to your home base," she said, her hand flitting over his notebook and the photos of the old schoolhouse. "Is this one of your projects?"

"Not yet. I'm working up a bid for it, hoping to go to contract next month."

"Portland, right?" She lifted a photo, her fingers long and slim, her nails short. No polish or prettiness. None of that sweet-smelling lotion that Kendra used to keep her hands soft and smooth. "I spent summers there when I was in college, interning at an accounting firm. It's a cool city, very pretty and lots of things to do."

"You didn't want to stay?"

"Why would I?" She looked up from the photos, her eyes that deep violet blue that made him want to look and just keep on looking.

"Because it's a cool city with lots of things to do?"

She shrugged, her attention on the photos again. "Portland isn't home."

"Any place can be home if you want it to be."

"That's exactly it." She replaced the photos and stood so that they were just inches apart, the crown of her head barely reaching his chin. "I don't want to make my home anywhere else. You may think that Benevolence is too small, too quaint, too —"

"I never said any of those things."

"You didn't have to. You moved away, and you didn't come back."

"Come back to what? You've always had a home here, Adeline. You've always had family and a community that loves you. I've always had a shack filled with junk and a reputation for being *one of those Jefferson boys.*"

"Trust me," she murmured, walking to Tiny and trying to tug him to his feet. "That is not what you have a reputation for."

"No?" He moved in next to her, his hands brushing hers as he grabbed the dog by its scruff. "Maybe you should tell me what I do have a reputation for, then."

"I'm not sure you can handle it, Sinclair." She grunted as the dog finally lumbered up, then dropped back down again. "What with all your successes, you just might get like Randal Custard."

"A head so big I can't fit through a door-way?"

"Exactly."

"Now I'm really curious." He stepped over the dog, moving into Adeline's space because she was there, and he was, and that smile made him think of all the things he was missing being a bachelor, all the things he'd enjoyed about being part of a couple.

"So tell me, Adeline," he murmured, his hands settling on her shoulders, his thumbs sliding along the silky column of her neck. "What *are* people saying about me?"

"It would take me an hour to cover every-thing." She ducked away from his hands, her cheeks bright red. "Neither of us has the time for that."

"I could make the time."

"I couldn't. I have a dozen things to finish tonight. Tiny," she called to the dog as she half ran to the front door, "we need to go."

The dog stayed right where he was, belly up, tail thumping.

"Tiny!" She tried again, her cheeks still blazing, her gaze darting from the dog, to the floor, to the couch. Everywhere in the room except for Sinclair.

"You can leave him here," he said, and she finally met his eyes.

"He'll drive you crazy."

167

"Maybe."

"And Janelle —"

"Do you really care what Janelle thinks?" He took a step toward her, smiling as she backed away. "There's no need to be nervous, Adeline."

"Who says I'm nervous?"

"If you back up any further, you're going to go through the door."

"Look, Sinclair," she said, swiping a stray piece of hair off her cheek, "I'm going to be blunt. I don't have time for chitchat, and I don't have time for games."

"What games?"

"The kind where you look at me like I'm a glossy piece of Lamont family fudge, and you're a starving man. The kind where you tell me all kinds of things that I want to hear because you're hoping to get something that I'm not going to give."

"If I were going to tell you things you wanted to hear, I wouldn't be talking about your mother or your dog. I'd be talking about the way your hair looks in the moonlight or the way your eyes glow when you're smiling. I'd be telling you that there aren't many women who'd take over a chocolate shop for their grandfather or wear an ugly orange dress for their grandmother's friend."

"There are plenty of women who'd do both those things," she countered, but he wasn't in the mood for a debate. He wasn't really in the mood for a conversation. He'd been in Benevolence for too long, listening to Gavin for too many hours at a time. He was starting to feel antsy, and that wasn't a good thing. Not when a woman like Adeline was standing in front of him.

"That's not the point, Adeline," he responded. "The point is, I'm not into chitchat, and I'm not into games. If I were, I'd be doing more than thinking about kissing you."

That was it.

She was off like a shot, opening the door and racing out onto the landing, calling to Tiny as she went.

The dog didn't respond.

Not a surprise. The mutt had a mind of his own.

Sinclair could have followed Adeline, but there wasn't much to add to what had already been said. He *didn't* play games, and he *didn't* do chitchat. And he *did* want to taste her lips, feel her smooth skin under his palms.

He wasn't going to act on either thing, because Adeline didn't seem like the kind of woman who'd be happy for a week or two, and he wasn't the kind of guy who planned to give more than that.

The dog whined as he closed the door.

"You made your choice, Tiny," he muttered, dropping into the chair and eyeing the pile of photos and the computer file. "So have I. Now we're both stuck with it."

Tiny lumbered across the room and dropped down next to Sinclair's feet.

He ignored the dog the same way he was ignoring the voice inside his head that was telling him to go downstairs, walk into Chocolate Haven's kitchen, and show Adeline just exactly what would happen if either of them was willing to take a little time out for games.

CHAPTER SEVEN

Three dozen chocolate favors complete. Thirty-eight dozen plus to go. Adeline carefully slid a box onto the pantry shelf she'd cleared, peeking inside it to make sure the favors were as pretty as they'd been when she'd packed them.

They were perfect.

That should have been enough to make her smile, but her legs hurt from her run, her knees hurt from her fall, and Tiny was still upstairs with Sinclair. That situation had some positives. First, Tiny wasn't home alone. Second, he wasn't wandering around the neighborhood getting into trouble. Third, Sandy had been so relieved when Adeline called to tell her that she'd found Tiny, that she'd promised to watch him the next time her husband was out of town.

Those were all good things.

Great even.

On the flip side, at some point Adeline

was going to have to retrieve the puppy. That would mean facing Sinclair, and that wasn't something she was in the mood to do.

Not that she didn't like Sinclair. She did. That was the problem. She liked him enough that *like* could turn to something else if she let it. A few more smiles, a few more heated glances, one more second of his thumbs sliding along her skin, and she'd be chasing after him the same way she'd chased after Adam a hundred eons ago. She knew exactly how that would turn out.

She wasn't going there.

Not in a million years.

She stalked back into the kitchen, eyed the tempered milk chocolate that she'd left on the counter. It looked gorgeous — silky and smooth and creamy. She didn't taste it. Just poured it into molds that had already been piped with dark chocolate, set the timer for the molds, and left the lot sitting where it was. She'd learned from trial and error that messing with the molds after she poured the chocolate led to disaster.

She flipped through Granddad's clipboard, checking the list of candies that she had to make for the following day, then compared it to a dozen online orders that had come in and needed to be filled. How

Byron had managed to keep the place running on his own, she didn't know. As far as she could see, Chocolate Haven was a multi-employee business.

Maybe she should have realized that before her grandfather ended up in the hospital.

She frowned. She'd never thought of herself as selfish or self-absorbed. Maybe she'd just been blind to what was going on right in front of her face. After all, she'd been stopping in at Chocolate Haven every Monday and Thursday for as long as she could remember, and even in the days leading up to Byron's fall she hadn't noticed him being anything other than cheerful and happy. Overwhelmed? She'd have said he wasn't. Not even a bit. But Byron was a proud man. He probably wouldn't have admitted to being overwhelmed even if he was.

She measured sugar into a large pot, added butter, and started melting it down. The recipe card for caramel nougat was in the box on the counter. She didn't have to pull it out. She'd made the candies dozens of times since her grandfather's accident. It had taken a few trial runs to get it right, but she'd finally gotten the hang of it. She watched as the sugar bubbled and turned a beautiful deep brown.

Someone knocked on the front door as she added marshmallow fluff to the caramel, then folded it in with chopped peanuts and vanilla that she'd made from her grandmother's recipe book — vodka and vanilla bean. Simple as could be, but more flavorful than store-bought.

Whoever it was knocked again. She ignored the summons. The shop was closed. Anyone who was anyone who knew or needed her would come around to the back and walk in.

She had dozens of small cupcake wrappers sitting on trays, and she pulled on disposable gloves and scooped nougat out of the pan with a tiny melon baller. She smoothed it with her palms, dropped it into the white wrapper. She'd have three dozen when she finished.

Someone pounded on the back door, and she screamed, nearly dropping the nougat ball she was smoothing.

"Hold on!" she shouted, setting the ball into a wrapper and tossing the gloves into the trash. It couldn't be May or Janelle. Both would have walked in without knocking. She doubted it was Sinclair. He'd have knocked on the back door first rather than walking around to the front.

She opened the door, expecting to see someone she knew. Maybe a friend who'd stopped in to say hello or a customer hoping to buy some chocolate after hours. Instead she saw a teenage boy, his dark hair hanging to his shoulders, his gaze direct. She didn't recognize him, and that surprised her. She was familiar with most of the families in Benevolence, knew most of the people by name who lived there. Those whose names she didn't know, she could have easily picked out of a lineup.

This kid, though, was a complete stranger.

She hadn't ever seen him before, and that made her nervous. Sure, strangers came to Benevolence. The town had a pretty healthy tourist season. This wasn't it. Even if it had been, most tourists wouldn't knock on a closed shop door.

"Can I help you?" she asked, doing her best to look relaxed and unintimidated. Not that the kid was trying to be intimidating. He looked as uncomfortable as she felt, his hands hanging limp at his sides, his jacket a few inches too short in the sleeves. His khaki pants were short too, just barely touching the top of his scuffed dress shoes.

"I saw your sign," the kid said, his Adam's apple bobbing up and down beneath the buttoned collar of a wrinkled button-down shirt.

"My sign?"

"About needing help," he said quietly. He had a deep voice for how young he looked, and a direct gaze that made her think that maybe she'd misjudged his age.

"You're looking for a job?" She hadn't planned to sound so surprised, but that's how the words came out. Like the poor kid didn't look like he had any business inquiring about a sign she'd posted for the public to see.

To his credit, his gaze never wavered. "Yes, ma'am. I am."

"Do you have experience in the kitchen?"

"I cooked for my mom when she was sick. Other than that, no."

It was an honest answer, and she appreciated that.

If he'd been one of the local teens, maybe one of the kids who came in after school to buy a couple bucks' worth of sweets for his girlfriend, she'd have had him fill out an application. She could train someone who was willing to learn. God knew she'd been training herself for the past few weeks!

This kid wasn't someone she knew, though. She had no idea where he'd come from or how he'd happened upon her HELP

WANTED sign. "Any paid work experience?"

"I was a busser at Denny's in Houston. I can give you the manager's contact information for a reference."

"Houston is a long way from here," she pointed out as if either of them could have any doubt about that.

"My mom died a couple of months ago. I didn't have any other family in Houston, so I decided to spend some time with my dad. He lives in Ellensburg. I packed everything I had and drove there, but Dad and I don't see things the same way, and I decided to head back to Houston."

It was a pat answer, a rehearsed one, and for the first time since she'd opened the door, he glanced away.

"You're young to be driving across the country alone." She knew she should send him on his way. He had no experience and his story seemed too pat, but it was freezing out and he was standing there in his too-short pants and lightweight jacket, and she couldn't make herself tell him to go.

"I'm eighteen, ma'am. Nineteen in a month." He pulled a wallet from his pocket, opened it so that she could see his driver's license. The photo was obviously him, the birthdate matching what he'd said.

"Well, Chase Lyons," she said, reading his

name off the license. "You sure look young."

He cocked his head to the side, studied her for a moment. "So do you, but you're running this shop."

"It's my grandfather's shop. I'm just filling in while he recovers from an injury."

"Doesn't matter whose shop it is, ma'am. I still need a job, and you're still looking for help. I don't know anything about chocolate except how to eat it, but I'm a quick study."

"How long are you planning to stay in Benevolence?"

"Long enough to earn the money to put a new carburetor in my Corvette so I can get back to Houston."

"You have a Corvette?"

"Nineteen seventy-four." For the first time since she opened the door, he smiled. "Belonged to my grandfather. He gave it to my mom before he passed. She gave it to me before . . ." He shook his head, the smile fading. "Anyway, the carburetor is shot. I made it to the campsite outside of town. You know it?"

"Sun Valley?" The place had been around since the fifties and attracted RV enthusiasts year-round, the two-thousand-acre campground was the perfect place for travelers to park for a night or two.

"I guess. I was too busy pushing the

178

Corvette to pay much attention to the sign. The guy who owns it is letting me park in the lot until I can get the car fixed. Should only cost me a few hundred bucks."

"It won't take you long to earn that amount, and I need help until my grand-father is able to return." That was the perfect excuse to send Chase away, and she latched onto it.

"I'll need money for gas too, ma'am. And food."

"There are a few other places in town that are hiring. They could probably use you for a week or two."

"I put in an application at the hardware store this afternoon, but the owner didn't seem all that enthusiastic about hiring a stranger. Same for the gas station. They need a janitor, but they said they've got plenty of local high school kids applying." His teeth chattered, and he tugged the edges of his jacket together.

She almost told him to zip it up, but then she realized the zipper was broken, the fabric threadbare. There was a tiny rip in the shoulder that had been patched with large stitches.

It reminded her of Marvin Smith's jacket. The one his wife, Millie, hated with a passion and was constantly threatening to toss.

Only Marvin's jacket had a rip in the right cuff.

She eyed Chase's cuff, saw the rip in it. For a moment, she had a clear image of the teen climbing into Dumpsters, trying to find clothes that would work for a job interview. It made her heart hurt, made her want to drag him inside, feed him a hot meal, offer him enough money to get him back where he was going.

She pushed the image away, because she knew what she *shouldn't* do. She shouldn't make him another one of her projects.

"There are a lot of kids who need jobs," she managed to say.

"Have they applied here?"

"Not yet, but I'm sure they will once they hear about the job opening."

He nodded, his shoulders slumping. "I can't suddenly become a local, ma'am, but I can promise you this: If you hire me, I'll stick around until your granddad is back. If that means staying for a few months, I'll stay." He shivered again, and she couldn't take it any longer. She stepped aside and motioned for him to come in.

"How about I make some hot chocolate, and we discuss it?"

"I'm here to apply for the job, not ask for charity."

"You're not asking for anything. I'm offering you something hot to drink because it's the polite thing to do, and because my mother raised me to be that way."

"My mother raised me to pay my own way. If I drink your hot chocolate —"

"Chase," she said, cutting him off, "it isn't charity to take a cup of hot chocolate that someone offers you. Now, go on in the service area. Sit at one of the tables. I'll have the hot chocolate for you in a few minutes."

"I *could* do that," he responded, pulling his hair into a ponytail and grabbing a hairnet from a box near the sink. "Or I could help you finish these things." He gestured to the caramel nougats. "Looks like the mix will harden if it's not shaped soon."

"It will, but I can make another batch."

"That would be a waste of good ingredients, ma'am," he responded as he scrubbed his hands, put on a pair of disposable gloves, and scooped nougat with the melon baller. "And that doesn't make any kind of business sense."

He was right about that.

She kept an eye on him as she set a small pot on the stove and poured milk into it. She let it simmer while she melted a couple squares of dark chocolate, mixed it into the milk, scooped in some sugar, and stirred. It

181

smelled good. Maybe even great. She wasn't drinking it, though. She had a dress to fit into, and she was getting closer to achieving that goal.

She glanced at the whiteboard. She'd rewritten the note about losing weight, and she imagined crossing that off the list. It was enough to make her smile, and if Chase hadn't been standing beside her, she might have hummed a few measures of "What a Wonderful World."

She grabbed Byron's lunch thermos, poured the chocolate into it. "Here you are," she said, handing it to Chase.

"Thank you." He set the thermos on the counter and went back to work, scooping up the last of the nougat and placing it into a wrapper.

"There! Finished!" he said triumphantly, his smile so broad and sincere that Addie couldn't help smiling in return.

"They look great."

"Where do you want me to put them?"

"The display case out front. This is part of tomorrow's inventory." She lifted one of the trays and led the way into the service area.

It didn't take long to fill the case. It took her even less time to decide to give Chase a chance. She needed help. He needed money.

It seemed like a win-win situation to her.

"That's it," she said as she placed the last nougat in the case. "Now, how about we sit down and talk for a minute?"

"You're interviewing me for the job?"

"I am."

"That's awesome, Ms. . . . ?"

"Lamont." She gestured to one of the wrought-iron tables that had been in the shop since its doors opened. "Go ahead and have a seat. I'll get the application from the office."

"Can I fill it out and bring it back?" he asked, glancing at his watch.

"Do you have somewhere else to be?"

"No, I just . . . don't want to take up any more of your time than necessary."

"You're not taking up my time, Chase. I need to fill this position. You're here. It only makes sense to let you apply." She hurried into the office, rifled through Byron's file cabinet until she found the application. Chase seemed like a good kid who'd had a rough time. She didn't think she was getting the whole story about how he'd wound up in Benevolence, but as long as his background check came up clean and he did the job he was paid for, she didn't mind giving him a place to work until he had the money to get back on his feet. Hopefully, he'd stick around until Byron was able to return. She wasn't counting on it. A person was either cut out for small-town life or he wasn't. If he wasn't, he'd feel smothered by the close-knit community, strangled by the expectations that came with that.

She'd seen it happen more times than she could count, people who came for a visit and decided to stay only to find that they couldn't handle the slow pace or the nosy neighbors. Just last year Miles Orson and his wife had sold their Victorian on Main Street. The one that they'd begged to buy, had put hundreds of thousands of dollars into, and had lived in for exactly two months and three days.

Right around the first day of the third month, Miles's wife, Shelley, had given him an ultimatum: *Get me out of this town or give me half of our assets.*

Miles had chosen to get out of town.

Most people in Benevolence thought he'd have been better off handing Shelley half his assets. Of course, they didn't know just how many assets the Orsons had. Since Addie had prepared their taxes for the two years it took for the house to become their home, she knew exactly how much he'd have been giving away.

The romantic part of her, the part that,

once upon a time, had believed in dreamy fairy-tale love, wanted to think that Miles had chosen love over geography. That part, the little bit that was left, liked to imagine that Miles and Shelley were the kind of couple that would last forever because they were meant to be.

The practical side of her figured that Miles and Shelley would be together for as long as it took Miles to find a way to keep all his assets and lose his wife.

Chase filled out the application quickly, printing his social security number, his previous home address and place of employment without hesitation. He took out his driver's license when she asked, allowed her to photocopy it, and then stood silently while she skimmed the information he'd provided.

It all looked good. She'd check his references, of course. He'd only listed two, his former employer and a transfer adviser at a community college.

"You were attending college in Houston?" she asked, and he nodded, his dark brown eyes deeply shadowed. He looked like he hadn't been sleeping well. She glanced at the blank spot where his current address should have been.

"Where are you staying, Chase?"

"In the 'Vette." His cheeks flushed as he said it.

"If I hire you, I can probably find someone willing to let you stay —"

"Ma'am, I don't need a place to stay," he interrupted, and for the first time since she'd opened the door, she could see the nearly nineteen years of life in his face. There was maturity there, a confidence that she hadn't noticed before.

"You can't keep sleeping in your car."

"I can until I have the money to do something else."

"In that case," she said before she could think about all the reasons why she shouldn't, "you're hired."

Chase grinned. "You won't regret this, ma'am."

"I will if you keep calling me ma'am. It makes me feel like a ninety-year-old woman. Call me Addie."

"Yes, ma'am," he said, and she laughed.

"Give me a minute to lock up the office, and I'll give you a ride back to Sun Valley."

"I walked here, and I can walk back," he said, pulling his jacket around his chest and heading to the back door.

"It's five miles in freezing weather, and you're not dressed for it. I'll give you a ride and pick you up in the morning. I usually start prepping for the day at five, but I won't need you until eight. How about I pick you up around seven forty-five?"

"I can walk," he responded as he opened the back door, letting bitter cold air waft in. "It's good for me."

"Not in this kind of weather," she said, but he was already out the door.

She grabbed her coat and ran after him.

He was gone. No sign of him in the parking lot or near the building. She jogged to the front of the shop, scanned Main Street but didn't see any sign of the teen.

"Shoot!" she muttered, running back to get her keys and coat. She turned the back doorknob, expecting the door to swing open. It didn't. She tried again. No luck.

"No. No, no, no, no!" She yanked harder, but the blasted door stayed closed. Her purse was inside. Her cell phone. Her keys.

"This sucks," she shouted to the heavens.

Tiny howled in response, and the apartment door opened.

"Everything okay out here?" Sinclair called from the landing.

"Just peachy," she responded, yanking at the door one last time. Had she turned the lock when she'd followed Chase?

She couldn't remember doing it, but she must have. Otherwise the door would still be unlocked, and she would be inside, not standing in the cold freezing her butt off.

"You sure?" Sinclair headed down the stairs, his boots clanging on the metal.

"Positive," she lied.

"Looks like you're locked out." He moved in close, tried the doorknob. "Seems to me that would be a problem."

"Janelle has a spare key. I'll just walk over and get it."

"Or I could open the door for you." He took something from his pocket.

"What's that?"

"Swiss Army knife. It comes in handy in situations like this." He nudged her out of the way, fiddled with the lock for about five seconds, and the door swung open.

Of course.

Sinclair seemed like that kind of guy. The kind who had a solution to every problem, the kind who'd be great on any team, working with any group, because he could solve any problem.

In other words, the exact opposite of Gavin.

"You made that look easy," she accused, and he shrugged, pressing a hand to her lower spine and urging her into the kitchen.

"It's an old lock. I run into them all the time in my line of work."

"Well, your expertise came in handy. Thanks." She eyed the doorknob. "I'm going to have to be more careful. You won't always be around to pick the lock for me."

"Being careful is good. Being prepared is better," he said, taking her hand and pulling her back to the door. "I'll show you how to open the door if you get locked out again."

"That's okay. I'll just make a few extra keys and wear one around my neck." Because there was no way on God's green earth she wanted to stand *this* close to the man.

"You know what I think?" he said, his breath ruffling her hair and making goose bumps rise on her arms.

"What?" she managed to say as he handed her his pocket knife.

"Being chicken doesn't suit you."

"I am not," she said, pivoting so that she was looking straight into his eyes. "Being chicken."

"Then why do you run away every time I get within a foot of you?"

"You're closer than a foot now," she pointed out, because he was only a couple of inches away, and she wasn't going to run. Mostly because there was nowhere to go. One direction was the closed door. The other direction, his chest. Which, she had to admit, was pretty fine-looking.

"I've noticed," he murmured.

Something about the way he said it made her pulse jump and her cheeks heat.

"You were going to teach me how to pick the lock?" she prodded, because she couldn't quite make herself step away.

"That's probably the safest thing I could be doing," he muttered, turning her around, his hands on her shoulders, his fingers warm through her T-shirt. And, God! She wanted to lean right into his chest, turn herself back around, pull his head down for that kiss that she'd almost gotten before . . .

Chase!

She'd almost forgotten about the teen.

Who was she kidding? Thanks to Sinclair, she *had* forgotten.

"Holy cow! I've got to find him." She grabbed her purse and keys.

"Find who?"

"The kid I hired. I was going to give him a ride to his car. That's how I got locked out of the shop."

"And he walked off while you tried to get back inside? I don't think that's a great quality in an employee."

"I turned to grab my coat and purse, and he left. He's walking, so I shouldn't have any trouble tracking him down."

"Or," he said, tugging her coat closed, his knuckles brushing her jaw as he pulled her hood up over her hair, "you could let him walk to his car since it seems like that's what he wants to do."

"His car is five miles outside of town at the campground. It's way too cold for anyone to walk that far."

He frowned. "He's parked at the campground?"

"His car broke down. He's looking for some extra cash to pay to get it fixed."

"Please tell me you're kidding," he said as they walked outside.

"Why would I be kidding?"

"You hired a complete stranger to work in your grandfather's shop?"

"People hire strangers all the time, Sinclair," she responded as she crossed the lot to her car. She knew he was following, could feel him like the hot sun on a cold day.

"Not in a town this size," he grumbled, reaching past her to open the car door. His arm brushed hers, and everything in her sprang to attention, her entire body just kind of responding as if he were everything she needed, all the things she'd ever wanted.

She had to leave. Now. Before she made a complete fool of herself, said something really stupid like *Can you please keep your distance, because I can't think when you're this close.*

"People in this town do all kinds of things that might surprise you," she replied, hopping in the car with every intention of closing the door and driving away.

Sinclair was standing in the way, though, so she shoved the keys in the ignition and turned on the car.

"How old is this kid?" he asked, leaning in so that the interior light splashed across the sharp angle of his jaw and the small scar above his brow. There was another scar near his ear, a thin line of white that angled into his hairline.

"Almost nineteen, and I really need to get going. He doesn't even have a winter coat, and it's below freezing out here."

"I'd better come with you."

It wasn't a question or a suggestion, but she'd passed the years of taking orders from people. "That's not necessary."

"It is if I'm going to get any sleep tonight, and since I didn't sleep worth a damn last night, I plan on it."

"There's no need for you to lose sleep —"

"Do you know how many women a year are killed by people they know?" He closed the door and she could have driven away, but he had a point.

She didn't particularly want to die, so she waited while he rounded the car and climbed in, then she turned on the radio and headed toward the edge of town.

CHAPTER EIGHT

Two hours.

That's how long they spent looking for the kid that Adeline had hired. They found his old Corvette parked exactly where he'd said it would be — in the vehicle parking area at Sun Valley.

The kid, who apparently went by the name of Chase, wasn't in the car. Adeline had insisted on looking through the windows even though it had been pretty damn clear there was no one in it.

She'd also insisted on talking to the campsite manager. Ryder Manchester hadn't been all that happy to be pulled away from the leggy blond he'd been entertaining in his double-wide, but he'd confirmed that the 'Vette was owned by a kid named Chase Lyons, who was paying him five dollars a day to park the car in the empty lot.

Highway robbery, in Sinclair's opinion. After all, the lot was empty and the Corvette wasn't bothering anyone. He'd kept his mouth shut, because this was Adeline's show. She'd hired the kid, and now she seemed to think it was her responsibility to make sure he was okay.

Only Chase was nowhere to be found.

After two hours, Sinclair felt like he could say that definitively. Adeline didn't seem as willing to give up. She stood outside Chocolate Haven, scanning Main Street as if the missing kid was suddenly going to turn up.

"You need to let it go, Adeline," he said, taking her elbow and leading her around the side of the building. "He's found a safe place to stay for the night. Maybe someone's barn or a shed."

"That's no place for a teenager to be," she argued.

"He's an adult."

"A young adult."

"Who isn't your responsibility."

"That doesn't mean I shouldn't be concerned."

He started up the stairs to the apartment. He'd left Tiny there. God only knew what the dog had gotten into while he was gone. "It seems to me that you borrow way more than your share of trouble from other people."

"What's that supposed to mean?"

"You've taken on the shop for your grand-father, the wedding for May. You agreed to let Byron stay with you while he recovers, and now you're worrying about a kid you met a couple of hours ago."

"And?" she demanded, moving in beside him as he unlocked the apartment door.

"And, maybe you have enough of your own stuff to worry about." He stepped into the apartment, bracing himself for whatever mess Tiny had left. Not a thing was out of place. Not a couch cushion or pillow. Not a piece of trash. Tiny lay next to the coffee table, his tail thumping the floor.

"Wow!" Adeline said as she walked into the apartment. "He's so . . . calm."

"We played fetch for an hour. I guess that wore him out." He didn't mention that Tiny had been fetching shoes from the bedroom and running around the apartment with them. That was need-to-know information, and she didn't need to know.

"You have the magic touch when it comes to him."

"He's just worn out from a long day."

"He's never worn out, but he sure looks content. Too bad we've got to get home. Come on, Tiny." She crouched, and the puppy lumbered over.

"Are you still planning to ship him to

Spokane tomorrow?"

"I left a message for my friend. He hasn't returned the call yet, so I guess Tiny has a reprieve. Of course, that means that Nehemiah is going to have to deal with him for another day." She scratched the puppy behind his ears, her expression tender and a little tired. She loved the ugly mutt, but that didn't mean she could do all the things for him that she needed to.

Sinclair understood that. He'd been on the receiving end of it when he was a kid. There was no doubt his parents had loved him, but they hadn't had much to give. They'd expended too much of their energy on each other and on the party scene they'd never quite grown out of. They'd been happy enough to give their sons what they needed but only if it didn't interfere with their plans. Weekends and holidays were the worst — loud parties in the basement while Sinclair and Gavin watched television until the wee hours of the morning.

Adeline? She'd had a different problem than he'd had with his folks. From what he'd seen since he'd been in town, all she did was work. Dawn to way past dusk, and he hadn't seen anyone stepping in to help her. Not Janelle. Not either of Adeline's sisters. Not friends, either. If anything, they added to her workload. That didn't seem to bother her. She just added to her list and kept on trucking.

Everyone had a breaking point, though. He had a feeling she was reaching hers.

"I'll take Tiny to my brother's place tomorrow," he found himself offering. He wasn't sure why. Or maybe he was. He liked Adeline. She worked hard. She cared a lot. He didn't want to see her break, and he didn't want to watch her realize that everyone who counted on her couldn't be counted on.

He thought that was the way things were heading: She would finally really need all the people she'd helped, and none of them would be there for her.

Could be he was just cynical.

He'd been called it enough times to think that it might be true.

"And do what with him?" She patted Tiny's head, a small frown line between her brows. "The last thing you need is a puppy under your feet all day."

"The last thing I need is to spend another day alone with Gavin. Tiny will be a nice distraction."

She cocked her head to the side, her braid flopping over her shoulder. Or what was left of her braid. Most of her hair fell in soft waves around her face.

He knew how silky it was, had felt it brush his knuckles and chin. His palms itched to touch it again, to feel the smooth glide of it.

"I don't think you need that kind of distraction," she said, her gaze on Tiny.

"I don't need a distraction at all, Adeline," he said, giving in to temptation and brushing the silky strands away from her cheeks.

She stilled, her violet eyes wide in a face that shouldn't have been beautiful but was. Eyes too big, chin too sharp, skin too fair, but somehow it worked itself into a quirky kind of gorgeousness that Sinclair would have had to be blind not to notice.

"No? Then probably Tiny should stay with Nehemiah," she said, her voice a little husky, her pulse beating frantically in the hollow of her throat. He could bend down and kiss that spot, taste the silky skin there, and he didn't think she'd protest. He sure as hell wouldn't.

But he didn't think it would stop with that one little kiss, that one small taste of chocolate and berries and quirky gorgeousness.

Didn't *think*?

He *knew* it wouldn't stop there.

He let his hands drop away, his fingers skimming along the firm muscles of her upper arms, the warm flesh of her wrists and palms.

"*Gavin* needs a distraction, something to keep his mind off Lauren and the baby," he said, his voice just as husky as hers had been.

"Right. Sounds good." She nearly sprinted for the door. "I'll bring him when I come to the shop in the morning. See you then. Come on, Tiny!" she shouted, racing down the stairs, the puppy chasing after her.

He wanted to tell her to be careful, but she was moving too fast, the metal clanging so loudly that he didn't think she'd hear.

He waited until she drove away, then closed the door and locked it. He'd finished the bid, sent it off to be read and discussed by the Portland City Council. There was more paperwork to do, but he'd had about enough of that, so he changed into running gear. The best way to refocus his thoughts was a high-level workout, and he did need to refocus.

He didn't know what it was about Adeline, but every time he was with her he forgot all the reasons why he'd vowed to remain single. He forgot all the drama that went with relationships, all the frustration of trying to fulfill someone's needs but never quite having what it took to do that. He

200

forgot that he wasn't really the kind of guy who did deep, meaningful relationships and that Adeline seemed like the kind of woman who wouldn't accept anything less.

Yeah. When he was with her, he forgot a lot of things.

Then she left, and he remembered.

And called himself every kind of fool for ever forgetting.

He pounded down Main Street, moving through town at a steady pace. It was quiet this time of night, most of the houses dark, the streetlights illuminating the road and sidewalk. No traffic distracted from the silence, no horns honking or people laughing. No chatter or congestion, just the moonlight and the solitude, and the hard run that demanded every bit of his energy.

He didn't realize where he was heading until he turned off Main Street and sprinted onto Highway 9. No sidewalk there, but the road was more a country lane than a main thoroughfare. Ten miles up, it spilled out onto the I-90. This section was quiet as a tomb, the pavement cracked from years of heavy use and little maintenance. The campground was a few miles ahead, a few lights gleaming through dense coniferous forest hinting at RVs that were parked for the night. Unlike the Jefferson property, Sun

Valley didn't have Spokane River frontage, but Leonard Galveston hadn't let that keep him from creating a successful camping site there. The way Sinclair's grandfather had told the story, Leonard had purchased the acreage for a song and a dance in the early sixties. He'd cut down a few trees, put up a sign, and the next thing the little town of Benevolence had known, they had a thriving campground just outside the town limits.

It had taken a lot more than that to make the place a success. Sinclair didn't need to know Leonard to know that. He knew firsthand how difficult it was to build a business from the ground up. He'd scrimped and saved and worked long hours every day of the week to make his restoration business profitable. It had taken five years to earn a good living. Three more to see all his hard work come to fruition.

Maybe if his grandfather had known just how much work a business took, maybe if he'd had the ability to do more than talk about all the things he wanted, the house and property could have been the bed and breakfast that Sinclair's grandmother had once dreamed of making it. He'd seen the plans, sketched out on little notepads that he'd found in a rolltop desk in his grandfather's bedroom. He'd left the desk there and left the pads right where he'd found them, because there was a tiny part of him that wanted to see that dream finally come true. His grandmother deserved that. She'd worked herself to death. Literally. Holding down three jobs so that she could pay the taxes on the property, pay off debt that her husband had accrued. That was another thing that Sinclair had learned while cleaning out the house. He'd found three journals shoved between the mattress and box spring of his grandmother's bed.

The last entry was dated a week before Maude had died of a massive stroke. Nearly three years to the day before Sinclair's parents died in a one-car accident caused by his father's drunk driving. Neither of Sinclair's parents had been wearing seat belts. Both had died instantly. Like Elijah, they'd both died with dozens of unfulfilled dreams — college educations, better jobs. Things they could have achieved if they'd put as much effort into that as they had into drinking.

He frowned.

He doubted his grandfather had known about Maude's journals.

If he had, he probably wouldn't have cared about all the dreams and disappointments scribbled on the yellowed pages. As far as Sinclair had been able to tell, his grandfather hadn't cared about much more than finding the next treasure that he could sell to the highest bidder.

Only all his treasures had been junk that no one wanted. Not even the junk collector in the next town over.

He shoved the memories aside, his legs burning from exertion, the muscle in his bad thigh cramping. His pace was a little too fast for the distance he needed to travel. Five miles to Sun Valley. Five miles back. An easy run, but his bum leg had been giving him problems, and if he tweaked it, he'd have to go back to physical therapy. Not something he had time for.

Not that he had time for *this.*

Going to check on a kid that he didn't know and hadn't ever met wasn't something he should be spending any amount of time doing, but he was doing it anyway. Partially for Adeline. If he found Chase in the 'Vette, he could call and let her know that the kid was safe.

His motivation wasn't completely altruistic, though. He wasn't buying the story that Chase had given Adeline. Someone traveling from Ellensburg to Houston had no reason to be within walking distance of

Benevolence. The quickest route would have taken Chase south. Not that Sinclair expected an eighteen-year-old to be good at navigation, but most people had a GPS on their phone and most knew how to use it.

Besides, Chase had made it from Houston to Ellensburg. He obviously knew what route to take.

So, why'd his 'Vette break down on a country highway that led to one of the smallest towns in Washington State?

That was a question Sinclair wanted an answer to.

As if it were his business. As if somehow he could make decisions for Adeline or change her mind about who she hired.

Sun Valley was just ahead, a huge well-lit sign welcoming travelers. The parking lot was as empty as it had been earlier, the only car parked there the old Corvette. A sweet ride, that car. One that had been taken good care of. The paint gleamed in the street-light, the tire rims nearly white. Not a dent or ding on the body of the car. Sinclair had noticed that earlier. He'd also noticed the plate number. He had a friend with the state police. He might be willing to run the number. Just to make sure the car wasn't stolen and that the kid wasn't on the run.

He approached the vehicle cautiously.

Anyone sleeping in a car would be hyper-alert for danger, and the last thing Sinclair wanted was a bullet through the heart. He'd faced plenty of enemy fire, and he knew the dangers of war. He also knew the dangers of his home turf. The streets were safe enough. As long as a guy was smart.

He glanced in the passenger window. Still empty. No sign that anyone had been there since Sinclair and Adeline left. A blanket still lay on the passenger seat, a small backpack on top of it. From Sinclair's angle, it looked pink. An odd color choice for a guy when Sinclair was a kid, but teens nowadays weren't as stuck on the gender-specific colors and sports and clothes. Could be Chase liked pink, or it could be the pack was another color.

Curious, Sinclair pulled out the mini Maglight he always carried, focused it on the interior of the 'Vette. Yep. Pink. The blanket was white and worn. There was nothing in the driver's seat. The car was a coupe rather than a convertible, the back window full of what looked like stuffed animals.

Weird collection for an eighteen-year-old who owned a 'Vette.

The pink backpack he could have chalked up to personal preference, but he didn't know many eighteen-year-old guys who carted stuffed animals around in their Corvettes.

He walked to the back of the car, snapped a picture of the plate number, and forwarded it to his friend. If the vehicle had been stolen, Damien would know it, and he'd take care of the problem.

He shoved the phone and Maglight back into his jacket pocket, stretched a kink out of his back and kneaded the muscles in his thigh. They'd loosened up a little, but it was going to be a long run back to town.

Might as well start now.

He was halfway across the parking lot, just working up to stride, when lights flashed at the entrance of the lot, and a car pulled in.

Not just any car. A Benevolence deputy's car. No lights flashing or sirens blaring, but Sinclair had no doubt it was there for him.

He stopped, waited as the cruiser rolled up.

It parked a few feet away, the deputy taking his sweet time getting out. By the time he did, Sinclair's feet were frozen, his hands so cold he wanted to shove them in his pockets. He figured the deputy wouldn't appreciate that, so he waited impatiently while the guy rounded the cruiser, his uniform hat shading his face and hiding his features.

A flashlight beam landed straight in Sinclair's eyes.

"I got a call about someone breaking into cars. You that guy?" the officer asked, his voice vaguely familiar.

If Sinclair hadn't been blinded by the light, he might have recognized the face. As it was, he was still freezing cold and slightly pissed, because he was pretty sure Ryder had seen his light and called the sheriff. "I was just out for a run, Deputy."

"Running from where?"

"Town."

"You don't look like anyone I . . ." The deputy's voice trailed off, and the light dropped. "Sinclair Jefferson?" he asked, a hint of surprised pleasure in his voice.

"That's right."

"I heard you were back in town, man! It's been a long time." He strode forward. Tall, lean, short-cropped blond hair, and a scar that bisected his cheek from eye to jaw.

"Jax?" Sinclair knew he sounded as surprised as he felt. Jax Gordon had moved in with his uncle and aunt during the middle of seventh grade. Sinclair had heard about him before he'd seen him, rumors of his entire family being murdered whispered through the seventh grade class for weeks before Jax had arrived. When he'd finally shown up, he'd plopped himself down at the desk next to Sinclair's, the slash on his face still raw, the marks from the stitches visible.

He'd looked about as angry as a twelve-year-old could be, and he'd had enough attitude to keep everyone away. Even the teachers had avoided him. He'd been smart, though, studying rather than causing trouble, working in the library during recess and after school. That's where they'd first connected. Sinclair had been hiding from the gossips who were talking about how his father had killed his mother. He'd known it was true, but he'd figured no one but his family had any right to discuss the accident. He'd also thought his mother had had some responsibility for her death. She'd been drinking too, had allowed her husband to drive, and hadn't worn a seat belt.

It didn't matter, though, that his parents' stupidity had killed them. He'd felt obligated to defend what little honor the Jefferson family had. He'd already been in two fights over it, and if he got in a third, he was facing suspension. Three days home from school was a nightmare when the home you lived in had ceilings covered in mildew and stacks of moldy newspapers filling almost every surface. He'd walked into the library, found a book on architecture, and sat at an empty table. He hadn't realized that Jax was at a desk a few feet away until he'd heard pages rustling.

They hadn't spoken that day or the day after.

It had taken nearly a month before Sinclair was curious enough about the silent kid with the ugly scar to ask what he was reading. It had been a book about law enforcement, a huge tome that Jax had checked out of the town library and carried in his backpack every day. His father, he'd explained one day months after they'd first spoken, had been a police officer.

That was the beginning of a friendship that had lasted until they'd both left town.

"Surprised?" Jax asked, shaking Sinclair's hand. He still had the strongest grip of any guy Sinclair knew, still had the most direct gaze of anyone he'd ever met. When he looked at a person, it was as if he saw everything, and when he finally offered someone friendship, he was loyal to a fault.

"You left town about six minutes before I did, so yeah. I guess I am surprised to see you here."

"Left. Returned." Jax shrugged. He'd never been much for sharing personal information. As far as Sinclair knew, he'd never confided the truth about his injury to anyone. Even Sinclair didn't know all the details. It had been an act of revenge. Drug related. Jax's father had been killed defending his family. That was all Jax had ever said, and Sinclair had never been the kind of person to dig for things someone didn't want revealed. He had his own secrets and shadows, and he didn't want anyone poking at them.

"You accomplished your goal?" he asked, because that was the only way Jax would have returned. From the time they'd met until Jax had gotten in his old Ford truck and headed to California, the one thing he'd wanted, the one thing he'd planned and dreamed and desired, was to make the person who'd killed his family pay for it. Everything — every book, every test, every long run, or weight-lifting session — was done with that in mind.

"He's in jail," Jax said simply. "And Aunt Vera needed help around the house after Jim's stroke, so I decided to move back."

"I didn't realize Jim had a stroke."

"Because you haven't been over to visit them since you returned." There was no accusation in the words, but then, Jax was never accusatory. He made statements and he let people come to their own conclusions.

Sinclair's conclusion was that he should have visited the Gordons. They'd been good to him. He'd just been too bitter when he was a kid, too determined to get out of town and start a new life to realize it.

"How's he doing?"

"Not bad considering he almost died." Jax shoved his hands in his coat pockets, rocking back and forth on his toes the way he had when they were kids and he was getting ready to say something difficult. "I came back while he was in the hospital. Seemed to me that this was the right place to stay. Like you said, I'd accomplished my goal. Also got divorced along the way, so I didn't have much holding me to San Diego."

"You were married?"

"Don't sound so surprised. I may be damaged goods, but there are plenty of women who think I'm a pretty good catch."

"You know I wasn't thinking about the scar," Sinclair said. He'd stopped thinking about it after the first few months of their friendship. After a couple more months, he'd stopped seeing it. Jax had just been Jax — driven, serious, a little too somber for most kids their age.

Sinclair had liked that about him.

Or maybe he'd just liked that they both had their hang-ups and their baggage.

"Neither was I." Jax laughed. "You know how I am. Nose to the grindstone, oblivious to anything but the goal. Piper didn't seem to mind until she did. By the time I realized it, it was too late."

"I'm sorry," he said, because there wasn't a whole lot else he could say.

"I was too until I learned she'd been seeing my partner for a couple of months before she walked out."

"Ouch."

"Yeah. Sucked, but at least I didn't end the relationship thinking there was something that could be salvaged in it." He shrugged again. "When Vera called to say Jim was in the hospital, I got on a plane and flew to Spokane. Spent three months there while Jim was in the hospital. That was six months ago."

"And now you're in Benevolence and planning to stay?"

"Guilty as charged." He grinned. "But then, I never hated this town the way you did."

"I didn't hate it." Not much, anyway.

Jax laughed, the sound ringing through the quiet night. "I'm calling bullshit on that. From the day we met until the day I left town, leaving was all you ever talked about."

"Truer words were never spoken, brother,

213

but it was my grandfather's house I was most interested in escaping."

"Kind of funny that we've both ended up where we didn't want to be," Jax said. "Or maybe not funny. Maybe just . . . interesting."

"I didn't end up back here. I came to help my brother, and I'm leaving when I'm done," Sinclair said, because he had no intention of sticking around, and he didn't want to think about what it meant that he and Jax were both in Benevolence after they'd fought so hard to leave it.

"Good plan," Jax said. "How about you come for dinner tomorrow night? We can talk about it more then. Jim and Vera would love to see you. Vera's been talking about you nonstop since you got to town."

"I'll be working. I need to get my brother's crap in order. Lauren is due to have that baby any day —"

"I'll call bullshit on that too," Jax said, cutting him off. "You have time, if you want to. And you owe me, since I took the rap for setting fire to that old outhouse on your granddad's property."

"I needed some way to force my grandfather to get our plumbing fixed."

"And I was willing to take the fall so your grandfather wouldn't ship you to military school. I was grounded for a month for that one, remember?"

How could he forget?

It had been a record cold winter, and Gavin had been sick for most of it. Sinclair had argued with his grandfather about the merits of having a plumber come in to fix their only functioning bathroom. His grandfather had insisted the outhouse was just fine.

It wasn't fine when a kid the age Gavin had been had to walk a half mile in five-degree weather, but that hadn't changed anything. Their grandfather didn't want to spend money on indoor plumbing, and Sinclair hadn't been able to fix the problem.

He had finally had all he could take of it.

He'd set fire to the outhouse.

It had burned way more quickly than he'd imagined it would, and his grandfather had been way angrier than Sinclair had expected. If Jax hadn't stepped in and sworn that he'd accidentally set the outhouse on fire while smoking a cigarette, Sinclair would have been shipped away.

Which wouldn't have been a bad option if he hadn't been afraid to leave Gavin alone in that rattrap of a house. "You're calling that debt in *now*?" he asked.

"You going to refuse to pay it? Because

we're standing here in this parking lot, and I did get a call about a trespasser. Seems to me, I could cart you in . . . ask you a bunch of questions that would waste time for both of us."

"You wouldn't."

"Probably not." He shoved his hands deep into his pockets, rocked back on his heels. "But you do owe me, and I'm pretty desperate to get my aunt and uncle to stop worrying about my life."

"What's to worry about? You're living in their hometown, in their basement, and —"

"Hold it!" Jax raised a hand. "Just so we're clear, I'm not living in their basement. I've got my own place. Little Victorian on Monroe. Used to be Mary Pickford's place."

"The old witch with a million cats?" He remembered the house as much as he'd remembered the woman who used to scream at them to stay on the sidewalk. A two-story Victorian that sat on a double lot at the corner of Monroe and Second Avenue, the place had smelled of cat piss and tuna, and so had the woman who'd owned it.

"Mary died six years ago. I got the place for a steal because it had been empty for so long."

"Empty because it's nearly impossible to

get the smell of cat piss out of floors and walls." Sinclair had been tasked with doing it on more than one occasion and had had to rip out drywall, pull up floorboards, and basically gut every house that required it.

"Isn't that the truth," Jax agreed. "It took me a month to replace all the floors and re-plaster the walls. So, you coming to dinner tomorrow or not?"

"You haven't given me much of a choice."

"We always have choices, Sinclair. Just matters what we do with them. So, you coming? I'll need to tell Vera if you are."

"I'll come," he conceded, because he liked Vera and Jim, and he should have visited them long before now. He guessed he'd forgotten how much they'd done for him, how many times they'd sent home food or offered a quiet place to study after school.

He hadn't wanted their charity, but they hadn't made it seem like that's what they were offering.

"Good. She serves dinner at six. On the dot. Bring Adeline with you, if you want."

"Adeline?"

"Don't play dumb, Sinclair. There's not a red-blooded man in this town who doesn't know who she is."

"I'm not playing dumb. I'm wondering why you want me to bring my landlord's granddaughter to Vera's."

"Because she's gorgeous?"

"And?"

"And, I'm thinking this might not be a bad time to start getting back in the dating game."

Jax might be thinking that, but Sinclair was thinking he might want to wait a little longer. Adeline deserved to be more than a rebound relationship. "Since when are you a game player?"

"Turn of phrase, Sinclair," he responded easily, his gaze drifting to the Corvette. "You were looking in the Corvette. Ryder was sure you were planning to steal it."

"I was looking for the owner."

"You want to make him an offer? It's a pretty sweet ride."

"I want to talk to him."

"About?"

"Nothing in particular. I'm just curious."

"I can tell you this. His name is Chase Lyons. Eighteen. From Houston. No record. Not even a speeding ticket. Got named to the two-year-college honor society last year. Had a write-up in a Houston paper."

"You've spoken with him?"

"Ran the plates. Did a little research. I like to know who's hanging around town. Not that there's been any complaints about him. He's applied for a couple of jobs, but other than that, he keeps to himself."

"How long has he been here?"

"Three weeks. Maybe four."

"That's a long time to be living in his car."

"Who told you he was living in the car?"

"That was the impression Adeline got when he applied for a job."

"I think he's staying in one of the outbuildings. There are half a dozen of them on the property, and I don't think Ryder checks them more than once a year. I've thought about looking, but I call attention to what the kid is doing and he'll end up having to pay Ryder for using a building that has no heat, no water, and no comfortable place to sleep. Since he doesn't have the cash, I've just left things alone. I have been looking for him around town, though. I figured I'd offer him a loan or a place to crash while he earns the money he needs. Vera and Jim could sure use a little help around the house. Unfortunately, the kid is as elusive as hell. I've only seen him once, and when he saw me, he headed in the other direction."

"You think he has something to hide?"

"As long as there's no warrant out on him and he stays out of trouble, I don't care."

"If you want to talk to him, I know where

you'll be able to find him. He starts working at Chocolate Haven tomorrow."

"Good to know, and a good excuse to stop
by and say hello to Adeline. She sure has
grown up a lot since our high school days."
He walked back to his cruiser, opened the
passenger door. "Climb in. I'll give you a
ride back to town."

Sinclair had planned to finish his run, but
he thought his time might be better spent
reconnecting with Jax. Especially since Jax
seemed intent on connecting with Adeline.

She needed a date to May's wedding, and
Jax was looking for someone to hook up
with. It shouldn't have mattered to Sinclair
one way or another, but it did.

He got in the car, fastened his seat belt,
answered a few dozen questions about his
career, and asked a lot more about Jax's. It
was like old times, only better because they
both had their lives heading in the direction
they wanted. Jax seemed about as happy as
a clam to be back in Benevolence working
for the sheriff's department. He substituted
at the high school, taught self-defense
classes at the community center. He was,
Sinclair thought, everything he'd planned
to be when they were growing up.

Which was great for him, and would be
great for Adeline.

She deserved someone like Jax. Someone focused and determined and who loved the town as much as she did.

Sinclair still didn't like the idea, but then, if he let himself, he could picture the hollow of her throat, the way her pulse thrummed there. He could still feel the warmth of her skin, the silky smoothness of her hair.

Yeah. If he let himself, he could think of a dozen reasons why Jax and Adeline shouldn't go out.

But the only real reason was that he wanted to be the one to ask her. He wanted to be the one picking her up at her house, touching her lower spine as they walked to his truck.

Jax turned into Chocolate Haven's back lot, pulled up in front of the door. "All right, man. See you tomorrow."

"See you then." He got out of the car, frowning when he realized there was a light shining from the apartment again. "Damn," he muttered. "I can't be getting that forgetful."

"What's wrong?" Jax leaned across the seat, eyeing the building.

"This is the second time I left the apartment dark and came back to the lights being on."

"You think someone is in there?"

"No, but I'd like to know why that light keeps going on." He headed toward the stairs and wasn't surprised when he heard the cruiser door open and close.

Jax walked up the stairs behind him.

It seemed a little like old times and felt an awful lot like being home.

CHAPTER NINE

Lack of sleep did funny things to people. Like making them want to shove a dozen chocolate bonbons down the gaping cleavage of Millicent Montgomery. Which was exactly what Addie wanted to do.

She gritted her teeth instead, replacing the half dozen dark-chocolate caramels Millicent had said she wanted and taking out the newly requested vanilla creams. It was the fifth change in as many minutes, and Addie was about ready to blow a fuse.

She didn't want the forty-year-old to know it.

Letting her impatience get the best of her wasn't going to keep Chocolate Haven in business.

But Millicent had married well. Twice. She had the money to prove it. In her opinion, that made her a little better than the rest of the town. That, also in Millicent's opinion, gave her license to be picky, demanding, and a general pain in the butt.

"You do have the best chocolate in the state, but I much prefer it when Byron is here," Millicent said, her breasts heaving beneath a corseted top that was pulled so tight, Addie was surprised the implants beneath it didn't pop.

Poor Chase stood a couple of feet away, his face deep red, his gaze averted. First he'd been chastised for not switching out Millicent's chocolate choices fast enough. Now he was being treated to a generous view of the woman's over-inflated and tanned boobs.

His mother had raised him right. He kept his eyes down as he tried to help Addie pull the new requests. He was fumbling for the chocolates, though, and managed to drop two on the floor.

"Maybe," Addie said as she placed the last chocolate in the box, "you should wait to come in again until Byron returns."

"Humph!" Millicent replied. "Is that any way to run a business? Being rude to a customer?"

"I'm not being rude. I'm just making a suggestion." And wishing like heck that Millicent *would* wait to return when Byron was back. She wouldn't. The woman loved chocolate more than she'd loved either of her husbands.

"I don't need a suggestion. I know exactly what I want." Millicent frowned, leaning toward the display case, her cleavage as deep and dark as an ocean trench. "Although . . ."

Great! Here we go again!

Addie thought she heard Chase groan.

"Maybe you can switch out a few of those and give me chocolate mint bars instead."

"I'll do it," Chase said quickly, probably sensing how close Addie was to telling Millicent where she could shove her pound of chocolates.

He took the box from her hands, his face still red, his hands steady as he exchanged chocolates, each one set into the box *just exactly right.*

Of course.

Addie had been working with him for three days, and she'd discovered that he was a quick learner — bonbon making, chocolate tempering — everything she taught him, he soaked up like a sponge. She'd also learned that he held himself to a very high standard. He didn't like making mistakes. A shame, because that was the quickest way to learn. She didn't know him well enough to say that, so she'd just let him work slowly through every task. The process may have been more challenging for Addie than it was for him. She had that list hanging on the wall in the kitchen, mocking her with all the things that needed to be done in the next few days, and she could have rolled bonbons in cocoa powder sixteen times faster than Chase.

"I'm not sure how I feel about this," Millicent said as she watched Chase.

"Feel about what?" Addie asked, the words coming out just a little sharper than she'd intended. She'd spent half the night sewing the blasted zipper into the horrid dress. She'd finally managed to finish at two in the morning. There were a couple little buckles in the fabric, a few tiny little runs in the glossy sheen. She just hoped to God that May didn't notice.

"You having your hired help fill orders for me. If you're unhappy serving me, Adeline" — Millicent huffed, her breasts nearly spilling out — "I can take my business somewhere else."

"There's a Rite Aid in the next town over," Chase volunteered. "They sell chocolate."

Millicent speared him with a look that could have made a grown man cry. His cheeks were still red, his gaze firmly planted on her face, but Chase didn't look intimidated.

"If I wanted drug store chocolate, I could have gone to the five-and-dime. I was in the mood for something more decadent, something richer." She rolled her R, and Chase smirked.

Millicent scowled.

"Millicent," Addie bit out, "do you want to add anything to your order?"

"I'm not even sure I want the chocolate at this point." She crossed her arms over her chest. "Really, Adeline, Byron would never treat a customer like this."

"Byron isn't here." The words just slipped out, and Millicent stiffened.

"Young lady, you don't have to be rude."

"I'm not being rude. I'm being honest."

"It is not working to your advantage today. I was going to take another dozen chocolates, but I guess I'll make do with what you've packed, because I just really do not have time for people's disrespect."

Neither did Addie, but she kept her big mouth shut, closed the lid of the chocolate box, and used the big gold sticker to seal it closed.

"Here you are," she said, and Millicent snatched it from her hand, dropped a twenty onto the counter, and left.

"Six-dollar-and-fifty-four-cent tip," Chase said.

Addie rang the order up, took the change from the cash register, and handed it to him. "You're quick with the numbers, Chase."

"I love math. I also love science and English. I guess I'm a school geek." He smiled, but he didn't look happy. He looked exhausted, his face pale, his eyes shadowed.

"You know, Chase, I've got a spare room at my place. It's not going to be used until my grandfather is released from the hospital. Maybe the end of next week. You could stay there until he does, and then we can either clean out my attic and make a room for you there, or you could sleep on the couch until you're able to get your car fixed."

He looked surprised and a little terrified, his gaze shifting away for a moment before settling on her again.

She counted to five, counted to five again, and he still hadn't responded. "It's not a trick question, Chase, and you're not going to get fired if you say no. I just hate to think of you sleeping outside or in that tiny car of yours."

"It's not that I don't appreciate your offer, I just . . ." He shook his head. "It's better if I just keep doing what I'm doing."

"Well, you know the offer stands. Anytime you want to take me up on it, you can."

He nodded, his lips pressed tightly together, his eyes lowered.

There was something going on.

She hadn't been able to put her finger on it, but he wasn't being completely upfront about where he was going at night, what he was doing after the shop closed. Sinclair insisted that he hadn't been sleeping in the 'Vette. He'd been out there a couple times, and had never seen Chase there.

Adeline thought she should probably be worried about that, but she wasn't. Chase was punctual, industrious, and focused. He also liked to eat. Not the chocolate that she offered every day, the snacks that she brought. The first day, she'd offered him pretzels. He'd taken both the snack-sized bags she'd given him, devouring them so quickly that she'd offered him another. The second day, she'd brought a dozen sandwiches, chips, and two boxes of granola bars. He'd eaten two of the sandwiches and then sheepishly asked if he could take a couple when he left for the day.

He obviously hadn't been kidding when he'd said he was out of money. The kid ate like a starving man, probably because he *was* starving. His jeans hung from narrow hips, his button-down shirt bagging around his shoulders. She wanted nothing more than to put a little meat on his bones and a smile on his face.

She'd held out the tip, but he pushed it away.

"I didn't earn it."

She stuffed it into his shirt pocket. "Anyone who can put up with Millicent deserves way more than this."

"*You* put up with her."

"I get paid more than you." Not exactly the truth. She wasn't getting paid anything. All the checks that Byron insisted on writing her were being put through the office shredder.

"No, you don't." His comment surprised her, and she looked up from the bonbons that she was repositioning in the case.

"What do you mean by that?"

"I saw you put the check through the shredder yesterday."

"Just because I don't take the money, doesn't mean I'm not being paid."

"And just because I put up with someone for five minutes, doesn't mean I get to take this money." He took it from his pocket and slid it into the tip jar on the counter.

"Look, Chase —"

"More customers coming," he said, nodding toward the door. "Looks like that police officer. You want to handle it or should I?"

"I'll handle it if you'll pull that taffy we started," she said, mostly because she was sick to death of making candy. She and Chase had filled twenty Internet orders in the past two days. They'd filled the display cases, helped twenty second-graders roll bonbons, made three dozen blue lollipops for Dixie Walker's baby gender-reveal party.

Chase didn't seem to be tired of the process yet, but she sure as heck was.

Chase hurried into the kitchen, disappearing a couple of seconds before the door opened and Jax Gordon walked in.

"Morning, Addie," he called as he sauntered to the counter.

And sauntered was exactly how she'd describe it. He had more confidence than anyone had a right to. He was also one of the nicest guys Addie had ever met.

"Good morning, Jax. No work today?"

"What clued you in? The jeans, or the T-shirt and flannel jacket?"

"The lack of gun belt and firearm."

"It's my day off. I'm helping Jim put down a new tile floor and thought I'd pick up some chocolates for Vera before I headed over there."

"What do you think she'd like?"

"Just give me a dozen of whatever you like

most," he said, his gaze drifting to the hallway that led to the kitchen. "Kid still working out for you?"

"Yes. Are you still hoping he won't?" He and Sinclair both seemed to be worried about Chase. Neither believed the teen's story. Adeline didn't either, but she liked Chase, and she was willing to give him a chance.

"Who said I was hoping that?"

"I just get the impression that you'll be happy when he finally leaves town."

"I don't care how long the kid stays here, just as long as while he's here, he stays out of trouble."

"So far he's been a model employee." She reached into the display case and grabbed four milk chocolate bonbons and put them in a box, added a few caramel pecan logs and a piece of white chocolate bark. Vera loved Lamont fudge, but Addie didn't have any of that to give, so she substituted five soft brittle squares — Vera's second favorite.

"How long is he planning to be in town?" Jax was still staring at the hallway.

"Until he has enough money to get his car fixed."

"I can help him with that."

"He won't take your charity. He wouldn't even take the tip Millicent left." She gestured to the tip jar. "He also agreed to help out until Byron returns. Even if his car is fixed, he won't be able to leave."

"You might be better off hiring someone local."

"Why?" she demanded, handing him the filled chocolate box.

"Because you have no idea what his long-term work potential is. He could steal you blind and —"

"Shhh!" she hissed. "He might be listening."

"I don't care if he is. He's got a clean record, but I'm not sure how he ended up in Benevolence. I'd like to find out. Maybe I should go back there and ask." He handed her a twenty, probably would have headed down the hall, but she blocked his path.

"Can you wait and ask him another time? I'm swamped, he's not causing anyone around here any trouble, and —"

The bell above the shop door rang, and Sinclair walked in.

He didn't have Tiny with him. Which was a relief.

Or maybe not.

"Did Tiny escape?" she asked.

He smiled, and her heart did a funny little flip that she did *not* appreciate.

"No. He and Gavin are hiking. They were

both driving me crazy, so I sent them off together."

"Sorry about that. If you want, I can go get him."

"Tiny or Gavin? Because I'd much rather you take my brother off my hands than the dog." His gaze shifted to Jax, and he nodded. "Did you ask her?"

"I was getting to it."

"Getting to what?" She didn't like the look that passed between the two, and she braced herself.

"What time did you come back to the shop after you took Tiny home last night?"

"Around eleven." She'd decided to run to Walmart to hunt for an orange zipper. That had taken time. Lots of it. She'd puttered around looking for things she didn't need because she hadn't wanted to return to the shop. "Why?"

"The office light in your granddad's place was on again," Jax said.

"This is what?" Addie's stomach churned with unease. "The third time?"

"Yeah," Sinclair muttered, his eyes dark with irritation. "And it's really starting to bug me."

"Did you change the lock?"

"Yesterday." He raked his hand through his hair. "If someone was there, they got in another way."

"You're sure you turned the light off?"

"I'm pretty good about things like that."

He was pretty good about a lot of things.

It was on the tip of her tongue to say it, but he shoved his hands into his jacket pockets and continued speaking. "Is your mom the real estate agent representing the property next door?"

"May's shop? Yes."

"Do you think she'd be willing to let us take a look inside?"

"Janelle is always willing to show a property."

"We're not interested in seeing the property," Jax said. "We want to take a look at the door that leads into Byron's property. If someone is getting into the place, that's how he's doing it."

She hadn't thought about that.

Now that she was, it made sense: Byron seeing someone in the apartment, the door closing when she walked in, the random lights turned on when they should have been off. All of it could be attributed to someone entering the apartment through that door.

Why someone would want to do that, she didn't know. Once, she could understand, but Byron didn't keep valuables in the apartment. All the family's antiques and heirlooms were at Janelle's place, all Alice's old jewelry was in a safety deposit box at the bank. Even if there had been valuables in the apartment, it seemed like a thief would have taken what he wanted, and not returned.

"What do you think you're going to find?" she asked. "Someone squatting in the building?"

"I don't know." Jax opened the box of chocolates and pulled out a bonbon. She'd swirled the glossy top with a thin line of hazelnut spread. She used to love bonbons. She used to love fudge. Now just looking at the piece of chocolate made her want to puke. "But I went home last night, and I started thinking about your grandfather and how he keeps insisting that someone was in the apartment the day he fell, and it makes me wonder . . ." He bit into the bonbon, moaned softly. "This place makes the best chocolate I've ever eaten."

"I'll tell my grandfather you said so."

"You driving out to see him today?" Jax finished off the bonbon and reached into the box for another one. If he kept going, there wouldn't be any left for Vera.

She didn't point it out, because she was in

236

a foul mood and didn't want to take it out on Jax.

"I'm hoping to." The hospital was in Spokane. A good hour-and-a-half drive. She'd planned to make the trip the previous day and the day before that, but she'd gotten caught up in . . . stuff. Dresses that didn't fit, zippers that were broken, fudge that couldn't be made properly. Running and accounting and doing a bunch of crap that really wasn't more important than Byron.

"Is he at Sacred Heart?" Sinclair asked.

"Yes. He's had three surgeries, so that was the best place for him."

"I'd like to go see him, so if you do go tonight, let me know. We can drive out together," Sinclair said.

She thought about that for about two seconds — about being in the car with Sinclair for nearly three hours. It didn't seem like a good idea. As a matter of fact, it seemed like a horrible idea. There were all kinds of trouble she could get into in three hours, all kinds of conversations that they could have, questions she could ask, things that she could learn about a guy that she really should be avoiding.

I probably won't go. That's what she meant to say.

Instead, "Sounds good," slipped out.

He smiled. "I have to do a little more work at Gavin's place. We've got a delivery scheduled. I'll pick you up after that. Maybe seven. Sound good?"

It sounded kind of like a date, and dating wasn't something Addie was interested in doing. "I —"

The door opened, the bell rang, and a small group of women walked in. She didn't recognize any of them. All had variations of a short, curly hairstyle. All wore dark blue slacks, thick winter coats, and leather gloves.

"We made it!" one cried gleefully. "Chocolate Haven. The object of every chocolate fantasy I have ever had!" The woman rushed forward, her group rushing along with her.

In the midst of the chaos of women calling out their chocolate orders, Sinclair and Jax disappeared and Chase appeared, boxes in hand, gloves on. He began filling orders, and she began ringing them up, the shop resounding with a dozen voices all chattering at once.

She gathered that the group was from Montana, that they'd been driving all night to come to Chocolate Haven for their March birthdays. All because one of them had been there with her parents years ago and had never forgotten biting into a piece of Lamont fudge.

She'd heard variations on the story many times since she'd taken over the shop. For some reason, today it made her a little maudlin, a little more tired than she already was. Chocolate Haven wasn't just a shop. It was a legacy.

So far, no one had walked out empty-handed. Everyone who'd come for fudge had gone home with something, but that first bite of fudge . . . it was something people wanted to relive.

Addie hadn't been able to accommodate any of them.

God! She hoped she didn't destroy the place before Byron was released from the hospital. She hoped that she wasn't ruining what three generations of Lamonts had built and babied and grown. She hoped more than anything that Byron would be back soon, taking over the shop, doing all the things that everyone who came to Chocolate Haven expected. Because she sure as hell wasn't doing it.

She swallowed back a hard lump that seemed to have settled right in the middle of her throat, handed the last box to the last costumer, and headed back to the kitchen to try the fudge recipe. One. More. Time.

■ ■ ■ ■

Sinclair had never been good at waiting.

He tapped his fingers on the mahogany table in Janelle's real estate office and eyed Jax. He liked the guy. He always had, but he hadn't been all that happy to see him in Chocolate Haven. He should have kept walking, gone into the apartment to replace the breakfast and lunch that Tiny had devoured on the way to his grandfather's house. That's what he'd planned. Grab some food and go back to work.

But he'd gone into Chocolate Haven instead.

And not just because he'd wanted to find out if Jax had spoken to Adeline about the light on in his apartment. Sure, he'd asked Jax to check in with her. He'd have handled it himself, but Adeline had dropped Tiny off that morning and run. She'd been there and gone so quickly, he'd barely had time to say good morning.

She was avoiding him.

Which was fine.

As long as she was also avoiding Jax.

That didn't seem to be the case, and he wasn't all that happy about the way it made him feel.

"You look about as happy as a turkey on Thanksgiving," Jax commented, pulling a chocolate out of the box he was holding and biting into it.

"I've got work to do at my brother's place."

"I've got work to do at Vera's, but I want to get in that building." Jax finished off the chocolate, set the box on the table, and stood. "You can head out, if you want. I'll wait for Janelle. I can call and let you know if I find anything."

"Do you really think you will?"

"I've got some suspicions."

"Do they have anything to do with Adeline's new assistant?"

"It did occur to me," Jax said, pacing to a window and looking out onto Main Street.

Janelle had a nice office. A really nice one. But then, from what Sinclair had heard, she did several millions of dollars' worth of sales a year.

Jax continued. "Things started going haywire in that apartment right around the time that boy's car broke down."

"Haywire how?" Sinclair eyed the box Jax had abandoned on the table and thought about snagging one of the chocolates. He hadn't eaten breakfast. Thanks to Tiny. And he was starving.

"You know that Byron fell down the stairs, right?"

"Yes."

"Did you know he said someone was in the apartment? According to the story he's telling, he saw someone standing in the hallway when he walked in the door. He ran outside to call for help, tripped, and nearly broke his neck."

"You checked things out?"

"James McDermott heard him calling for help and found him at the bottom of the stairs. As soon as he heard that someone was in the apartment, he ran up and searched. He found nothing."

"McDermott was sheriff when I was a kid, right?"

"Exactly. He knows what's what, and he said there was no sign of anyone. He even checked the door that goes into May's building. It was locked."

"Did he go in the building next door?"

"I think we all assumed that Byron was in shock. Maybe he'd hit his head when he fell or something." Jax shrugged. "Now I'm wishing we had."

"How long had Chase been hanging around at that point?"

"A few days. His car broke down, and he rolled it to the camp. Took a while, but eventually he started hanging around town asking for work."

"So, he's been in town for . . ."

"A few weeks."

"Anything missing from the apartment?"

"Nothing that Addie or Janelle noticed."

"You know," Sinclair said, a picture of Adeline running down the stairs in that orange dress suddenly filling his head, "the night Janelle brought me to see the apartment, Adeline insisted she'd heard a door close when she walked into the place."

"She didn't mention it to me."

"You guys see each other a lot?" he asked, and then wished he hadn't.

Jax smiled, his scar pulling just a little, his eyes filled with amusement.

"What's so funny?" Sinclair growled.

"I guess I just never figured you for the kind of guy who'd fall for a girl like Addie."

"What kind of girl would that be?" he asked, not nearly as amused by the conversation as his friend seemed to be.

"Small town. Simple. Uncomplicated."

"Adeline isn't simple."

"You have it worse than I thought. Good thing I found out now. I was planning on asking her to May's wedding."

"Go ahead. I've got no claim to her," Sinclair said, nearly choking on the words.

"I don't move in on a friend's territory. Claim or no. Besides, Willow was always more my type."

"She's coming in for the wedding?"

"With her fiancé," Jax said. "Hopefully the guy is good enough for her. Otherwise . . ." He smiled. "I just might decide to try my hand at wooing the oldest Lamont sister. As for you, if you're really interested, then you've got a long road ahead of you."

"I'm . . ." Not? That would be a lie, so he didn't say it. "I've got a home and business in Seattle."

"I heard. Mr. Successful. The one Jefferson to break the mold." Coming from anyone else, those would have been fighting words, but Jax knew more than anyone just what Sinclair's family was. He'd stood by Sinclair anyway. Always.

Funny how time and distance could make a person forget the things that were once important.

"I broke the mold, and I'm not planning to come back to a town that was very happy to keep me pressed into it."

"Give me a break," Jax said without heat. "You were a kid with a chip on your shoulder. The town, on the other hand, was always proud of you."

"Says who?"

"Me. I spent most of our formative years trying to live up to your stellar-ness."

That made Sinclair laugh. The fact was, they'd been neck and neck for class valedictorian. They'd both worked multiple jobs, both played sports, both had been fighting their own battles in their own ways, and making an impression while they did it.

"Is that laughter I hear in my office?" Janelle called, sashaying into the room with a broad smile and a little too much cheerfulness. "Sorry about the wait, gentlemen. I was meeting with another client."

She glanced at her watch. "My daughters will be in for the wedding this afternoon, and I need to get home and get their rooms ready, but I have a few minutes if you want to talk about May's property." She slapped a folder onto the desk, the photo of the three-story brownstone on the front of it.

"I think you have the wrong idea about why we're here," he said, lifting the folder anyway. The property was a nice one. Good location. Really nice example of the period architecture, the dormers on the top floor in excellent condition.

"My secretary said you wanted to take a look at the interior of the building. She thought you might be planning on opening an office here. It's a perfect location. Close to several historic areas that are desperate for restoration specialists." Her smile didn't falter, but she didn't look quite as peppy as she had when she'd walked in.

Jax interrupted. "Actually, Janelle, we want to see if the door that leads into Byron's apartment is locked."

"That's it?" She glanced at the folder, and Sinclair had the distinct impression she was thinking of ripping it from his hand. "Because I can assure you that it is. I walked through with May when she closed down the shop, and that's one of the things we checked."

"How long has it been since you were in there?" Jax asked.

"The last time I entered the property was the day I put the sign out front." She frowned, the tiny lines on her forehead deepening. "Actually, that's not true. I did two showings that first week. Both to people in town. Neither panned out, but that's business. Anyway" — she sighed — "the door was never unlocked, so it couldn't possibly be unlocked now."

"I'd like to check anyway," Jax said gently. "For peace of mind more than anything."

"I really don't have a lot of time."

"It won't take long."

Unless they found something or someone.

Sinclair kept silent. He wasn't the deputy, and it wasn't his job to convince Janelle to unlock the door.

"I can call May," Jax suggested. "I'm sure she wouldn't mind letting us in."

"Her wedding is a few days away." Janelle grabbed a coat from a hook near the door, took her purse from a file cabinet. "If we're going to do this, let's do it."

She marched through the doorway like she was going to the gallows.

Sinclair followed.

He didn't care that she was unhappy. He needed to get more sleep, and worrying about the damn door opening in the middle of the night was not helping him get it.

Once he knew for sure that the thing was locked tight and that Byron's place was inaccessible through it, maybe all the nightmares would stay away for a while.

"You okay, man?" Jax asked as they walked outside.

"Right as rain," he lied.

"Sure," Jax responded.

That was it. Just *sure*.

But there was something in his eyes that said he understood.

Janelle, on the other hand, was oblivious.

She hurried along Main Street, waving at a few people as she went. Head up, steps brisk, she looked determined and just a little annoyed as she passed Chocolate Haven, then punched numbers into a lockbox that hung from the doorknob of May's former store.

She pulled out a key, unlocked the door, and led them into a huge room. Empty of everything but a few shelves, it had a parquet floor that had probably been installed in the seventies, pink walls that were a little dingy, and spiral stairs that led up to the second floor.

A mess.

That was Sinclair's first thought and his second.

His third thought was that he could fix it.

He could tear down a dividing wall that separated the large room from a small kitchen behind it; he could pull up the parquet and reveal hardwood that peeked out at the edges of the room.

He could tear down the ugly spiral stairs and replace them with something more original to the design.

His fourth thought?

That he was crazy to be thinking about anything but getting upstairs and checking on the door.

"Careful on these stairs," Janelle called as she ascended them. "The people who had the building before May were hippies. They wanted to start a commune here in Benevolence, so they bought a few old buildings and *fixed them up.*"

The emphasis on the last words told Sinclair exactly what she thought of the job the hippies had done.

"The place smelled like pot and dog when she bought it, but she managed to make it a very profitable business. Up here," she said as they walked into another gutted room, "was just storage for her shop. I hate to think about what it was before she bought it."

He hated to think of it too.

The room had been ripped apart, plaster pulled off the walls so that the studs were visible beneath. A few old trunks sat against one wall, burn marks in the cracked leather.

He imagined using those trunks in the building after it was brought back to life, but pulled himself away from the thought.

He wasn't going to buy property in Benevolence. He wasn't going to restore it. He sure as hell wasn't going to open an office in the town.

He was intrigued, though. The building had potential, a narrow hallway leading into what must have once been bedrooms. Three were empty, the wood floor as old as the building.

He followed Janelle into one, waiting as she turned on an overhead light. It flickered listlessly in the gray and dingy drop ceiling that had probably been installed around the same time the hippy commune had moved in.

"Really, this building was a little too big for May. Half the rooms weren't used. This being one of them." She bypassed a beanbag chair that had its stuffing spilling out, and opened a closet door.

She stood completely still and silent for a couple of heartbeats too long.

"Is something wrong?" Jax asked, peering over her shoulder and blocking Sinclair's view.

"No. It's just . . ." She bent and lifted something, turning it in her hand.

It looked like a stuffed bear. Or maybe it was a cat. Sinclair wasn't all that up on kids' toys. This one looked old, though. He knew that. The fabric was threadbare, the fur long gone.

"A kid's toy," Jax said, taking it from Janelle and studying it. "Was this here be-fore?"

"I . . . don't remember it being here, but I wasn't looking all that carefully."

Sinclair glanced in the closet. The far wall

had been painted neon orange, the door centered in it bright green. The floor was bare. Not a box. Not a shoe. Nothing. "I don't think it would have been difficult for you to see, Janelle. The closet is empty."

"May and I were together. I just peeked in, checked the lock, and walked away." She frowned. "I'm sure I just missed seeing it. Nothing else makes sense."

"It all makes perfect sense if someone has been in here," Jax responded. "Aside from the front entrance, is there another way in and out of the building?"

"The back door. There's also a fire escape off the back, but that hasn't been used in years. I don't know if it even functions."

"Want to show me both?" Jax headed back across the room, and Janelle followed.

Sinclair stayed where he was.

Neither had tried the door, so he did. It unlocked when he turned the knob. He re-locked it, tried again, and got the same result. He opened the door, tried the one that led into Byron's apartment. It opened easily.

Footsteps tapped on the floor behind him, and Jax whistled.

"Looks like we found our entrance point," he said.

"What's . . ." Janelle's voice trailed off.

251

"What in the world?"

She walked into the closet, crowding in next to Sinclair, her perfume a little too cloying for the space. "I can't believe you were able to get in here."

"The locks don't seem to work properly," he said.

"I'm sure they were working when May and I did our walk-through." She pushed the lock on the doorknob and turned the handle. The lock opened immediately.

"The back door was unlocked too," Jax said, walking into the apartment. "Seems like access to Byron's place was easy enough, if someone wanted to get in."

"Get in for what? Nothing has ever been taken." Sinclair glanced around the office. It looked just the way he'd left it — clean desk with a few work papers piled on one corner, his guitar leaning against the wall. He walked into the hallway, searched the bedroom, the bathroom, the living room. As far as he could tell, nothing had been touched.

Same as always.

"Your guess is as good as mine. I'm think-ing it has something to do with this" — Jax tossed the stuffed toy into the air and caught it — "and I'm also thinking it has something to do with Chase. You've seen the inside of his Corvette. Thing has dozens of stuffed animals shoved into it."

"You think Chase has been staying in the building?" Sinclair asked, ignoring Janelle's frown. She looked more irritated than concerned. He doubted she appreciated being pulled away from her schedule to deal with a problem that wasn't quite a problem. If Chase had been staying in the building, if he had been entering Byron's apartment, he hadn't done any damage, taken anything, or created any real problems.

Unless Sinclair counted the scare that had caused Byron to fall down the stairs.

"I think" — Jax eyed the open doors and then the toy he was holding — "there's a good possibility someone has been in that building. Whether or not it was Chase . . . I'm going to have a little chat with him, see if I can pin down where he's been sleeping at night. I'm also going to call the sheriff. He may want to send another guy over since I'm not officially on duty. I'll be back in a few minutes." He hurried from the room, and Sinclair walked back to the closet.

He didn't like the idea that someone could easily access the apartment. He liked it even less that someone probably had, but he couldn't discount the idea, couldn't quite convince himself that it hadn't happened.

"Is May's building heated?" he asked, testing the locks again. They weren't broken. They also weren't designed to keep properties secure.

He walked back through the closet and into the room beyond. There was no evidence of a squatter. No blankets, no discarded food wrappers, nothing to hint at someone using the property long-term.

"Yes, but she keeps the thermostat set low. She's very frugal, and spending money to keep the place warm when she won't be in it doesn't make sense to her."

"It wouldn't make sense to me either." He headed into the hall, trying hard not to notice the thick crown molding or the hand-carved window casings.

The more he looked, the more evidence of the building's past was revealed. He found those things intriguing. He always did. The past lived in the tiny details of places like this. Nicks in the old wood floor. Cracks in the mantel of a boarded-up fireplace that he found in another room. There were a few paintings on the walls in one of the bigger bedrooms. One looked like it had been created during a drug-induced psychosis, the colors so bright they hurt his eyes. The others were old oil paintings. One of a woman with dark hair and even darker eyes dressed in Victorian attire — dark dress with full sleeves and a low neckline. She held a book in one hand and a cup of tea in the other. He was certain that the fireplace behind her in the picture was the one he'd seen in the other room.

"That's Lily Wilson." Janelle ran her hand along the top of the intricately carved frame, frowning at the layer of dust she removed. "She was married to McArthur Wilson. He owned the textile mill outside of town in the late eighteen hundreds. He built the brownstone right around the time my in-laws built Chocolate Haven; Lily hated living out in the middle of nowhere. She wanted to be in town, right in the center of activity."

"She was a beautiful woman."

"And a very generous one. After McArthur died, she donated ten thousand dollars to build the local library. That was a lot of money back in the day." She glanced at her watch. "I don't want to rush things, Sinclair, but I've got to get home soon. I'm going to leave the key with Jax and have him lock up, but if you don't mind . . ."

She stopped short of asking him to leave.

He should have taken the hint and gone.

He had no intention of doing anything with the property.

He certainly wasn't going to buy it.

That would be an investment in a town that he'd always despised.

But he wanted to see the rest of the property, look at the upper level where the servants had once slept. He had a feeling there'd be more of the building's past there, larger glimpses of what it had once been, a clearer view of what it could be.

"Shit," he murmured, because he knew what was happening, and he was helpless to stop it. He was getting pulled in, just the same way he had dozens of times before.

Some of the guys he worked with said he had a sixth sense when it came to properties. He knew just the ones to choose that would turn the highest profit and make the biggest impact. This place? It could be a showstopper one day, and God help him, he just couldn't seem to turn away from it.

"What's that?" Janelle said, glancing at her watch again, her high-heeled foot tapping on a shag carpet that he was sure hid mahogany floors.

"I don't want to keep you," he responded, touching the old window, his fingers trailing over pitted glass. "But I'd like to see the rest of the building."

"I don't have time —"

"I may be interested in restoring it," he

said, cutting her off.

Her entire demeanor changed. No more impatience. No more tapping toes or glances at her watch.

She smiled, brushing wisps of hair back into whatever fancy hairdo she had. The gesture reminded him of Adeline, but her smile was more predatory than her daughter's could ever be.

"In that case," she nearly purred, "follow me."

CHAPTER TEN

Addie noticed the sheriff's car right around the time Chase returned from the break he'd asked for.

Fifteen minutes to grab a cup of coffee.

She'd allowed it because he'd arrived early, and because the shop had been empty, the first rush of the day over. Things would pick up again at lunchtime, but for now, things were quiet.

Except for the sheriff's car which was parked right in front of the shop.

She watched as Kane Rainier got out, his sheriff's uniform crisp and clean, his shoes gleaming in the sun as he passed the shop door and headed . . .

To May's shop?

That's where it looked like he was going.

She pressed her face against the storefront window, watching as he walked in May's front door.

"Everything okay?" Chase asked as he carried peanut clusters from the kitchen.

"I don't know. The sheriff is next door."

"Really?"

There was a hint of fear in Chase's voice, and she turned to face him.

"Don't worry, he's not going to lock you up," she joked.

"Why would he?" he asked, his gaze dropping as he placed the peanut clusters in the display case.

"Relax. It was a joke."

"Oh. Sorry. Sometimes I'm a little too serious."

"I've only known you a couple of days, but I could have told you that was a fact."

He smiled. The tray was empty, the display case filled with beautiful gleaming chocolates.

It was good to have help.

Great to have help, actually.

She'd been able to keep up on the inventory and fill all the Internet orders. Things were working out swimmingly. She just hoped to heaven Chase wasn't some sort of criminal, because that would screw things up for both of them.

"What's next?" he asked. "Want me to do more of the wedding favors?"

"Sure," she responded, distracted by the sheriff's car, a little worried about what it might mean. May had closed down the shop over a month ago, and the place had been empty since then. As far as Adeline knew, no crime had been committed on the property, but . . . she'd been a little too busy to notice if there had been. Sinclair and Jax had said they were going to ask Janelle to let them into the property. Had they found something? Drugs? Guns? Squatters?

A body?

She pressed her face closer to the glass, trying to see into the shop next door. It was impossible, of course.

"I'll finish the milk chocolates," Chase said as he headed back to the kitchen. "We only have a hundred more of those to make."

"Actually . . ." She stopped him. "Can you watch the front of the house for a few minutes? I want to see what's going on next door. You have my cell phone number. If anything comes up that you don't think you can handle, give me a ring."

He hesitated, then nodded. "Okay. Sure. I can handle that."

"Don't look so scared, Chase. You're not going to get slammed with customers. If you do, just take one order at a time."

She was taking a chance, leaving him there alone. She knew that. Not a chance of him

260

messing things up. A chance that he might take all the money from the register and leave town.

She barely knew the kid, after all.

Jax had said he had a clean record, though, and she figured if Chase were going to steal to fund his trip home, he'd have done it his first day on the job.

Outside, the bright day had grown even brighter, the sun glinting off the sidewalk and gleaming in the windows of May's old shop. The storefront display had once been filled with fabrics and sewing doodads. Often May would hang dresses that she'd made or quilts that someone in the community had fashioned. She'd sold those on commission and had made a tidy little sum from tourists who'd come for the hiking or rafting or for the chocolates, and who'd wanted to bring a piece of Benevolence home with them.

It seemed a little sad to see the windows empty.

Time marches on. That's what May had said when she'd decided to close down. People didn't sew like they once had. They didn't value quality either. They went to Walmart to buy their fabrics and their buttons. They purchased cheap threads instead of the good quality stuff she offered.

Mostly, Addie thought, it had been love that had made May close the business down. She'd made plenty of money in her lifetime, and she wanted to enjoy being a wife.

Late in life, but it was something she'd always dreamed of.

That's another thing May had said.

She'd also said that Addie should find herself a man, that everything that was wrong in her life would be right if she did.

That had made Addie laugh, because nothing had been wrong in her life. Even if something had been, there was no way any man was going to solve the problem.

She bypassed the empty windows and opened the shop door.

The place smelled musty.

Not surprising since no one had been in it for a month.

Janelle had been excited to list the property, certain the place would sell for a pretty penny.

Only it hadn't sold.

The empty building seemed to mock Main Street. In all the years Addie had been alive, she couldn't remember a shop ever staying empty for longer than it took a new owner to move in.

"Hello?" she called, her feet tapping on

the old parquet floor. "Where is everyone?"

"Is that you, Addie?" her mother responded.

Great. Perfect.

Addie had been doing everything in her power to avoid Janelle, because she wanted to avoid the thing she hadn't dared think about — dinner with her sisters.

It was coming. She knew it. Felt it the way other people felt storms blowing in, deep in her bones. Adeline would be there, sitting at one end of the table, her sisters sitting on either side with their significant others close by. Janelle would be at the other end, overseeing the whole thing, a beatific smile on her face.

Until she looked at Adeline.

Her one holdout, the only daughter who didn't have someone in her life.

Adeline loved her sisters. She loved her mom. The three of them together, though? Right before a wedding? When two of the three Lamont girls were in serious committed relationships and Addie was . . . not?

It didn't sound like fun.

It sounded like torture.

"Addie!?" Janelle called again, a hint of impatience in her voice.

"Right here," she called back.

"Good! I planned to stop in and see you.

This will save me some time." Janelle descended the spiral staircase, her high heels clicking on the rungs.

Sinclair was right behind her.

And, God! He looked good.

Just like he had when he'd stopped in Chocolate Haven.

Just like he did every time she saw him.

He smiled, and her cheeks flamed. She felt the heat just kind of creeping up her face, and she couldn't do a thing about it.

No way was she going to let Janelle get any ideas.

"Hello again, Adeline," Sinclair said.

"Again?" Janelle raised one of her perfectly groomed brows.

"He stopped in the shop earlier. To ask about the lights in Byron's apartment," Adeline hurried to reply, because Janelle had a look in her eyes that might have been speculation, and Adeline did not want to go there.

"*His* apartment," Janelle chided. "He's paying for it." She turned her attention to Sinclair, offering one of the smarmy smiles she used when she was trying to convince someone of something. "What do you think, Sinclair? She's beautiful, isn't she?"

For one heart-stopping moment, Addie thought Janelle was talking about her.

Then her mother touched the wall, looked up at the ceiling. "Buildings like this are hard to find in towns like Benevolence."

The building. She was talking about the building.

Thank God!

"Hard to find on the market," he agreed, his gaze focused on Addie. "And you're right, she's very beautiful."

Maybe it was the way his gaze shifted, drifting from Adeline's eyes to her lips and making the journey back up again. Or maybe it was the smile that just touched the corners of his mouth.

Or the gleam in his eyes.

Whatever the case, her face got even hotter, and she thought that if he said one more word, gave her one more look like the one he just had, she might just spontaneously combust.

"Beautiful *and* a good investment," Janelle continued, completely oblivious to the undercurrent that seemed to pulse through the air. "If you restored it, you could rent it out. There are plenty of people in town who aren't in a position to buy but would love to rent the storefront."

He nodded, but his gaze never wavered, his focus so intense, Addie looked away.

"I saw the sheriff come in," she said, her

voice squeaking just a little. She cleared her throat, tried again. "Is something wrong?"

"Jax is concerned that we've had a squatter here. The back door was unlocked and it looks like someone had access to your grandfather's apartment," Janelle responded.

"Don't you think someone would have noticed if a squatter was wandering in and out of the building?" She eyed the cavernous space, tried to imagine someone using it as a crash pad for a night or two or more. It was a little cold, but probably a lot better than sleeping outside.

Or in a car.

A Corvette?

The thought chilled her, a bunch of puzzle pieces suddenly slipping into place.

"Not if the person used the back door and came and went after you left for the night," Janelle responded. "That back parking lot faces the green, and no one is there after dark."

She didn't sound all that concerned, but Addie?

She was worried.

Not about the squatter but about who that person might be. Chase had his Corvette and no money. No food, either. From the way he'd been eating the snacks she kept in

266

the shop, she'd say it had been a while since he'd had a good meal.

"No worries, though," Janelle continued. "Whoever it was isn't here now, and we're going to padlock that back door and place a NO TRESPASSING sign on it. I think that should keep the hooligan out."

"Hooligan?" Addie repeated, barely managing to hold back laughter. "Does anyone use that word anymore?"

Janelle huffed. "I do. And it is completely appropriate to the situation."

Sinclair's lips twitched.

His really nice lips that she had almost kissed and that she would kiss if given another opportunity.

Which was precisely the reason why she needed to stay away from the guy.

Despite what May thought, despite what Janelle thought, despite what every person she knew seemed to think, Addie did not need a man in her life.

"What else would you call someone who lives in a property that isn't his?" Janelle continued.

"Desperate?" Sinclair said, all his amusement gone.

"Well," Janelle replied, "we do have charitable organizations willing to help those who are struggling. Breaking into an empty building and using it for shelter . . . that's just wrong." She glanced at her watch. "I have to get home. We're all having dinner together at six, Adeline. I'm sure you'll have time to stop in for a while. You're invited too, Sinclair. I'm sure Willow would love to reconnect with you."

"I'm not sure when I'll finish work for the day," he said, and she nodded.

"Stop in any time. If you can't make it for dinner, you can join us for dessert. I bought a beautiful cream pie from the bakery and a lovely coffee to go with it. Seven would be a perfect time for that. We can discuss the property a little more then, after you've had some time to think about it."

She headed outside, her pace brisk. No doubt she assumed that Sinclair would show up for dessert and the discussion. People usually did what Janelle wanted.

"Your mother," Sinclair said once Janelle disappeared, "is a force to be reckoned with."

"Isn't that the truth?" she sighed.

"Were you making chocolate?" he asked, rubbing at a spot on her cheekbone. "Or bathing in it?"

She laughed, her skin tingling where he'd touched it, her stomach twisting with the kind of longing she had never ever wanted to feel again. "The fudge didn't set. I guess it splattered when I tossed it in the trash."

"Chocolate is a good look on you," he murmured, leaning forward and running his finger along her neck.

"More chocolate?" she asked, her voice thick.

"No," he said simply. No excuse. No explanation, and his finger just kind of stayed right where it was, resting lightly at the hollow of her throat.

She could have moved away.

She should have, but she just stood there like a ninny, looking into his eyes.

"Sinclair!" Jax called from somewhere above. "Get your ass up here. We found something."

That was it. The spell broke. The heat disappeared.

Sinclair jogged up the stairs, and Addie followed, her heart racing.

She could fall for this guy.

She could fall harder than she'd ever fallen with Adam, because she was an adult, mature enough to know what she wanted and what she didn't. Mature enough to be looking for something more than what she'd had before.

"This way," Jax said, leading them through the hallway and to a door. It opened into a stairwell.

Funny that Adeline had never been on the third floor of the building. She'd worked for May when she was in high school, restocking shelves and ringing up customers, but she'd been too caught up in teenage things to think much about the building that the fabric store was housed in.

Now she was curious.

Old wallpaper decorated the walls — muted flowers that had probably once been vibrant and lovely. At the top of the stairs, a landing opened into three rooms. Kane Rainier stood on the threshold of one, a camera in hand. A transplant from Seattle, he'd been working in law enforcement there before applying for a position as a deputy in Benevolence. That had been six years ago. He'd moved up the ranks quickly because he was a great guy, fair and hardworking. It hadn't surprised anyone when he'd been named sheriff. Sometimes, though, Addie wondered why he'd chosen to leave everything he had, everything he knew in Seattle, to settle in a town he'd never even visited.

She'd asked him once, and he'd just smiled and told her it was the chocolate that had convinced him.

"Looks like someone has been here for a while," he said, stepping aside so that Sinclair could look inside.

Addie pressed in close, peering around his arm and eying the interior of the room.

A bed of blankets lay on the floor. No pillow, but there was a small suitcase sitting in one corner. Beside it, several empty cracker packages had been abandoned.

She knew the brand of crackers.

They were her grandfather's favorite.

As a matter of fact, he usually kept his pantry stocked with them.

Her heart skipped a beat, and she eased under Sinclair's arm, trying to see if there was anything else in the room that might have been Byron's. One of the blankets could have been his. The boxes of cereal that sat under the window? They were Byron's favorite too.

"Whoever it is," she said, her stomach hollow with anxiety because she knew . . . *knew* . . . it was Chase, "may have gotten some of the food from Byron's place."

And, maybe, a blanket.

She glanced around the room.

And a towel or two.

"I think we all know who it is," Jax growled. "That kid has definitely outstayed his welcome."

"You don't know that Chase was involved," she argued, even though they both did know.

"How about we go ask?" Kane said calmly.

That was what she'd noticed first about him — how calm he always was. Nothing seemed to faze him. Ornery drunks, petty thieves, drug addicts, wife beaters, Kane handled them all with remarkable aplomb. He knew how to be tough and compassionate, and that was a necessary thing in a town the size of Benevolence.

"How about we do." Jax headed for the stairs, but Kane pulled him up short.

"It's your day off, and your aunt is expecting you. I'll handle this." It wasn't a command, but it wasn't a suggestion either.

Jax's jaw tightened but he nodded. "Let me know what he says."

He stalked away. Obviously not happy, but too respectful to argue with his boss.

"Okay," Kane said. "Here's how we're going to play this. No accusations. I'm just going to take Chase into Byron's office and ask him where he's been staying. We'll see if he admits to squatting on the property. If he does, I think we can call this a kid's mistake. If he lies . . ." He shrugged. "Maybe he's not as nice a kid as people keep telling me."

"He *is* a nice kid," Addie insisted, but Kane was already heading downstairs.

Sinclair touched her back, urging her to follow.

"It's going to be fine," he said.

She hoped he was right.

She really did.

The kid was smart.

He admitted everything. His car had broken down near the campsite sometime around midnight. No one was around, but he could see lights from town, so he'd walked there.

By the time he'd hit Main Street, he was freezing. He saw the FOR SALE sign on May's shop and tried the front and back doors. The back had been unlocked, so he'd walked in to get warm.

The rest, as Chase told Byron over the phone, was history.

Sinclair wasn't sure he should be listening to Chase confess his crimes, but after the sheriff talked to the kid, he'd insisted that Chase call Byron and May.

There was only one landline in the shop. It was in the kitchen, where they were all congregated, the sheriff staring Chase down as he spoke to Byron, Addie pretending to be busy making fudge, only she'd scooped so many cups of sugar in the bowl, he thought it was going to be more like rock candy than chocolate.

Sinclair didn't pretend anything.

He was there.

He was listening.

And he was impressed by the way Chase presented the facts. There were no excuses. He explained how he'd gone into Byron's apartment and gotten some crackers. Later he'd taken cereal. He'd intended to leave money to repay him, but — and this was the hard part, the part where Chase's voice broke and Addie let out a little sob — Byron had seen Chase in the hall one night, run outside, and fallen.

The kid obviously felt guilty.

He promised all kinds of things over the phone, and Sinclair didn't think it was because he wanted to keep from going to jail. He'd work for free, he'd paint the shop, he'd clean Byron's apartment every day for the rest of his life. He'd even take care of the elderly man when he got out of the hospital.

It was as sincere an apology as Sinclair had ever heard.

When Chase finally ran out of words, he listened for a minute, nodded. "Okay. Sure, Mr. Lamont. I really appreciate it. Okay."

He handed the phone to Addie, and then

ran into the restroom and slammed the door.

Sinclair had a feeling he was crying, but at eighteen, he was too proud to let anyone see it.

Sinclair? He'd learned to cry in public right around the time he'd knelt by the side of one of his comrades and held his hand while he was dying.

"I agree," Adeline spoke into the silence. "Yes. Of course. Monday? That's . . . a little sooner than I expected. No. Of course I'm not backing out. I said you could stay with me, and you can." She listened for a minute, frowned. "Granddad, relax. I'll take care of it. Right. See you tonight."

She held the phone out to the sheriff. "He wants to speak with you."

She walked out of the room without another word.

Sinclair followed because he'd heard what he wanted to, and because he had to get back to work, but first . . .

Adeline.

Yeah. She'd been on his mind a little too much.

He could try to avoid her, or he could go with his gut, spend a little more time getting to know the person she really was.

The way he saw things, that would either

make him want more or it would clear his head, make him see the truth so that he could go back to Seattle and move on. No regrets. No doubts.

She was at the register when he walked into the service area, back to him, her red braid falling to the middle of her shoulders.

She heard him coming. He knew it, but she didn't turn.

"What did your grandfather say?" he asked, and she finally turned, her eyes a little red. No tears, but he thought they were there just waiting to fall.

"He completely forgives Chase. Of course. He said mistakes happen, and the fact that he owned up to what he did really impressed Byron. He could have lied and said he had nothing to do with Granddad's fall. No one was there, and there would have been no way to prove what had happened. We're going to float Chase a loan so he can get his car repaired and a place to stay."

"He could skip town with the money." But Sinclair didn't think he would. He thought Chase was the kind of kid who'd stick around and pay off his debts.

"Granddad says any kid who has the courage to confess to what Chase did, will stick around long enough to repay a loan."

"I think your grandfather is right."

She nodded, but all the good humor that was usually in her face and in her eyes was missing. She looked sad and tired and a little too overwhelmed for Sinclair's liking.

"What's wrong?" he asked, taking her hand and tugging her closer. They were just inches apart, and he could see the blond tips to her red lashes, the beginning of fine lines near the corners of her eyes.

"I just . . ." She shook her head.

"What?"

"Feel bad for everyone. Chase. My grandfather." She paused, laughed. "Me."

"Is running the shop that difficult?"

"Filling my grandfather's shoes is," she responded, reaching up to brush something from his shoulder. "Dust," she said. "May's place is a mess."

"It's a diamond in the rough."

"You're not really planning to buy it?"

"I'm thinking about it."

"Why?" she asked, and he could think of a dozen reasons. Most of them about profit and margin, but the thing that mattered most had nothing to do with any of those things.

"Because it deserves to be restored. It deserves to look like what it did when Lily Wilson lived in it."

"Mom told you about her, huh?" She

smiled, a little of the sadness lifting.

"There's a portrait of her in one of the rooms."

"One of the only ones the hippies didn't get to. There are about a dozen others painted over in bright colors. The town historian is hoping to have them restored one day. She says they belong in the Wilson house. Lily's husband adored her. Probably because she was so much younger than he was."

"Her husband was old?"

"Mom didn't tell you the whole story. It was quite the scandal. Lily was the other woman before she was the wife." She stood on her toes and whispered in his ear. "People say that he never divorced his first wife. Just sent her off to live in Seattle so that he could live with gorgeous Lily."

"Lily the lady who funded the library?"

"One and the same." She backed up, and he was sorry she'd moved away, sorry that her warm breath wasn't still whispering against his skin. "People in Benevolence aren't sure whether to love her or hate her. She did a lot for the community though, so I choose to believe she really loved her husband and that she really believed he was divorced when she married him."

"You like to think the best about everyone, don't you?" he asked, and she sighed.

"It's gotten me into some trouble, but yes. I guess I do."

"You make it sound like a bad thing."

"Only when the people you believe the best about aren't worthy of it."

"There's a story there," he said, cupping her face in his hands, looking into her eyes. "I'd like to hear it."

"Why?" she asked, her cheeks pink but her gaze direct.

"Because I want to get to know you better," he admitted. He'd never been one to beat around the bush. Not in business and not in relationships.

"Again, I'm going to ask why. You'll be here for a couple of weeks, and then you'll leave, and I'll still be here doing the same thing I've been doing for my entire adult life."

"If you're not happy —"

"I'm very happy," she said, cutting him off. "That's the problem. I like life in this little town. I don't want anything different. Someone like you . . ." She shook her head. "You'd always want more, and you'd never find it here. Not in any piece of property or person or family."

"You're assuming a lot, Adeline." He let his hands drift to her nape, let his fingers slide along soft warm flesh, and he thought that maybe, even in a town like Benevolence, home could be made or found or discovered.

"I'm assuming because I've seen it before. Been there, done that. Not going to repeat it."

He wanted to ask her who she'd been there with. That brainy guy she'd hung out with when she was a kid?

Alec? Adam?

The bell rang and a group of teenagers ran in, giggling and laughing as they joked about how much chocolate they could eat.

Adeline got busy ringing up orders, and Sinclair figured he should get busy at his brother's place.

He didn't want to go, though.

He wanted to stay for a while, watch Adeline laugh and chat with the people who came into the shop, see what it was about this life and this place that she loved so much.

Because he wouldn't mind finding what she had. Wouldn't mind being as certain as Adeline that he was exactly where he wanted to be with exactly the people he wanted to spend his time with.

Chapter Eleven

Gavin returned Tiny at five thirty.

Adeline pretended that she wasn't disappointed that Sinclair hadn't been the one to bring the puppy back.

She was good at pretending: pretending she was doing just fine running the shop, pretending that she was excited about being in May's wedding, pretending that it didn't matter that she still didn't have a date to the nuptials.

Pretending that she was excited about having dinner at her mother's house.

Scratch that.

She wasn't excited about it, and she didn't care if Janelle knew it. If she could have thought of a good excuse not to go, she would have. Sadly, she'd come up blank, so she'd given Chase the closing checklist and left.

He had her cell phone number. If he had any trouble, he was supposed to call. Otherwise, he'd close at six, make a few dozen white chocolate wedding favors, and then head over to Adeline's place. She'd given him a key, because that had been part of the agreement he'd drawn up with the sheriff. Byron and May wouldn't press charges, the sheriff's department wouldn't press charges, but there were some things Chase had to do while he was in town. One of them was find a place to stay.

Addie had offered that. She'd also given him three weeks' pay up front.

He'd been unhappy, but the sheriff had taken him to the bank, watched as he'd deposited the check, and then taken him to have the new carburetor ordered.

She didn't know what the two had talked about while they were gone, but Chase was quiet when he returned. He'd stayed quiet all day, and she was worried that maybe he'd do exactly what Byron and Sinclair said he wouldn't: run.

One more thing to add to her list of worries.

She tugged on black slacks and slipped on a sweater set that Willow had sent her for Christmas. Cashmere. Definitely not something she could run through the wash. It was pretty, though, the color a muted purple that Addie would never have chosen for herself.

Her cell phone rang, and she glanced at the caller ID.

Janelle. Of course, because it was quarter of six, and Adeline wasn't there.

Too bad.

Dinner was being served at six. She'd be there at six. Hopefully her mother would be too busy picking her future son-in-laws' brains to ask Adeline about her date for the wedding.

She grabbed her pumps from the closet.

Pump?

There was only one sitting on the rack.

She looked under the bed, went in the office, searched it.

No sign of the shoe.

She had another pair, but they were bright red stilettos that Brenna had given her for her birthday.

Not quite her style.

"Tiny!" she called. "You didn't get in my closet while I was in the shower, did you?"

The puppy trotted in, a massacred shoe hanging limply from his mouth.

"You did!" she shouted, and poor Tiny scrambled under the bed, the shoe still in his mouth.

Or he tried.

Only his head went under.

His butt hung out, his tail thumping wildly.

"This is not a game!" she yelled. "I have to be at Mom's house in five minutes, and you've destroyed the only pair of heels I can actually walk in."

Tiny's tail thumped even more wildly.

"Darn it, Tiny! I need this like I need another hole in my head." She reached into the closet, grabbed the first thing her hand landed on. A dress of some sort. Soft gray. "I can't wear red and purple either. You know what my mother will do. Comment on the choice in front of the girls' handsome, successful dates. You know? The thing I don't have!?" she shouted, irritated way out of proportion to the crime.

It was just a black pump, after all.

And not an expensive one.

But, God!

She was tired, and she had to go to dinner and then to the hospital, and when she got home an eighteen-year-old kid was going to be there.

She discarded the slacks and sweater, tossing both onto the bed, then tugged on the dress she'd pulled out. Another one of Willow's picks, it slid over her breasts and hips, clinging to every curve she had.

She scowled at her reflection as she shoved her feet into the stilettos. On one of her sisters the look would have worked. She just looked like a kid playing dress up.

She ran a brush through her hair, put on lipstick and a little blush, dragged Tiny from the bedroom, and slammed the door.

"Go ahead," she told him. "Enjoy the leather shoe, but we have company coming over tonight, so you're going into the laundry room until I can introduce you."

A little dog food, and Tiny was convinced that the laundry room was the place to be. She put a sign on the door so that Chase would know not to open it, and ran outside, her ankles wobbling as she hurried to her car.

She was already two minutes late.

Janelle was probably sitting at the table, talking about how thoughtless Addie was being.

"Shit," she breathed, as she buckled her seat belt and skidded out onto the road. "Shit, shit, shit."

Nehemiah was out on his front porch.

He waved as she drove by, and she slowed down, because she'd hate to hit an elderly person or a kid or even a dog just because she was in a mood and driving too fast.

She pulled up in front of Janelle's house

ten minutes late, limped up the driveway in heels that were never meant to be worn by someone like her, and walked into the house that she'd always felt just a little out of place in.

She heard voices.

Just as she'd predicted, everyone was gathered in the dining room.

"Is that you, Adeline?!" Janelle called.

"Who else would it be?" she murmured, then called, "Yes. Sorry I'm late. The shop —"

"Come on in and sit down. Dinner is getting cold."

Right.

Dinner.

She walked into the dining room, the space glowing with candlelight and ambience, the table nearly overflowing with food. A wine bucket sat at one end of the table, the silver gleaming in the dim light.

There was a couple on either side of the rectangular table. Brenna and Dan. Willow and Ken. Beautiful and handsome . . . every single one of them.

Both sisters stood as she walked in, both ran to her.

And then they were all hugging the way they'd done hundreds of times before, and it seemed as if all the years when they hadn't really been part of each other's lives didn't exist.

"I've missed you both," she said, pulling back to look at them. Willow looked tired, her cheeks even more hollow than usual, her eyes shadowed. Brenna looked . . . tense, as if she wanted to be anywhere but there.

Join the crowd, Addie wanted to say, but two men that she barely knew were watching, so she kept her mouth shut.

"Dan. Ken. How are you?" she asked.

That was enough to open the flood gates.

Ken loved to talk about his real estate business, and Janelle loved to join in. Next thing Addie knew, everyone was eating and chatting and it was almost like being a normal family except that neither of her sisters seemed thrilled to be there.

She met Willow's eyes, wanted to reach over and touch her hand, ask what was wrong and why, when her life seemed perfect, she looked like she wanted to cry.

"How are things going for you, Addie?" Willow asked, picking at the salmon that a caterer had prepared.

"Great," she lied. "The shop is running pretty smoothly."

Janelle interrupted her conversation with Ken to cut in. "You know that Byron is being released on Monday, right?"

"Yes. I know."

"And you know that he is refusing to go to the convalescent center?"

"I know that too."

"He told me that he is staying with you."

Uh-oh. They were moving into dangerous territory. There was nothing Adeline could do but walk right into it. "That's right."

"I wish that you had informed me of that fact. I had to pull strings to get him into Good Sam's. People went to a lot of effort to make sure there was a spot, and —"

"Granddad is a grown man," Brenna interrupted. "I think he's perfectly capable of deciding where he wants to recover."

"That's easy for you to say, Brenna," Janelle said. "You're not the one who is going to be taking care of him. Adeline is."

"If she wants to do it, I still don't see what the problem is." Brenna wasn't going to back down. She never did.

Adeline had always loved that about her, the way that she fought for what she believed in, went after everything wholeheartedly. She was the youngest and the toughest.

Dan leaned over, whispered something in her ear, and she frowned, reaching for her glass of wine.

After that, she didn't say a word, just

shoved salmon into her mouth like she'd never eaten before.

Addie, on the other hand, was picking at the fish, the salad, the bread, the couscous. She didn't want to call attention to her diet, but she couldn't afford to eat the massive amount of food her mother had piled on her plate.

"As I was saying," Janelle continued, "Byron is going to need a lot of help, and Addie won't be home much. She's so busy with the shop and with her accounting business. Dan, did I tell you that she is an accountant?"

"I believe you did," he said, smiling at Adeline.

She should have liked the guy. Her sister loved him, for crying out loud!

But the handful of times she'd talked to him, she'd found him to be a little too bigheaded, a little too confident, and a little too fake. Four years after he'd started dating Brenna, he still hadn't given her a ring. Adeline had a feeling tonight was the night. That was the way he was, the kind of guy who'd want to make a big deal out of the moment, have people watching his grand gesture.

If he really knew Brenna, he'd have known she didn't like being in the limelight. Just because she'd modeled in New York and in Europe didn't mean she liked everyone knowing her business.

All in all, she was a private person who didn't share much of herself with anyone.

Maybe not even Dan.

Addie eyed the guy.

"And you're a plastic surgeon," she said, because she'd rather not talk about her accounting job when she was sitting with an attorney, a doctor, a model, and a real estate mogul.

"I am. Shocking that your sister and I ever met, considering that she refuses to let me do any work on her."

Maybe it was supposed to be funny.

Addie wasn't laughing.

Neither was Brenna.

Her full lips were pinched tight, her fingers wrapped around the stem of the wineglass like it was Dan's neck and she wanted to break it. "Not a good topic for the dinner table," she said tightly, and Addie wondered if things were okay between the two of them. She'd never liked Dan, but from the moment Brenna met him at a modeling gig, she'd been smitten with the guy.

"A joke, honey," Dan said, patting her shoulder and smirking like she was too stupid to understand things. "Relax."

"I am relaxed," she bit out, but anyone sitting at the table could see it wasn't true.

"How about we have some dessert?" Janelle said, ringing a small silver bell that sat next to her plate.

Seconds later, the catering team was there, clearing plates and refilling water glasses.

One more course, and Addie could make her excuses and leave.

She'd catch up with her sisters when their mother wasn't around.

And when talkative Dan and Ken weren't there.

And when all of them were relaxed enough to really connect.

Which might be several decades from then.

She frowned, sipping her water and half listening as Dan described the facelift he'd given a celebrity whose name he could not mention.

She barely noticed when the doorbell rang, didn't pay much attention when her mother left the table. She was too busy eyeing the cream pies that the caterer had brought in.

Pies as in plural. As in more than one.

As in, she wanted to dive headfirst into the coconut one, because Janelle had gotten it from the local bakery, and Addie knew exactly how the coconut cream pie would taste.

She was salivating. Seriously. And if she didn't leave the table, she might just pull the entire pie onto her plate and dig in.

She stood. "I think I'll go see if Mom has any diet soda," she said to anyone who was listening, and then she ran into the kitchen.

Sinclair had been inside the Lamont house once or twice when he was a kid knocking on doors and begging for work because he'd needed money to buy food. Janelle had let him cut the grass a few times. On really hot days, she'd invite him into the kitchen for a cold glass of pop or some water.

The place was as posh and perfect as he remembered, everything in its place, and everyone looking stunning. Willow and Brenna hadn't changed much. They still had Lamont red hair and blue eyes. Both were classically pretty. Beautiful, really, but not nearly as intriguing as Adeline.

"Where is your sister?" Janelle asked, gesturing for Sinclair to sit in a chair beside Willow.

He waited, because he wanted to know where Adeline was too.

She was the reason he'd come.

Not the property that he'd been thinking about while he cleaned out his grandfather's mess, not the hope of some amazing desserts. He'd come because he hadn't heard the rest of Adeline's story about the guy she'd been down the road with.

He wanted to hear it.

He wanted to listen to her talk about the guy that Gavin said had been an asshole in the first degree.

Yeah. Sinclair had asked.

He'd picked his brother's brain while they'd cleaned out their grandmother's dresser. A dresser filled with things that had surprised Sinclair. Pretty baubles and trinkets, nice quality antique jewelry, old photos of people long gone.

He'd put everything in boxes and brought it to the apartment. He had a feeling a few of the pieces had value. He had a friend who was in the antique business. She lived in Seattle, but might be willing to drive in to see the things he'd been finding. All the junk his grandfather had collected had hidden some really nice pieces.

"Addie went to get some diet soda," Brenna said, standing and stretching. She was tall. Just a few inches shy of Sinclair's height and as lean as a racehorse. "She should be back in a minute."

"Diet soda? With a meal like this? The girl is addicted to the stuff." Janelle shook her head, obviously disgusted by her middle daughter's choice. "I'd better go talk to her. She'll probably bring the entire bottle to the table."

"God forbid," Willow intoned, and Janelle frowned.

"We had salmon, Willow. And couscous. And asparagus salad."

"I know what we had, Mother, but I don't see why Adeline can't have what she wants to drink."

"I agree with Willow," the man sitting next to her said. He looked to be around Sinclair's age, his blond hair cut in some trendy style, his clothes obviously expensive.

"I'm sure you do, Ken," Janelle said with a broad smile. "She's your fiancée. I'd be disappointed if you did anything else."

"Not just because of that," Ken said. "She's a beautiful, intelligent woman, and I appreciate her insight." He smiled at Willow, and she lowered her gaze, poked at a piece of pie her mother had set in front of her.

It didn't take a hell of a lot of insight to see that she wasn't buying the phony compliment, but far be it from Sinclair to point it out.

"One of the things I like about you, Ken,"

Janelle continued, Adeline apparently forgotten in Janelle's bid to impress Willow's husband-to-be, "is that you are supportive of Willow. I'm sure that being in a relationship with a prosecuting attorney isn't always easy, but . . ."

Sinclair walked out of the room, following the sound of clanging pans into the kitchen.

Four people were there. Three of them wore black slacks and shirts. Adeline wore a dress made of some kind of soft fabric that hugged every one of her beautiful curves.

He could have crossed the room right then, slid his hands along her sides and let them settle at the narrow curve of her waist. He could have pulled her into his arms and kissed her the way he'd been wanting to do just about from the moment he'd seen her, but she looked miserable, her red hair hanging limply around her face, her expression grim.

"Troubles?" he asked.

She shrugged, walking out the back door and onto a wraparound porch that looked out onto a well-lit yard. Small lights on either side of a paved path led the way to a beautiful gazebo, but Adeline stayed where she was, shivering in the crisp cold breeze.

"Maybe outside isn't the best idea," Sinclair murmured, rubbing his hands along her arms.

"I'd rather freeze than spend another minute at that table."

"Your mother?"

"My sisters. They aren't happy. Neither am I, because I can't stand the men in their lives."

"I heard that Willow was engaged," he said.

"You heard right. I'm still in denial, because Ken is one of the most obnoxious men I've ever met, and I've met a lot of them."

"According to Gavin, you dated one of them," he responded, and she met his eyes, the long fall of her hair sliding over her shoulder and resting against the sweet curve of her breasts.

"Gavin has a big mouth," she replied, stalking to the porch railing and staring out into the yard. "But I can't say he's wrong. Adam wasn't exactly a winner."

"He was the short guy who liked to wear bow ties and spout useless facts, right?"

She laughed. "I thought the bow tie was cute and the useless facts fascinating."

"Until?"

"Until he decided that there were more exciting things than this town and the people who lived here. And me."

"How long did you two date?" he asked, and she turned to face him.

"Why are you asking, Sinclair?"

"Because I'm curious."

"About a decade-old relationship that didn't work out?"

"About you." He took a step closer, inhaled the clean air, the subtle scent of winter that still clung to it. Chocolate. Berries. Adeline. All of it mixed together in some heady aroma that he couldn't resist.

His hands found their way to her waist, slid around so that his palms rested against the curve of her lower spine.

"I think we had this conversation earlier," she said, but she didn't move away.

If she had, he'd have backed off. If she'd said one word that indicated she wasn't just as curious as he was, just as interested, he'd have gone back inside.

"We started the conversation earlier, but we didn't finish it," he replied, brushing a lock of hair from the side of her neck and leaning down to press his lips to the spot his fingers had caressed. Warm smooth skin and a hint of chocolate, and every thought in his head flew away.

"God, Adeline," he murmured. "You are gorgeous."

"My sisters are gorgeous, I'm —"

He stopped the words with a kiss that should have been light and simple. Just a brush of the lips to seal in the words he didn't want to hear.

It wasn't enough.

Nothing would ever be enough when it came to Adeline.

He dragged her in, her soft curves as addictive as her lips, and when she moaned, he was lost. Lips against lips, body against body, just thin fabric between them. Her hands on his arms and then his waist.

"Adeline!?" Janelle called.

Sinclair broke away, his breath heaving as he looked into Adeline's eyes.

She looked as dazed as he felt.

"Damn," he muttered, and she laughed shakily.

"That's one way to put it."

"Adeline?! Sinclair?!?" Janelle walked out the back door. "There you both are! Dan is about to make an announcement, but he wants the whole family there when he does."

"Granddad isn't here," Adeline pointed out, and Janelle frowned.

"Please don't ruin this for your sister by mentioning that," she snapped. "This is her moment, and I want it to be as perfect as it can be."

"Another engagement, huh?" Adeline said,

her body seeming to shrink in on itself as she followed her mother into the house.

"Yes. Dan has been planning it for a month. I even helped him choose the ring." She sounded . . . giddy. Not a word that Sinclair would normally use to describe Janelle, but that's exactly what she seemed to be.

"Something simple, I hope. You know that —"

Janelle cut her off. "Adeline, your sister has very sophisticated taste. Simple doesn't suit her. Now, hurry up! I've got my camera ready to record the moment."

"Of course you do," Adeline muttered as her mother hurried into the dining room.

"Don't be bitter, Adeline," he said, taking her hand and pressing a quick kiss to her palm. "It doesn't suit you."

"I'm not bitter, I'm . . . irritated. Mom doesn't care who any of us marry. As long as we marry."

"I think you're wrong about that." Janelle was a lot of things, but she wasn't stupid. Maybe she was caught up in the moment. Maybe she wasn't seeing the forest for the trees. Eventually, though, if a guy wasn't good to her daughter, she wasn't going to put up with him. "I think she wants the three of you to be happy, and I think that she equates marriage and family to that."

"I think . . ." She frowned. "You're right, but I still find this whole farce annoying."

She stomped away.

Or tried to.

Her heel caught on a fancy oriental throw rug, and she tripped.

He grabbed her before she could fall into a sideboard filled with antique glass.

"Careful," he murmured, his hands refusing to release her waist. "You take out that glass display, and your mother will have a lot more to complain about than your diet soda addiction."

"Addiction? Is that the word she used?"

"Yes."

"Maybe I should take up smoking or . . . illegal drugs. That would give her something real to complain about. Or I could become an alcoholic and wander around town plastered all the time."

"Like my grandfather used to do," he said, the words harsher than he'd intended.

"Oh God! No! I wasn't —"

"I know. Sorry. Being back here . . ." He shook his head, irritated with himself for being overly sensitive. "Turns me into the kid I was before I left."

She cocked her head to the side, studying him for several heartbeats. "You were a great kid, Sinclair. Everyone in town thought so. You were the only one who wasn't sure of it."

Then she turned on her heel and marched into the dining room.

He followed, her words filling his head, mixing with the ones Jax had spoken. *Everyone in town was proud of you.*

Maybe.

If he thought about it enough, remembered the people who'd cheered him on, helped him out, offered him jobs so that he could buy the things he and his brother needed, Sinclair had to admit that people in town had cared.

He'd been the one with the chip on his shoulder.

He'd been the one who'd felt out of place.

He wasn't sure how he felt now.

Maybe like he was finally figuring out where he belonged.

CHAPTER TWELVE

Addie couldn't stop thinking about the kiss.

Not during Dan's proposal. Not as she dutifully oohed and aahed over the huge diamond and sapphire ring he slid onto Brenna's finger. Not as they all made a toast to Dan and Brenna's happiness.

A toast that Sinclair had made with a glass of apple juice.

She'd filed that piece of information away for another time, and then . . . she'd thought about the kiss.

Because she just couldn't stop reliving the way his lips had felt, the warmth of his hands, the way her toes had curled inside the stilettos.

She and Sinclair discussed a lot of things during the long drive to the hospital, but neither had mentioned the kiss.

Now Addie was sitting in Byron's hospital room, nursing a lukewarm cup of coffee and trying really hard not to think about the one thing she couldn't stop thinking about.

It would have been a lot easier to do if Sinclair hadn't been sitting right beside her, his thigh pressed against hers as they listened to Byron complain about the hospital, the food, the nurses.

"I mean, really, doll," Byron said for what seemed like the hundredth time. "Shouldn't they let an old man rest?"

"You're not an old man, Granddad," she replied, and he scowled, poking at the button on the bed rail and raising his head a little more.

"I am old, and I'm getting older every day that I have to lie in this damn bed." He'd lost a little weight since he'd been admitted to the hospital, and his eyes had lost some of their spark. The salt-and-pepper hair he'd had for as long as Addie could remember seemed grayer, his skin colorless.

"You'll be home on Monday. In a nice quiet room with —"

"That kid hovering over me, right?" He poked her arm like he always did when he wanted to make sure he had her attention.

"Chase won't hover if you don't want him to."

"I sure as hell don't! I may be old, but I can take care of myself. Am I right, Sinclair?" he demanded.

Sinclair nodded. "It's obvious that you can."

"I knew I liked you, kid, and I'd like you even better if you'd go to the Riverfront Mall and buy me a couple of cigars."

"You can't smoke in the hospital," Addie protested.

"There's a designated area right outside. I'll just wheel myself over there and have myself a nice smoke, maybe a little whiskey."

Sinclair laughed.

Adeline wasn't amused.

Knowing Byron, he'd been plotting ways to get cigars and whiskey for hours. Maybe even days.

"Who else did you hit up for cigars?"

"A couple of the nurses. I offered a hundred dollars, but no one took me up on the offer. Now, Jack . . . he was more than willing to bring me a couple. You know how Jack is. Right, doll?" He poked her again. "Got me a stash of booze too."

"Please tell me you're kidding," she said, but she knew he wasn't. Jack Withcott and Byron had been friends for decades. They'd grown up together, worked on the town council together. They argued, debated, and spent plenty of summer evenings sitting on Jack's porch with a glass of whiskey and a couple of cigars.

"Why would I kid about something like that?" Byron grinned.

"Where'd you stash the stuff?" she demanded, getting down on her hands and knees to look under the bed. She thought she saw something up near the head of the bed, and she shimmied under, tugging her dress back into place as it rode up her thigh.

She snagged a small box, dragged it out, and opened it. Sure enough, there were a dozen nice quality cigars inside it. "I can't believe Jack did this."

"Believe it, kid." Byron leaned back, his hands behind his head, his eyes gleaming with amusement. "The booze is in the closet."

"Granddad! Seriously, you can't drink and smoke while you're recovering."

"Never said I did either of those things. I just left the possibility open." He eyed Sinclair, smiled a smile that could only mean trouble. "So, you came to visit because you wanted to see how I was doing, huh?"

"That's right."

"Had nothing to do with the fact that you got to spend an hour and a half in a car with my beautiful granddaughter?"

"Granddad!" she protested, but things had already spiraled way out of her control. Byron was like a dog with a bone . . . or

Tiny with a shoe. Once he got hold of something, there was no letting go.

"What? It's a valid question." He shifted his attention to Sinclair again. "You going to answer?"

"It definitely had something to do with that," Sinclair responded bluntly.

Which, of course, was going to win him about a thousand brownie points with Byron.

"Hmm." Byron nodded. "Good answer. You go get me some coffee, Adeline. I want to talk to Sinclair."

"About what?" she asked, because there was no way ever that she was leaving the two of them alone together.

"A project that I'm interested in him doing."

"What kind of project?" she demanded.

He smirked. "That's for me to know and you to find out."

"Granddad, seriously, I came all the way out here to visit with you. I'm not running for coffee so that you can spend fifteen minutes picking Sinclair's brains about his intentions."

"I said a project, Adeline. Not a miracle. Only the good Lord can do those."

"What's that supposed to mean?"

"You're jaded. We all know it. That scumbag Adam did a number on you, and there's nothing any man can ever do that will convince you that other men won't do the same. Talking to Sinclair about his intentions would be a waste of time for both of us because you are obviously determined to stay single and —"

"I'll get the coffee." She thrust the cigars into Sinclair's hands and ran from the room.

God! Her family!

They were all nuts.

Or maybe she was the crazy one, because the entire time Byron had been talking, she'd been thinking about how immature she'd been when she'd dated Adam, about how she hadn't really known what she wanted. If she had, she would have been looking for someone who was honest about the way he felt, who didn't just jump on board with her dreams because he wanted to be with her.

She would have been looking for someone who saw who she really was. Not who he wanted her to be.

Someone like . . .

Nope!

She wasn't going there.

She was not going to think about all the wonderful qualities Sinclair had. She wasn't going to imagine that maybe he was what she should have been looking for when she'd been too young to understand what forever really meant.

She ran down the corridor, found a vending machine, and shoved quarters in it. Her hands were shaking and her heart was racing, and she didn't know why. Or maybe she did.

She'd spent a lot of time thinking she'd stay single.

She'd put up walls and barriers, refused invitations, stayed busy with activities that didn't include dates. Somehow, some way, the walls had come down, and she was seeing possibilities again.

She didn't want that, because she didn't want to be hurt again. She also didn't want to look like Willow had at dinner — tired and worn out and unsure. She didn't want to accept a ring like she thought Brenna might have, because the family was looking on and she'd been in the relationship so long she didn't know how to be out of it.

What Adeline wanted was the kind of love Mary Sue had had. She wanted a man who'd love her with the kind of longevity that Nehemiah had exhibited, through good and bad and thick and thin and everything in between.

She wanted the happily-ever-after, the

forever and ever.

She wanted it, but she didn't really believe she could ever have it.

She grabbed the cup, sloshing coffee over her hand as she hurried back to the room. Sinclair and Byron were deep in conversation, a piece of paper on the small table beside the bed, both of them bent over it.

Something about the picture they made hit her in the heart. Maybe it was Byron's bony shoulders beneath faded blue flannel pajamas, or the way he was smiling as if he and Sinclair were already good friends. Or . . . it could have been Sinclair, studying the paper as if it were the most interesting thing he'd ever seen. Whatever the case, seeing them together made her think of family the way it used to be, before her father had died and her mother had gotten busy and her sisters had run.

She was tired.

That was the problem.

Otherwise she'd have just walked across the room, looked at the paper, asked what they were doing.

Instead, she set Byron's coffee on the table, walked to the window, and pulled back thick drapes. There wasn't much to see — just the parking garage and the lights of the city, the gleaming columns of a church spire. She could have walked there from the hospital, sat in one of the pews, just . . . listened for a few minutes. To her heartbeat, to her thoughts, to the way her soul stirred when she finally had a chance to just *be.*

Maybe that's what she'd do. Take a walk downtown. Do a little shopping. Brenna's birthday was a month away. Maybe she could find her something exotic and fun. A nice outfit or a pair of shoes.

Or, she could just give her the ones she had on her feet.

The ones that made walking nearly impossible.

She glanced down, eyeing the glossy red leather. Brenna would know they were a re-gifted item, seeing as how Brenna had been the one to give them to Addie.

So maybe Addie would just hand them to her after the wedding, tell her they'd look much better on her. They did wear the same size shoe.

Everything else? Not so much. Brenna had always been tall and reed-thin. Adeline . . . well, she wasn't tall, and she'd had curves. She had curves. She would always have curves.

"Everything okay, doll?" Byron said, and she turned, pasting on a smile and doing everything she could to look cheerful and happy.

"Just admiring the view."

"Of the parking garage?" Byron snorted, then patted the bed. "Come sit next to me. I want you to see this."

"What?" She limped to the bed, her feet screaming that giving the shoes back to Brenna was absolutely the right idea.

"I've been thinking that maybe those stairs in that apartment are going to be too much for me. You know" — he glanced away, his gaze skittering across the room before he met her eyes again — "even after I finish rehab."

"I'm sure you'll be fine, Granddad." Thinking about him giving up the apartment he'd lived in since Alice's death made her throat tight and her head hurt.

Sure, he was getting up there in years, but Byron was *not* old.

"Kid," he said, lifting her hand the way he always did when he had something serious to say, "we both know I won't be fine. A guy my age breaks his femur and lives to tell about it, and he'd be stupid not to start thinking about things like moving to a place that's a little more accommodating of his age."

"What place?" Was he thinking of moving

away from Benevolence? She didn't know if she could pretend to support him if he was. She didn't know if she could act like she was happy.

"The Bradford place."

It took about three seconds for the words to sink in.

When they did, she jumped off the bed, paced back to the window, tried to figure out a way to say what needed to be said without stepping on Byron's toes. "Granddad, there is no way on God's green earth you can move into that place."

She tried to keep her voice calm.

God, how she tried!

But . . . *the Bradford place?*

It had been empty for two decades and had been neglected for way longer than that. Vines had grown through broken windows, the old wrought-iron fence that had once surrounded the property had fallen over. She was pretty certain the roof was about to cave in, and Storm Snyder insisted rats were breeding in the overgrown yard. He lived in the house next door and claimed he'd had to put out enough rat poison to kill the entire world population of rodents, but the rats were still there.

"Not now I can't, but with a little work . . ."

"A *little*!?" So much for calm. So much for cool. She sounded like a banshee screaming through the darkness.

"Okay," Byron conceded, not at all upset by her outburst. "More than a little, but it's not like I don't have the money to do it. Your grandma had a life insurance policy, you know."

"Yes." Janelle had mentioned it on more than one occasion. She thought Byron should use it to retire. Adeline could have told her that no Lamont ever retired from Chocolate Haven. They worked until they died or until someone else could take over. Even then, they had a hand in the business.

"Then you know I have the funds. It's not like I'd be taking out a loan."

It didn't matter if he was taking out a loan or paying cash or getting the place for free, the Bradford house was a money pit. It would take several life insurance policies to bring it into habitable condition, and she wasn't even sure it could be done.

"I couldn't stomach spending the money after Alice died," Byron continued. "It didn't make sense that I would enjoy what was gained from her death, so I invested it, and it just kept getting bigger."

"That's nice, Granddad, but do you really think Grandma would want you to put all

313

of it into a house when you could live with me or Mom?"

"Your mother wouldn't have me if I paid her rent."

"That's not true!"

"It is. She likes that house tidy and organized, and that's just not my style. As for you . . ." He shrugged. "You have your own life to live, and you don't need me hanging around cramping your style."

"You wouldn't be, Granddad. I'd love to have you." It was true. She would. She and Byron had always gotten along well. She had the spare room and could expand into the attic if she wanted to. A nice master suite upstairs would allow them both to have privacy and space. She could hire someone, have the job done in a couple of weeks.

It seemed like a good plan. A great one, even. Or, at least, a heck of a lot better than him buying a crumbling house and rat-infested property.

But Byron shook his head. "Here's the deal, kid. I'm old enough to make my own decisions, and this is what I've decided. If Sinclair says he can save the place, I'm going to buy it, and I'm going to save it."

"I —"

"Alice was born there. Never told you

that, did I?"

"No," she responded, all her fight suddenly gone.

"She was. Spent the first eighteen years of her life there. Then we got married, and she moved into the Lamont place with me. Her parents stayed around for a while, but when they moved to Florida, they sold the house to Sammy Bradford. It was a pretty little place then. Alice and I watched it deteriorate. She used to talk about buying it and fixing it up again. Maybe giving it to one of you girls." He shrugged as if it didn't matter, but she knew it did. "Once she died, I thought about doing it myself, but time got away from me. I've been lying here in this bed for a long time, doll, and I've been thinking that if I want to do something, there's no better time than now."

"But . . . the Bradford place," she muttered, and he grinned.

"It's a project. That's for sure."

"So . . . you're going to buy it?" She tried to wrap her head around that — her grandfather living in a house again. Her grandparents had given up the Lamont house when Willow was born, moved into a nice-sized Victorian on Monroe.

When Alice died, Byron had put that house on the market and moved into the apartment above the shop. He'd said he didn't need anything more. She'd thought he hadn't wanted to live in a place he'd once shared with the woman he'd loved for more than five decades.

"If Sinclair thinks it can be saved, I am."

"I'll go by the place tomorrow, Byron," Sinclair said, folding the paper and putting it in his wallet. "Who is it listed with?"

"Janelle. Of course," Byron said. "My daughter-in-law has a real estate monopoly in this town."

"Not surprising," Sinclair said easily, kneading the muscle above his right knee. "It's too small a town to have more than one Realtor's office."

"She has two people working with her, Granddad," Adeline said. "Sinclair should probably call one of them to show the property."

"Why?" Byron snapped. "You think I have to hide this from your mother? That's not the way I work, kid. I'm buying this property, and Janelle may as well know it up front."

"That's not —"

"Knock-knock," a nurse called from the open doorway. "Time for your meds, Byron."

"It can wait, Lydia," he responded. "I've

316

got visitors."

"It can't wait." She rolled a cart in, her gray hair pulled back into a neat bun, her eyes bright and clear in a lined and pretty face. She had to be in her sixties, but moved like a woman a decade younger.

"Sorry to have to do this, folks," she said. "But I'm going to have to boot you out. I need to check his incision."

"She's lying. She's not sorry."

Lydia chuckled. "You're right, Byron. Making people leave their loved ones gives me a secret thrill."

Byron grinned. "I like you, Lydia. You've got spunk."

"I also have a dozen other patients who need their medicine." She took a cup off a tray, handed it to Byron.

Adeline knew that was her cue to go.

She had a lot more to say, though. About the Bradford property and Byron buying it, about the shop, the fudge, the disastrous encounter with Millicent that morning.

"I guess we'd better head out," Sinclair prodded, and she nodded, moving close to the bed as Lydia wrapped a blood-pressure cuff around Byron's arm.

"I'll stop by after the wedding," she promised, leaning over to kiss his cheek.

"It'll be late, doll. I don't want you driving all the way out here by yourself. Just wait until Monday and come. I'll be leaving this joint then, and we can go have a burger and a beer."

"No beer while you're on this medicine," Lydia chided.

"Killjoy," he muttered, but he was smiling.

That was good, and Adeline should have been happy to leave him there, but the talk about Alice and the house she'd grown up in, that had done something to her heart, and she hovered by his bed, watching as Lydia took Byron's blood pressure.

"Doll," Byron finally said, "you need to go. You look exhausted, and you've got a long ride ahead of you."

"I'm okay," she said, but she wasn't sure that she was.

The long days and nights were catching up to her. She could admit that to herself, but she'd never admit it to Byron. He'd worry and that was the last thing he should be doing. "And I am coming after the wedding. I'll fill you in on all the details."

"It isn't safe for a beautiful young woman to be driving around at midnight."

"It's perfectly safe."

He scowled. "Now you listen here —"

"I'll bring her," Sinclair cut in. "I plan to

take some photos of the house, and I'll want you to look at them before you make your decision."

"I don't need you to take me," Adeline argued, because spending more time alone with Sinclair? She wanted that more than she wanted to eat a cheeseburger and bucketful of onion rings. "It will be late, and —"

"Late for both of us. Janelle gave me an invitation to the wedding. She said May asked her to deliver it."

"That's . . . nice."

"I think so. I've also been thinking," he said, ushering her into the hallway, "that since neither of us have dates, we may as well go together."

"To the wedding?" she squeaked.

He smiled. "That is what we've been discussing."

"I know, but . . ." She could think of a dozen reasons why it wasn't a good idea.

She could almost feel her heart breaking.

Sure, they hadn't gotten to that point yet.

One kiss did not a committed relationship make, but God! If she fell for him, if she let herself even imagine that they might have more than a kiss and a few dates, she also had to imagine that soul-aching, breath-catching moment when it all ended and she was left alone again.

"But what?" He jabbed the elevator button, his jaw tight. "We're two dateless people heading to an eighty-year-old's —"

"Seventy-six."

"Does it matter, Adeline?" He ran a hand down his jaw. He needed to shave. Or maybe not. He looked good with stubble on his chin. "My point is that both of us are going alone, so why shouldn't we go together?"

"People will get the wrong idea."

"What idea would that be?" he asked as the elevator doors opened.

"That we're a couple," she replied, stepping into the empty elevator and wishing that it was filled with people. She didn't want to have this conversation with Sinclair. Not now. Not ever.

"And?"

"We're not."

"We could change that," he said, moving into her space, his hands suddenly on her waist and then her back.

She was in his arms again, all the arguments against going with him flittering away. "I —"

"You know what the best part of us going together would be, Adeline?" he whispered, his lips brushing her ear, his hands smoothing up her spine.

She wanted to burrow in, inhale the heady masculine scent of him, drink in all his warmth.

"What?" she managed to say as his lips trailed along her neck, found the spot right at the hollow of her throat.

"I get to avoid all the single-and-available women who are going to be at the wedding, and you get to cross something off your list."

That surprised a laugh out of her, and he smiled. "That's better."

"What?"

"You." The doors opened, and he urged her out into the hospital lobby.

"What about me?"

"You worry too much."

"I never worry. As a matter of fact, I have a reputation in my family for being very relaxed."

"In comparison to who?" They reached his truck, and he opened the door. "Janelle? Because, much as I like your mother, she's a little high strung."

"Only since my father died."

"And that was how long ago? Twenty years?"

"Eighteen," she replied, climbing into the truck, the dress riding up her thighs.

She tried to tug it back into place, but the

fabric had a mind of its own.

"Don't bother on my account," Sinclair murmured, his palm skimming her thigh.

And her mind?

It went completely blank, every thought swiped away with that one light touch.

He closed the door, rounded the car, and she still couldn't think of anything but his palm on her thigh.

Sinclair started the truck engine, hiked up the heat, and did *not* reach out and touch Adeline's thigh again. Tempting as it was — and it was very tempting — she seemed like she needed something different.

Maybe just a willing ear, someone to say all the things that she hadn't said in the hospital. She'd been upset by Byron's plan. She'd argued a little, thrown out a few other suggestions, and then she'd bit her lip and kept silent.

That said a lot about Adeline. It said a lot about how much she loved her grandfather. Sinclair wouldn't mind having that kind of love focused on him. He wouldn't mind feeling like the person he loved, loved him the same way. With Kendra, the relationship had been about mutual benefit. They'd both been about offering an equal amount, contributing the same. Fifty-fifty. That's what Kendra had said, and what Sinclair had been happy to agree to. He had a feeling real love required more. He had a feeling it was about giving 150 percent. And then giving more.

He grabbed gloves from the center console and zipped his coat. It was colder than any place had a right to be at this time of year. Twenty degrees if the truck's thermometer was to be believed.

"Your blood has gone thin, Sinclair," Adeline said with a quiet laugh. "You've been away too long."

"I guess I have." And he guessed he would have stayed away if Gavin hadn't begged him to come. If that had been the case, he'd be sitting in his apartment, looking out over Puget Sound, the world muted by glass and steel. That should have been the first thing on his mind — to get back to that quiet place, that clean and organized space. He'd worked his whole life to have a home like that — sterile, clean, organized. Only it had never really seemed like home. It was more a place to stay when he wasn't traveling for a job. The steel and glass? It didn't have the character and charm of the properties he worked on.

"And *I* guess you can't wait to get back to a warmer climate," Adeline commented as he pulled out of the hospital parking lot.

"I'm not in as much of a hurry as I thought I was."

"No?" She tugged her dress down, covering a quarter of an inch more of her beautiful thigh.

"There's a lot of work that can be done in this town. A lot more than I thought there would be."

"Every town has properties that need work," she pointed out, and he knew she was right, but in his memories, Benevolence was perfect, every property pristine and beautiful.

"I guess I just never realized Benevolence was like every town."

"What did you think it was?" she asked. "Mayberry?"

He laughed. "Something like that."

"And now?"

"Like I said, there's work to do, and I'd like to do it."

"Byron's project?"

"Among others."

"I hate to tell you this, Sinclair," she said, "but that property is not going to be salvageable."

"Your grandfather wants to try, and I'm not going to tell him it's impossible unless it is," he said gently, because it was the

324

truth, but he didn't think she'd want to hear it.

"My mother —"

"Adeline. How about we not talk about what your mother wants. It doesn't play into this."

"Right," she muttered. "Bad habit."

"Bad habits can be broken."

"Like you and drinking?" she asked. "Sorry. I noticed the juice during the toast, and . . . Bad assumption."

"Correct assumption," he admitted, because he saw no sense in hiding it. "I come from a long line of alcoholics. I realized a few years ago that I was heading down the same road. I didn't want to go there, so I gave up drinking. I have a sip of wine once in a while, but never a whole glass of anything."

"I'm still sorry. I shouldn't have brought it up."

"You can bring up anything you want." He let himself do what *he'd* been wanting to, let his hand drop to her thigh, his fingers sliding along firm flesh and taut muscle.

"Sinclair —"

"How about, just for now, you don't worry about what could happen and just accept what is?"

"Is that what you're doing?"

"With you?" he asked, because he thought it was. He didn't want to think about tomorrow or the next day. Not when he had Adeline beside him now.

"With Benevolence."

"What do you mean?"

"A few days ago, you seemed determined to leave town as quickly as possible."

"A few days ago, I was."

"What changed?"

"Me? When I was a kid, I felt like a charity case. I was the kid whose father had driven drunk and killed himself and his wife. I was the boy who had to live in a pigsty of a house. I was the one whispered about at church and at the library. I hated it, and that made me hate the town. Now that I'm older, I can see Benevolence for what it is."

"What's that?"

"A little town with a lot of heart. People care. At the time, that felt like pity and judgment. Now it just feels like what it was — people worrying about two kids who really didn't have much to go home to."

"You want to know something?" she said quietly, her fingers brushing over his knuckles, there and gone so quickly he barely felt them.

"I want to know everything," he responded, and she laughed.

"Trust me. You don't, but I'll tell you this one thing. I used to envy Gavin. He never had any pressure put on him. I remember one time, he got an honors award for getting a C in algebra. I had an A in that class, and I got squat. Except a lecture from my mom on the dangers of being too book smart and not people-smart enough."

"You must have gotten plenty of other awards."

"No. Not one. Willow won the regional spelling bee. She was the captain of a debate team that never lost. She had more academic awards than I can even remember. And Brenna? She was a cheerleader, Ms. Popular. A model. Most likely to achieve anything and everything. I was just . . . me."

He thought about that for a minute, about the way it must have felt to be sandwiched between Willow and Brenna. They'd both been popular in school. He didn't remember much about Brenna except that she'd been the talk of the freshman crowd during his senior year. A cheerleader with a 4.0 GPA, she'd already been modeling for a couple of years. Willow had been volunteering at the local hospital, tutoring calculus, and working as a secretary for the town's only attorney.

And Adeline?

He had no idea what she'd been doing.

He vaguely remembered seeing her walking through the hallway at school. She'd usually worn baggy jeans and ugly sweaters and pulled her hair back in braids that hadn't been able to contain her curls. "You're the only sister who stayed in town," he pointed out.

"Ironic, isn't it? The sister least likely to make her mark on the town was the one who stayed."

"I don't think that's the way people around here think of you."

"It isn't. But it's been a long day, and I'm ready for it to end. Only it can't, because I've got to go home and get Chase settled in."

"I think he's old enough to settle himself in."

"I know, but I haven't introduced him to Tiny yet, and I want to put clean sheets on the guest bed, set up some ground rules. That kind of thing."

"Unless he's asleep when you get there. This is the first time he's had a bed to sleep in in weeks. He's probably going to take advantage of it."

"Poor kid," she murmured, reaching down and pulling off one of her heels and then the other. They weren't the kind of shoes he'd ever have imagined her wearing, but she'd sure as hell made them work. "He's had a rough road."

"He made some poor choices. That's what got him into the mess he found himself in. If he'd asked for help, your grandfather wouldn't be in the hospital and Chase wouldn't be obligated to a hundred hours of community service before he leaves town."

"Would you have asked for help at his age?" she asked. "If I remember correctly, you had three jobs and never once told anyone that you were using the money to patch up the house you were living in."

"Who told you that?"

"Gavin. He said that every cent you had went into keeping that house from falling in on your heads. He also said that you sent him money until he graduated high school, and that you offered to pay for his college."

"He should have taken me up on it. Or, better yet, worked harder at school and at sports and paid for it himself."

"He was going to night school for a while. Then Lauren got pregnant, and he decided he'd better try to get a second job so she could stay home with the baby."

That was news to Sinclair. Gavin hadn't

mentioned anything about college, and he certainly hadn't seemed intent on finding another job. "That doesn't sound like my brother."

"Then you don't know him very well. He might have big dreams about writing a novel and becoming a millionaire off it, but he's not a total slacker."

He snorted.

"He's not, Sinclair. He's nearly finished his AA degree. A few more credits, and he'll be done."

"He didn't mention that to me."

"Maybe he wanted to finish and surprise you. Or maybe he was afraid that he wouldn't finish, and you'd be disappointed."

That was more likely the case.

Sinclair had always been more of a father to Gavin than an older brother. "I would have been disappointed, but I also would have been proud of him for giving it a go. I've always thought he could do well if he put his mind to it. His problem is he never puts his mind to it."

"Lauren has been good for him. He's been a lot more focused since they got married."

"She's good for him, but he's not good for her. That's the pattern of my family's story. Men who meet women who can support and take care of them." He'd said more than he'd intended, the words tinged with bitterness.

"She's not supporting him. I already told you, he does web design. And he's good for her, Sinclair. She's a smart woman, and she wouldn't have married him if he weren't."

"Don't kid yourself, Adeline. Plenty of smart people marry people who aren't good for them. Look at my mother — she liked to party, but she was a hard worker. And my grandmother? I didn't know her well, but I've been going through the house, looking at some of the things she collected. She had a keen eye and the smarts to hide valuables from my grandfather. It didn't do her any good, of course. She worked herself to death. At least that's the way I've always heard it."

"I'm not going to argue the point, but I'd like to think there are more smart people who marry smart than don't."

"Why? Are you planning a big wedding sometime in the future?"

She let out a snort of laughter. "Please! I gave up that idea years ago. The way I see it, I'll be happy to spend the rest of my life in my own little house by myself."

Adeline spending her life alone seemed about as right as a sunrise without sun or a winter without snow.

"You're giving up on the idea of love because one guy broke your heart?"

"I'm not giving up on the idea of love. I think love is great. I think it's a wonderful thing for people who want it. I don't."

"You may change your mind when the right guy comes along."

"What would that look like, Sinclair? Because I don't have any idea. Is the right guy the one who tells a woman she's beautiful every day? Is he the one who buys flowers just because, or calls in the middle of the day to check in? Is he the one who listens to all of a woman's cockamamie ideas and tries to support her goals even if he doesn't agree with them?"

"I'm a man, Adeline, so I have no idea what the right guy would look like," he said. "But if I had to venture a guess, I'd say he'd be the one who held her hand when she had no one else, the one who stood beside her when she was crying and laughing and all the times in between. Mostly, though, I'd think that the right guy would be the one who'd spend a lifetime with a woman and still think she was the most beautiful and fascinating person he'd ever met."

"A lifetime is a long time, Sinclair," she said so quietly he almost didn't hear, "to take to figure out whether someone is the right person or not."

"How could it take anything less? Being the right person for someone isn't a five-minute deal. Not in my mind. It's an all-out, forever kind of thing. Good and bad, better and worse, sickness and health, until death comes and steals one of you away."

"Is that why you're single? Because you don't think anyone could be that person for you?"

"I'm single because I only want to be with someone if I can be that person for her." He exited the highway, merged onto the country road that led toward Benevolence. They still had a long ride ahead of them, the two-lane highway dark and silent.

Sparse clouds drifted in from the horizon, shrouding the mountains that lay to the east and west.

There was something comforting about those mountains and that vista. Something beautiful and familiar. He couldn't say he'd missed it when he'd been in Seattle. The west side of the state had its own kind of beauty, and he'd been too busy building his business to miss anything about the town he'd left behind.

He *could* say that he hadn't appreciated the view when he was a kid. He'd been too busy rushing toward something different to appreciate what was there.

He didn't want to do that anymore. He didn't want to be so busy trying not to be one of *those Jeffersons* that he missed out on being something better.

An interesting thought. One he needed to delve into a little more. For now, he'd enjoy the moment, the mountains, the woman beside him.

He switched on the radio, turned it to an oldies station, and smiled as Adeline's quirky off-key voice filled the truck.

CHAPTER THIRTEEN

The few days before the wedding flew by. And when Addie said flew, she meant it. She and Chase spent fifteen hours a day at the shop. When they weren't there, they were at the house, getting the attic fixed up and ready for Chase to move into. There'd been a lot of stuff piled in the finished part of the house's upper level. Stuff from previous owners, shoved in boxes and forgotten for years. She and Chase had carted it through a narrow doorway and into the bonus room.

Or what Janelle called a bonus room.

Adeline called it storage. Now the eight-by-ten area was packed so tight with stuff there was only a few feet of walking space in it. The other part of the attic was larger, the walls covered with 1950s wallpaper, the floor nothing but plywood over ceiling joist. Eventually, Adeline would put down padding and carpet, but all she had time for was moving in the bed that Janelle had lent and the dresser that May had donated to the cause.

She'd had Chase hang curtains over the dormer windows and had given him a chair from the living room. There was no television, no computer, nothing that most kids his age would want to have, but he didn't seem to mind.

That was good, because there wasn't much she could do to make the place more comfortable. Not today anyway. It was finally the day May had spent close to eighty years of her life dreaming of. The wedding, and Adeline was supposed to be at Janelle's house by six to get her hair and nails done by Doris and her team.

God help her, because no one else seemed willing to.

She'd begged Janelle to intervene and talk May into using someone else, but for once in her life, Janelle had decided to keep her opinions to herself. She loved May like an aunt, and she didn't want to do anything that would take away from her special day.

That was great. It was wonderful. For May. For Addie? Not so much.

She glanced at the clock on her dresser. Five thirty. She had twenty minutes to take a shower and get going.

"Chase!" she called, grabbing the orange dress from the closet.

"Yes, ma'am?" He appeared in the doorway, his hair slicked back, his face freshly scrubbed. He'd been staying with her for a couple of days, working with her for a few, and he was always on time, always polite, and always eager to please.

"Are you sure you can handle the shop on your own today?"

"Do I have a choice?" he asked, and she smiled. He had a sense of humor, and just a touch of sarcasm. She probably shouldn't have appreciated that as much as she did.

"Not really."

"Then I guess I'll be just fine."

"It takes two hours to prep for opening," she reminded him, because normally they'd have been out the door by five, Tiny in the car, ready to be dropped off with Sinclair.

Sinclair.

Someone she didn't want to think about when she was in the middle of a mad rush to get to her mother's place.

"I know, I just . . ." He glanced away. "Thought I'd wait until you left."

"I won't be out of here for twenty minutes or more, Chase. If you wait that long, you'll never get the shop opened in time."

He nodded. "Okay," he said, but he didn't

move away from the doorway.

"I've got a bunch of turkey and roast beef in the fridge if you want to make yourself a sandwich. There are chips in the pantry. Pack what you want," she prodded. Chase ate a lot. More than three people. She'd been to the store twice since he'd moved in. Once to stock up on food that the teen could eat and once to restock. If he stayed much longer, she'd go broke feeding him.

"You don't have to feed me all the time," he said as if he'd read her mind.

"I know, but you need to eat."

"I can pay my way, ma'am. That's why I needed a job, so I could do that." He reached into his back pocket and pulled out his wallet, offering her a twenty from it. "I know this isn't much, but it's all I have left until I get paid next."

"Then you keep it," she insisted, making a mental note to pay him a dollar extra an hour. She'd already given him an advance on the next few paychecks. Part of his agreement with the sheriff was that his pay would be garnished to repay what he owed.

It all made perfect sense, but every time she looked at him, she thought that he worked too hard, was too good an employee for her to withhold any of his pay.

"I can't do that and feel good about

myself." He pressed the money into her hand and backed away. "I guess I'd better go. I just wanted to tell you that I thought I heard mice in the attic last night. I'm going to put out some traps tonight."

"Mice?" She'd never had a problem with them before, and she wasn't all that excited to be having one now.

"Yeah. I wouldn't worry about it, but if you hear something scurrying around, that's probably what it is. I can go to the hardware store and get the traps for you, but . . ." He flushed, and she knew he was wishing he hadn't given her back the twenty. Not that twenty would be enough. If there were mice, she wanted a hundred traps up there.

"Take this," she said, handing the twenty back. "I have more in my wallet."

"It shouldn't cost more than this. I'll just get one or two."

"Get a dozen or more." She dug into her purse, pulled out two more twenties. "Keep the change."

"Adeline, I don't want your money. You're already doing too much for me."

It was the first time he'd used her first name, and that did something to her heart, made it soften in a way she hadn't expected. She liked Chase, but she hadn't been feeling anything but overwhelmed the past few days. Now she felt something almost . . . maternal?

That surprised her. He was nearly nineteen, not even close to young enough to be her son, but he was alone in the world and that made her want to keep him close, take care of him, make sure that he had the things he needed. "I owe you some extra pay for taking Tiny to Sinclair's this morning and for setting those traps. Now, hurry up and get out of here. Chocolate Haven has never opened late, and I don't want to start today."

He shuffled away, and she closed the door, rushed through her morning routine. She could not be late. Her mother was waiting at the house with her sisters, and they were all planning on trekking to May's together. Willow and Brenna weren't in the wedding, but they'd been invited for a bridal breakfast. Mimosas and breakfast casserole. God knew what was going to be in that, but Adeline had vowed to choke it down.

Hopefully May wouldn't drink more than a sip or two of her mimosa. The woman hadn't had an alcoholic beverage. Ever. This was a nod to the occasion, but there wouldn't be an occasion if the bride didn't show up for the wedding.

Addie yanked on yoga pants and a T-shirt.

No sense dressing up when she was just going to have to get undressed and into the orange monstrosity. She snagged that, grabbed her purse and keys, and ran into the hall. She'd left her shoes on the top shelf of the coat closet. Thank goodness Tiny hadn't gotten to them. May had had white satin shoes dyed to match the dress and had handed them to Addie at the rehearsal the previous night.

The only problem was that they didn't actually match the bridesmaid outfit. Addie hadn't thought it was possible for anything to be brighter and more garish than the dress, but the shoes were. Low-heeled pumps with huge bows on the toes, they were a strange neon orange that it actually hurt to look at. That might be for the best. Maybe the wedding guests would be so blinded by the shoes, they wouldn't notice the dress.

She opened the front door and had one foot out when she heard something in the attic. A kind of sliding shuffle that sounded more like a dozen rats than a few mice.

She should probably go check things out, see if maybe a raccoon or squirrel had gotten into the attic, but with her luck whatever was up there would attack the dress and tear it to shreds.

Or worse, tear *her* to shreds.

She scowled, yanking the door closed and locking it. She'd given Chase a key, so he'd be able to get in after he closed, but she wasn't sure she wanted him to go inside with whatever had taken up residence in the attic. She'd like to think that Tiny would chase it down and evict it, but Tiny was everyone's best friend. That included every dog, cat, donkey, goat, and pig in the area.

Besides, Tiny wasn't going to be home. Gavin had refused to go to the wedding without Lauren, and Lauren had refused to go to the wedding if the house wasn't ready. They were at a stalemate, neither willing to budge. That meant Gavin wasn't attending the wedding. He'd offered to keep Tiny for the night since May had promised that the reception was going on until the wee hours of the morning. Addie had a feeling it would end around nine.

Her phone beeped, warning her that time had run out. She was supposed to be at Janelle's place. Now.

She jumped into her car, would have sped away, but Nehemiah hobbled out onto his porch, waving frantically as she backed out of the driveway.

She couldn't ignore him, so she parked the car and jumped out again, leaving the orange dress and neon shoes on the seat.

"Good morning, Nehemiah," she called, and he gestured her over.

"Morning, Addie. You heading out for the wedding?"

"I am. Are you coming?"

"There's going to be free food," he responded, as if that answered the question. Maybe it did. Nehemiah loved to eat, but he wasn't all that fond of cooking. His wife had been the one who took care of meals. After her death, he'd taken to eating at the diner or buying frozen meals from the dollar store.

"Lots of it," she agreed. "May and a few friends made all the food. From what I hear it's going to be delicious."

"No doubt about that. Those women can cook." He patted his stomach and smiled. "But I didn't call you over here to discuss the wedding food."

"No?" she asked, resisting the urge to look at her watch.

"I saw that boy outside of your house last night."

"Boy?"

"The one who's working for you. Saw him wandering around with his girlfriend."

"He has a girlfriend?" That was news to Addie.

"He must, since I saw him walking around with her."

"Are you sure, Nehemiah? Chase and I came back here at the same time last night. There's no way he left the house without me knowing."

"That's what you think, Addie, but I can tell you right now, he was out there. I couldn't sleep, and I looked outside and there he was, walking with a girl."

"A girl?"

"Young woman. Short little thing. Reminded me of my wife. She was tiny, too. Remember? Never could buy clothes off the rack. She had to have them altered to fit."

Addie remembered.

"Anyway," he continued, "I saw them walking out here, just holding hands and looking like two lovebirds, and I started thinking maybe the boy needs a man to have a little talk with him. Set him straight on some things."

"You're sure it was Chase?"

"I have eyes in my head, don't I?"

"Yes, but I didn't hear Tiny, and I'm surprised that he wasn't barking his head off if someone was wandering around outside." Although, Tiny had been sleeping in her bedroom since Chase moved in, and he only barked when strangers were around.

"The dog knows Chase, and maybe he knows the girlfriend. You know how that mutt is. He's everyone's friend, and he's not going to just haul off and start barking for no reason." He said exactly what she was thinking, and she tried really hard not to glance at her watch.

She was late, getting later every minute, but she loved Nehemiah, and she didn't have the heart to cut the conversation short. "I guess if Chase has a girlfriend, that's his business, Nehemiah. He's an adult. He can do what he wants."

He nodded, running a hand over his hair and squinting up at the still-dark sky. "You're right about that, Addie, but like I said, I've been thinking that maybe he needs a man to talk to him about the important things in a relationship."

"What things?"

"How to treat a lady right, for one. How to make her feel like she matters. How to stand by her when no one else will."

His words were oddly reminiscent of the ones Sinclair had spoken on the way home from the hospital. Words she'd tried really hard to forget, because every time she remembered them, her heart went soft and she forgot why she wanted to stay single, why making an attempt at a relationship wasn't a good idea.

It wasn't that she didn't want to be hurt again. Or, not for the most part, anyway. It was just that the pain of a relationship gone wrong wasn't worth whatever the relationship provided. Companionship, friendship, shared experiences — she could have those with anyone. She didn't need a man to fill a place in her life.

Of course, if she were going to have one filling a space, she'd want Sinclair. In a big way. In a huge way. In a "my life is going to change forever because of him" way.

"If you want to talk to him," she said, pushing thoughts of Sinclair out of her head, "go ahead."

"You don't think he'll get defensive? Some kids his age would."

"Chase isn't like that." Not that she'd seen, and they'd been working together for hours at a time. Unlike a lot of kids his age, he took instruction well and seemed eager to learn everything he could about how to run a business. He had no attitude, no arrogance, and there'd been more than one occasion when she'd wished his mother was around so that Adeline could tell her what a great job she'd done.

Chase was making his mother proud, and that made Adeline smile. Which was nice, because she'd been up most of the night trying to smooth out the tiny puckers in the new dress zipper, pacing her room wishing to God she didn't have to attend the wedding, and praying that Sinclair didn't really expect to go with her.

He hadn't mentioned it in the past couple of days. But then, she'd been avoiding him the same way she'd been avoiding her mother.

"Good. Great. I'll talk to him tomorrow. Thanks, Addie. I'll see you at the wedding."

"You sure will," she murmured as he shuffled back inside.

As soon as his door closed, she was in the car, backing out of the driveway again. Not many people were on the road this time of the morning, and she made it to Janelle's house in a minute flat.

Which was twenty minutes late.

The door opened as she got out of the car, and Brenna ran outside, her hair perfect, her makeup gorgeous, her jeans so tight Addie wasn't quite sure how she'd managed to slide into them.

"Get in the car!" she shouted as she raced across the yard.

"What?!"

"In. The. Car," her sister enunciated. "Hurry."

"Why?"

"Because I have got to get some coffee. Some real stuff. Not that decaf organic crap Mom buys to impress the guys."

Coffee was coffee to Addie, but she got back in the car and unlocked the passenger door.

Brenna eyed the pile of orange satin lying on the passenger seat, lifted the dress, and examined it.

"Good God!" she breathed.

"I know."

"You're actually going to wear that?"

"I am."

"In front of everyone in town?" She laid the dress on the backseat and climbed in beside Addie, her coat lined with faux fur, her leather gloves the soft kind that cost a fortune. Even at around six in the morning, she looked perfect.

Addie, on the other hand, had dark circles under her eyes, not a stitch of makeup on her face, and was wearing clothes that she'd bought on sale right after Christmas three years ago.

"Yes."

"You are a much braver woman than I am." Brenna yanked the seat belt across her lap and buckled it, some soft, subtle, flowery perfume filling the car as she moved.

"Or a much stupider one," Addie responded.

"She's May. You couldn't have said no."

"Exactly."

"Don't worry, kid. You'll make it work."

"Kid? I'm nearly two years older than you."

"You're still a kid, because if you're grown up and mature, then I guess I have to be too."

Addie laughed, a dozen memories filling her head: late nights lying next to Brenna, both of them huddled in the same bed, whispering about all the wonderful things they wanted to do with their lives. Sunny days sitting in the gazebo, sharing lunch and secrets. She'd almost forgotten about those sweet days, about the way things had been before their father was diagnosed with brain cancer.

She eyed her sister — the perfect hair and makeup and body, the fancy ring and expensive clothes. Beneath it all, she was still Brenna, and Adeline missed the time they had once spent together.

"What?" Brenna asked. "Do I have something on my face?"

"I was just thinking about how close we used to be."

"Funny, I was thinking that too. The other

night, I was sitting in the gazebo, remembering the fun we had there. I've missed you, Adeline."

"Not enough to come home."

"That has nothing to do with love. I hope you know that." She touched Adeline's arm.

"I do." But it would have been nice to think that Brenna would return one day, that she could find her place in Benevolence the same way Adeline had. "I just wish that we didn't live so far apart. You've grown up and become mature, and we were apart during most of that."

"I know. I wish things could have been different, but . . . I had to leave. I couldn't stay here with the shadow of Dad's death hanging over me."

"Is that how it felt?" she asked as she drove toward the Daily Grind.

"I guess it did, but like you said, I've matured a lot. Maybe I was just selfish. Speaking of which . . . Sinclair Jefferson. Talk about growing up and maturing! Wow!"

"Wow what?"

"Don't play dumb, Addie. That man is hot, *and* he's smart, rich, accomplished. Altogether a good catch."

"You're in the market for a new guy?" Addie said, only half joking.

She expected Brenna to laugh the comment off, but her sister was silent as a tomb.

Addie waited as she turned onto Main Street, followed the road to Madison, and pulled up to the Daily Grind. No line this time of morning, but the light from the small coffee shop glowed softly. She pulled into their drive-through window, ordered six coffees — just in case other people in the house needed caffeine — and Brenna still hadn't said a word.

She handed the coffees to Brenna and drove back onto Main Street, the silence as thick as pea soup.

"You *are* in the market for a new guy," she accused, and Brenna shrugged, her hair pulled into a perfect chignon, her diamond earrings gleaming in the dashboard light.

"Oh my God! You are!" Addie repeated, and Brenna's face crumbled.

"If you say one word to anyone about this, I will never forgive you," she muttered.

"About what? What is going on?" Addie pulled into Chocolate Haven's parking lot and stopped the car.

"He's cheating on me," Brenna said, her voice cracking.

"Dan?" She sounded like an idiot. She knew she did. But she couldn't believe that anyone would cheat on Brenna.

"What other asshole have I spent four

years trying to please?" Brenna retorted. "I've been suspecting it for a while, so I hired a private detective —"

"You didn't."

"I did. She e-mailed me a bunch of stuff last night. Pictures and e-mails and receipts. I don't know what I'm going to do with all of it."

"Break up with the bastard," Addie said.

"It's not that easy."

"It is exactly as easy as you want to make it," Addie insisted. "If you don't want to face him —"

"Face him? We're attending the wedding together."

"Brenna, no. Just no."

"Mom expects it."

"Who cares?"

"I do. I've always been a disappointment to her, and I'm not going to make it worse by going to this damn wedding by myself."

"There are plenty of other people you could go with."

"None of them are my fiancé."

That did it. That was it. Enough was enough. Adeline was a lot of things, but she wasn't someone who was going to sit around and watch her sister make a colossal mistake. "You are breaking up with him. This morning. Not tonight. Not tomorrow. You're going in the house, you're telling him to pack his bags, and you're kicking him out."

"I can't do that."

"Then I'll do it."

Brenna huffed. "I'm not so much of a coward that I need my big sister to break up for me. I just want to wait until after the wedding, because Mom will be disappointed and she won't be able to hide it, and I'm not going to ruin May's day by making it about me and my poor choices in men."

"Just lie. Tell Mom that he got called away on business. He's a big-shot doctor. Surely someone somewhere needs a boob job, stat."

Brenna laughed. "Oh my God, Addie, I've missed you so much."

She leaned across the seat, pulled Adeline in for a hug.

They sat like that until Adeline's phone buzzed.

She backed up, her throat tight as she looked into Brenna's eyes. "It's Mom. I don't even have to look to know it. What are you going to do?"

"Text him and tell him to make his excuses and leave. I've got the goods on him, and since the woman he was with was one of his clients, it could ruin him. If he makes a scene, I'll do it."

"No, you won't."

"He doesn't know that." Brenna pulled out her cell phone and texted rapidly.

Adeline waited until she finished, then handed her a cup of coffee. "Drink up. You're going to need it."

"I'm going to need something a lot stronger than this," she replied, taking a sip and then grabbing Addie's hand.

She held on tight as Addie pulled onto the road and headed back to Janelle's.

Sinclair's leg hurt like hell, his head ached, and he'd been up most of the night fighting the demons. They were still chasing him as he cleared out the last of the upstairs bedroom, piled garbage into the Dumpster, and walked back into his grandfather's house.

It was still a mess, but it was clean, the smell of decay and rotting wood gone. No more mildew or mold downstairs. Gavin had done a fair job pulling down old plaster walls so that the wallboards could dry.

Sinclair had a team coming in on Monday to make sure the mold was eradicated. It was a big job and a very expensive one, but there was no way he could have Lauren move in with a baby if it wasn't done right.

"Lookin' good, bro. Right?" Gavin said as he walked down the stairs, a pile of old books in his arms, Tiny following along behind.

"Better than it did."

"Lauren is going to love it. I can't wait to show her."

"You're going to have to. The mold team doesn't come in until Monday."

"After that, I'll bring her through. Maybe seeing it like this will convince her to move back." He set the books on an old sideboard that they'd pulled from the kitchen. Probably dating from the mid-nineteenth century, it took up one wall of the foyer, the old wood dinged and damaged but still beautiful.

"We've come a long way, Gavin, but there's still a lot of work to do."

"I know it. I'm going to finish the kitchen floor while you're at the wedding. Then I'll start on the hallway upstairs."

"Or watch a ball game and drink a couple of beers?"

Gavin scowled, his normally cheerful expression gone. "What's that supposed to mean?"

"You were supposed to finish the kitchen floor last night." He shouldn't have pointed it out. Gavin had been working hard for most of the week, cleaning things out, taking Tiny for walks, doing everything he could to live up to Sinclair's expectations.

"I was at Lamaze classes with Lauren," he snapped, his dark eyes flashing. "When I got back, I decided to finish the sitting room. I'm pretty damn sure I told you that when you got here this morning, and I'm pretty damn sure you said I did a good job."

"You could have done both," Sinclair responded, digging himself deeper into the fight, and he wasn't even sure why.

"I'm not you, bro. Not some perfect working machine who never takes a break because he's too busy proving himself to people who don't matter to prove to the people who do that he's actually a human being," Gavin growled. "I'll go do the floor now. I'll do the hallway too, and when you get back here tomorrow morning, don't say one damn word to me."

He stomped away, and Sinclair almost followed him.

He needed to apologize, but Gavin was as hotheaded as their grandfather had been. Easygoing until he wasn't, and then he'd be completely unreasonable until he calmed down enough to think clearly.

He'd come back after the wedding, bring a pizza and an apology.

Hopefully, they'd both be in better moods by then.

He took the drive home a little too quickly, speeding along the quiet country road and into town. Chocolate Haven was still open when he arrived, and he could see Chase through the storefront window ringing up a customer.

He didn't stop in to say hello, just pulled around to the back, jogged up the stairs and into the apartment. He'd had his assistant ship one of his suits from Seattle. He pulled it from the closet, took a quick shower and got dressed, his bum leg aching the entire time.

He wanted to pop a pain pill, crawl into bed, and forget everything for a while, but he'd given up the narcotics around the same time he'd given up alcohol.

Plus, he had a date with Adeline to keep.

One that he thought she might be hoping he'd forgotten.

She'd been avoiding him since the kiss, sending Chase up to the apartment with the dog each morning, hiding in the kitchen anytime he entered the shop.

He wanted to know why, and he planned to find out.

Tonight was as good a time as any. Neither of them was working. Both of them were going to be at the wedding. Together. Because that was what they'd agreed to at the hospital, and Sinclair always did what he said he was going to.

He tugged his tie into place, eyed himself in the mirror.

He should have shaved, but he figured Adeline was at May's house getting gussied up for the wedding that was starting in less than an hour. According to Janelle, the wedding party was spending the entire day together, leaving the house at four thirty for the five o'clock nuptials.

He glanced at his watch.

He planned to pick Adeline up at May's house and drive her to the church. He planned to walk her in and let the entire town of Benevolence know they were together.

That was for her. Not because she needed it, but because she thought she did. Sure, she gave lip service to confidence and said she didn't care what anyone thought, but he'd seen her list, and he knew what she valued. What she valued was pleasing the people she loved.

This was going to please Janelle. It was going to please old Nehemiah and May and, probably, Adeline's sisters.

It was also going to please Sinclair, because he hadn't been able to stop thinking about the way her lips had tasted, the silky smoothness of her skin, the feeling of her soft curves melting against his body.

He pulled up in front of May's house and got out of the truck, strode across a lawn that had been landscaped to within an inch of its life. Every blade of grass was the same height; every bush, every plant had been matched exactly with another bush or plant. There were roses, cherry trees, something that looked like forsythia.

The door opened before he reached the front porch, and Janelle ran out. Dressed in a navy dress that might have been a little too short for a woman her age, she hurried down the porch stairs. "Thank goodness you came, Sinclair. I've been worried sick."

"About?"

"Brenna's fiancé had to leave very suddenly this morning. Some kind of emergency."

"Hopefully not life and death," he said. He hadn't liked Dan, but he didn't wish the guy ill.

"I think one of his highbrow clients was demanding some work. That poor man. It's difficult being a doctor."

"I'm sure it is."

"The problem is," Janelle continued, "now

Brenna doesn't have anyone to take her to the wedding."

"I'm sure she'll be fine," he responded as the door opened and Adeline walked onto the porch.

His heart stopped. He could swear it did. Stopped and stood still in his chest and then started back up again, speeding along at a pace that surprised him.

She smiled, her hair in some odd style that puffed up from the top of her head, her makeup garish on her pale skin. She looked like a rodeo clown, dressed in the brightest, most eye-searing outfit possible.

And she looked absolutely beautiful, her eyes still that same violet blue, her lips just as kissable beneath bright red lipstick. He wanted to grab a napkin, wipe the red off, and see the natural pink beneath. He wanted to tell her how gorgeous she looked, all her curves hugged by satiny fabric, but Janelle was still talking, saying something about how bad it would look for Brenna to attend the wedding alone.

"Mom," Adeline said, interrupting the monologue, "Brenna is fine with walking into the church alone."

"She says she is," Janelle replied. "But we both know how she is. She pretends things don't bother her, but deep inside she's very sensitive."

Adeline snorted. "She's about as sensitive as a great white shark."

"Why in the world would you say something like that?"

"Because it's true. Brenna is a great person. She's beautiful, caring, and fun, but she isn't sensitive. Not about stuff like this."

"You're wrong, and since Sinclair is here, I thought he could escort her to the church, walk her in, help her get settled. That way she won't have to go alone."

"No," Sinclair said, but not before Adeline's face fell, the sparkle in her eyes dimming.

"Pardon me?" Janelle said as if she couldn't quite believe what she'd heard.

"I said no. I'm not going to escort Brenna to the church. She can go with Willow and Ken if she's worried about walking into the wedding alone. I'm thinking Adeline is probably right, though. I don't think Brenna is going to have a problem walking into the church alone."

"That's because you don't understand what it's like to be a woman, Sinclair," Janelle said.

"I know what it's like to be a confident person, Janelle. Which Brenna is. I also know that if I had a choice between attending a social function alone or going with someone I barely knew, I'd go alone."

"I still think —"

Brenna barreled out onto the porch, her skirt definitely too short for a wedding in a place like Benevolence, the pink fabric barely covering her upper thighs. She had legs that went on for miles. Her loose-fitting white sweater sagged off of one shoulder, and she tugged it back into place, the gesture unconsciously sexy.

Yeah. She was beautiful.

But Adeline . . .

She was the real deal.

"What's going on out here?" Brenna demanded, whatever sensitivity Janelle thought she possessed well hidden. "Please tell me you are not begging Sinclair to take me to the wedding, Mother."

"I wasn't begging."

"But you asked? Is that what you're saying?"

"I'm sure that Dan wouldn't want you to go alone."

"You know about this much about Dan." She held her index finger and thumb so close together they almost touched.

"He's a wonderful man, Brenna, and he wants the best for you."

"I'm sure that the fact that he's a surgeon

362

makes you think he's somehow immune to the problems that plague the rest of us." Brenna nearly spit out the words. "But really, Mother, you know nothing. Can I take your car, Adeline?" she asked, whirling toward her sister.

"Sure." Adeline fished keys out of the small bag she was carrying. "But I'm going to need them to get back in my house."

"I'll hitch a ride back here with Willow and Ken. Right now, I just can't stomach anyone." She stalked away, her stilettos sinking into the grass.

"What," Janelle asked, watching as Brenna marched up the sidewalk, "has gotten into her?"

"Maybe she just wants to be left alone for a while," Adeline responded. "Maybe she doesn't want you hooking her up with someone the minute she boots . . ." She stopped, her cheeks going bright red.

"What?" Janelle shot Adeline a hard look, her lips pinched, her brow furrowed

"The minute Dan leaves town."

"You could be right." Janelle nodded as if to reassure herself. "She probably thinks it would be unseemly to be seen walking into church with someone who isn't her fiancé."

"Yeah. That's what it is," Adeline said, a hint of sarcasm in her voice.

"Is something bothering you, dear?" Janelle asked.

"Mom, look at me." Adeline lifted the hem of the dress, let it float back into place, touched the tip-top of her poufed hair. "*Everything* is bothering me."

"Well, get over it. For May's sake. You wouldn't want her to have to look at pictures of you scowling during the ceremony."

"Right. I wouldn't want that," Adeline muttered. "I'll just head back inside and wait with the rest of the giant pumpkins."

She probably would have done exactly what she'd said, but Sinclair snagged the back of her dress. "You didn't say hello," he said.

For about three seconds she just stood there, his hand on her dress, her back to him. Not one word. Not even any indication that she'd heard. Then she turned, slowly and carefully, as if she were afraid of making some terrible mistake.

"Hello," she said, her cheeks bright pink under even pinker blush. "And now that I've said it, I guess I can say good-bye."

"Don't be rude, Adeline," Janelle snapped, glancing at her watch and frowning. "Noah is going to be here any minute to pick me up. I'd better freshen up my makeup. See you at the wedding, Sinclair."

She didn't say good-bye to her daughter.

That was something Sinclair noticed.

He also noticed that Adeline looked about as pissed as a person could be.

"Our moods match," he commented, and she met his eyes, no smile in them, no sparkle.

"It's been a hell of a day, Sinclair, and I don't mean that in a good way."

"I can kind of see that." He touched a tendril of hair that had somehow managed to escape the hair-sprayed do.

"Can you?" She plucked at the huge ruffle that hung from her neckline. "Or are you being blinded by the neon brightness of my dress?"

"If I were going to be blinded by anything, it would be your smile," he said, linking his arm through hers and tugging her down the porch stairs. "Since you're not smiling, I'm pretty sure I'm seeing what's in front of me."

"A mess. This getup is downright embarrassing."

"Is May happy?"

"Yes."

"Then be happy for her." He opened the passenger-side door of the truck, lifted Adeline, and set her down on the seat.

"What was that for?" She scowled, another strand of hair escaping.

"My leg hurts, and I didn't feel like chasing you down," he responded. She sputtered something in reply, but he'd already closed the door.

The evening looked the same as it had when he'd driven up to May's, but it felt different when he got behind the wheel and started the truck's engine. It felt better. It felt like maybe he could make it through without a ten-mile run or an adrenaline-burning workout. It felt like he was going to be okay, and that was something he needed on days like today when everything piled up in his mind and threatened to drag him back to the dark days after the explosion.

CHAPTER FOURTEEN

Randal Custard had a field day during the ceremony at Benevolence Baptist Church.

Addie might have been facing the bride and groom, but she could hear the *snap-snap-snap* of the camera and the quiet swish of Randal's pen scribbling on paper.

There wasn't a doubt in her mind that she and her dress were going to be on the front page of the newspaper.

She couldn't make herself care.

Not much anyway.

The ceremony was beautiful. Despite the horrible color choices and the oversized ball gown that nearly drowned May's diminutive frame, despite the organist who couldn't seem to hit a right note and the people who whispered and giggled from their pews as the bride tripped down the aisle in sequins and beads and a beehive nearly as tall as she was, despite all the little things that weren't quite right, the wedding was beautiful.

It was obvious that May and Jim were in love. They stared into each other's eyes as they promised to love each other until death parted them.

The smile on May's face when Jim slid a ring onto her finger? It was enough to make every minute of work on the wedding favors, all the late nights and the stress, worth it. It even made Addie's early-morning and late-night jogs to fit into the dress worth it.

Is May happy? Sinclair had asked. *Then be happy for her.*

The words rang through her head as May slid a ring on Jim's finger, and she couldn't help herself, she glanced Sinclair's way. He sat between Janelle and Brenna, squeezed into one of the front pews. He wasn't watching the couple. He was watching Addie. Not with the smirk she'd seen on Randal's face when he was snapping pictures of her walking down the aisle. No, Sinclair had a soft smile that made her heart skip a beat.

She wanted to run to him, and she wanted to run from him, and she wanted a million things she knew she shouldn't.

Because she'd been down that road before.

She'd told Sinclair that, and she'd told herself that, but all the telling in the world didn't change how she felt.

The minister pronounced Jim and May husband and wife, and the couple kissed — a sweet and safe peck on the lips that made the guests and bridal party cheer.

Addie cheered along with them. She followed the couple back up the aisle; she stood in the receiving line shaking hands and smiling at nearly five hundred people. She was going through the motions, still thinking about Sinclair's smile and his words and the way it had felt to be in his arms.

When the last guest disappeared into the reception area, she headed in the opposite direction. There was no organization to the reception. Just food and fun. That's what May had said. Addie had already set up the favors, putting one on each of the paper placemats May had bought from the dollar store. Her job, she guessed, was done, and she doubted she'd be missed.

She grabbed the orange handbag that May had insisted the bridesmaids carry, slipped out the back door of the church, and walked through the dark yard until she found the playground that had been installed long before Addie was born. Just a swing set, a slide, and monkey bars.

She sat on one of the swings, cold wind

gusting through the empty yard, music drifting from the building. She was a few hundred yards from dozens of people she knew and cared about, but she'd never felt so alone in her entire life.

The church door opened, light splashing across the yard as someone walked outside.

She knew who it was.

She felt him like she felt the cold air and the soft breeze. He walked toward her, a slight hitch to his stride, settled onto the swing next to hers, and didn't say a word.

When he took off his suit jacket and dropped it around her shoulders, she wanted to cry from the beauty of that one simple gesture.

"Do you have to be so perfect?" she murmured, her gaze on the dry ground beneath the swing.

"I'm not even close to perfect, Adeline," he said, standing up and pulling her to her feet. "Do you hear the music?"

She hadn't really been listening, but now that he'd mentioned it, she did. "What a Wonderful World" drifted through the darkness.

"We could go inside and dance," he said. "Or we could dance in the moonlight."

"There is none tonight. The clouds are too thick," she pointed out, and he chuckled, tugging her into his arms and starting a slow, easy waltz.

Somehow her head found its way to his chest, and she was letting herself be swept along with the music and with the man. When his lips found hers, it was the most natural thing in the world, the most right thing, and she wanted to stay in that moment, dwell in that feeling forever.

Her cell phone buzzed.

She ignored it, because the song had changed to another slow, sweet oldie, and they were dancing again, swaying together, the darkness pressing them closer.

When it buzzed again, Sinclair pulled back, his eyes gleaming in the darkness. "Maybe you should answer it," he suggested, his voice husky.

"It's probably just my mother."

"Or your grandfather," he responded, and she knew she couldn't ignore a call from Byron. No matter how tempted she might be.

She fished her phone from the handbag, glanced at the caller ID and was surprised to see her home number.

"It must be Chase," she said.

"Is he still at the shop?" Sinclair asked, his hands sliding up her back and smoothing along her shoulders.

371

"He's home," she responded, not even quite sure what they were talking about, because everything about Sinclair? It was everything she wanted, and that was the only thing in her head and her heart.

"You should probably see what he wants," he murmured. His fingers glided along her collarbone.

For about six seconds, she couldn't think. All she could do was feel those warm fingers against her cool skin, feel the flutter of a dozen butterflies in her stomach.

"Addie?" he prodded, pulling a pin from her hair. A heavy strand fell over her shoulders. "Are you going to answer the phone?"

"Yes. Right. I am." She pressed the phone to her ear as he pulled out another pin. She probably should have told him to stop. She was already a mess. Her wild, curly hair newly freed from the beehive was going to be a nightmare to deal with, but . . . God! His fingers felt so good sliding through what had been a tight and painful hairstyle.

"Hello?" she managed to say as she answered the phone.

"Adeline!" Chase nearly shouted. "I need you to come home!"

He sounded panicked and terrified, and every warm fuzzy feeling she had disappeared.

"What's going on? Fire? Robbery? Death?"

"I can't explain on the phone. I just need you to come." He hung up, the quiet click followed by a silence so thick she could have choked on it.

"What's going on?" Sinclair asked as he pulled another pin from her hair. That must have been the one holding the horrible style in place, because suddenly hair was on her neck, in her face, on her shoulders.

"I don't know, but I need to find out." She thrust his suit jacket into his hands. "If you see my mother, can you tell her I had to go home?"

"It's going to be kind of hard to see her when I'm with you." He followed her around the side of the building.

She dug in the handbag, realized she didn't have her car keys. "I've got to find Brenna."

"Or we could go in my truck." He snagged her hand and dragged her across the parking lot to his truck.

It only took five minutes to get to the house.

It seemed to take a lifetime.

As soon as Sinclair pulled into the driveway, she was out of the truck, racing to the front door. Her ankle twisted thanks to shoes that were a half size too big and weighed down by the god-awful orange bows. She barely felt the pop and sting of it. She was too terrified of what she'd find on the other side of the door.

It swung open before she reached it, and Chase was there, his face pale as paper, his hair standing up in a hundred different directions.

"I don't know what to do!" he shouted, grabbing her hand and clutching it like she was a lifeline that was going to keep him from going under.

"I can't help you unless you tell me what's wrong." She was doing everything in her power to keep the panic out of her voice. She didn't smell smoke, didn't see blood, couldn't hear anything out of the ordinary.

"It's Larkin," he said, his voice so thick she thought he might have been crying. There were no tears in his eyes, though. No tears on his face. Just the kind of stark terror that made her heart shudder.

"You're going to have to be clearer, Chase. I still have no idea what you're talking about."

"Upstairs," he said, racing through the hall to the door that led to the attic stairwell. He took the steps two at a time, and she followed, the sound of Sinclair's shoes tapping on the stairs behind her.

She didn't know what she was expecting — a scene out of a horror movie maybe? With blood and guts and demons rising from the floorboards.

The room looked . . .

Fine.

Clean as a whistle. Nothing out of place.

The bed was still in the center of the room, a floor lamp she'd given Chase sitting beside it, a book on the floor. A pink book that looked like it had a pony on the cover.

She was so focused on that, so busy trying to figure out why an eighteen-year-old kid would be reading a book about ponies that she almost didn't notice the lump in the middle of the bed.

When she did, she blinked. Twice. The lump was still there, covered by blankets and hidden from view.

"Girlfriend?" Sinclair asked, and she finally got it. Finally understood what she was seeing. A person. Lying under the covers.

"God! No!" Chase muttered. "I don't have time for that kind of crap."

He tugged back the blankets, revealing a girl who looked to be about ten. Dressed in pink jeans and a white sweatshirt, her feet bare, her toenails painted sparkly red, she didn't move, didn't open her eyes. Blond hair. Pale skin. Bright pink cheeks.

"Larkin?" Chase said, his voice shaking. "Lark?"

He touched the girl's cheek, but she didn't move, and Addie's heart started pounding a slow, horrible beat. Was she dead?

Sinclair walked to the bed, touched the girl's forehead. "She's burning up."

"She's been sick for a couple of days. I gave her some Tylenol this morning, but when I tried to give her more this evening, she threw it up. Lark?" Chase tried again, shaking the girl's shoulder gently. "Can you hear me?"

She moaned.

That had to be a good sign.

Didn't it?

"I'll get some cool cloths, and we'll try the Tylenol again," Addie said, sprinting from the room and down the stairs.

She grabbed hand towels from the linen closet, doused them with lukewarm water, snagged the bottle of Tylenol from the medicine cabinet, and raced back to the attic.

Larkin was lying exactly where she'd been, limp in the middle of the bed, Chase hovering next to her, Sinclair a few feet away, talking on his phone.

"Let's cool her head first," she suggested, doing what she'd seen a couple of friends do with their feverish kids. A cool cloth on the forehead. One on the back of the neck. She swiped another on Lark's neck, and the girl opened her eyes.

"Mom?" she said, and Addie met Chase's eyes. He looked stricken, terrified, and defiant.

"Who is she?" Addie asked, and he rubbed the back of his neck, scuffed his foot on the throw rug. Looked about as comfortable as a cat in a dog kennel.

"My sister."

"Who are you hiding her from?" Sinclair cut in, tucking the phone into his pocket. "And you may as well be honest. I called the doctor, and he's on his way over. Whatever you're hiding, it's going to come to light."

"I'm not hiding anything," he replied, and Addie knew he was lying.

Sinclair must have too. He scowled, crossing the space between them in two short steps. "Look, kid. I'm no fool, and neither are you, so how about we treat each other with a little respect?"

"What's that supposed to mean?" Chase puffed up his skinny chest and lifted his chin. "I've been more than respectful to you."

"It means that I don't want to be lied to. Whatever you did, it can be dealt with. But only if you tell us the truth."

"You want to know the truth?" Chase spat out. "My father is a bastard. He beat the shit out of my mother every day of her life for ten years. When she finally left him, it was the best thing that ever happened to our family. When she died, I figured I'd take care of Larkin. I quit school, got a job, and then he showed up and decided he wanted to be part of my sister's life."

"So you ran with her?" Sinclair asked, taking the Tylenol from Addie's hand and reading the dosage information.

"I gave the piece of shit a chance," he growled, his eyes hot. "I believed every lie he told me about counseling and being a changed man. I thought he was going to step in and help out. I didn't even complain when he said he was moving Larkin up here. I thought it would be good for her to have a fresh start. Only every time she called me, she was crying. She wouldn't say why. But, like you said, I'm no fool. I finally quit my job and drove to his house. Larkin was home from school. She had a bruise on her cheek and finger marks on her neck."

"You should have called the police," Sinclair said.

"I told you," Chase said, his voice breaking, "I am not a fool. I called the police. I hotlined my dad. I did everything I could think of, and no one would listen. Larkin was too afraid to admit what was happening, and CPS is too overwhelmed and overworked to spend time pursuing every complaint they get."

"So you ran with her?"

"You're damn right, I did. I was taking her back to Houston when my 'Vette died." He touched his sister's forehead and frowned. "She's why I was staying in the building, and it's why I took the food. Not for me. For her. I can go without, but she's just a kid."

He was just a kid too.

That's what Addie was thinking.

She didn't say it. Her heart hurt too much, her mind buzzing with a million questions that needed to be asked. Later. After they got Larkin's fever under control.

"Run down and get a glass of water," she said. "We'll dissolve a half a Tylenol in it."

Chase hesitated, and then ran, his feet pounding on the stairs as he rushed to do what she'd asked.

■ ■ ■ ■

Years of being in the military had taught Sinclair a lot about how to respond during crises.

Thank God for that, because the little girl looked just about as sick as a person could be.

He took out his pocket knife, cut a Tylenol in half. The doctor had promised he'd be there soon, but Sinclair had seen grown men having febrile seizures, and he had no desire to see a child do the same.

"This is not good," Adeline muttered as she lifted the girl's sweatshirt and laid a wet cloth on her stomach.

"The fact that she's sick, or the fact that Chase was hiding her in your house?"

"Both. But mostly the sick part." She lifted the cloth she'd draped over Larkin's forehead and touched it. "She's really burning up."

"He should have told you about her sooner."

"Maybe, but he's eighteen." She replaced the cloth. "Kids that age make stupid mistakes."

"Running with your little sister is more than a little mistake. He could get his butt thrown in jail for that one."

"If his father had reported the girl missing, Kane would have known about it."

Probably. But that didn't mean Chase wasn't in trouble.

The kid bounded back into the room, water sloshing over the rim of the glass he was carrying. His face was pale as paper, his eyes hollow. He was scared out of his mind, and Sinclair didn't think any of the concern was for the trouble he was in.

That did something to Sinclair, made him want to help the kid and his sister.

"Calm down," he said, taking the glass from Chase's hand. "Panicking isn't going to change anything."

"I know, but I promised my mother I'd take care of her. I swore that I'd make sure she was okay." His voice broke, but he didn't cry, his eyes hot and dry, his gaze focused on his sister.

"You've done the best you could with what you had." Adeline patted his shoulder, the thick satiny fabric of the dress swishing as she moved.

"I should never have let my father take her. I should have petitioned the court for custody. It's what my mom wanted. I was named guardian in her will. But working and taking care of a kid" — he swallowed hard — "it's hard. Way harder than I thought."

"She'll be okay," Adeline said. "And once she's better, we'll get everything figured out."

"If I'm not in jail for kidnapping."

Obviously, he knew the ramifications of what he'd done.

He'd done it anyway, and Sinclair had to have some respect for that. It took guts to take on the responsibility Chase had. If his story checked out, if everything he'd told them was true, Sinclair would do what he could to make sure Chase and his sister had the support they needed.

"How about we worry about all that after —"

The doorbell rang, cutting off Adeline's words.

She sprinted down the stairs, returned moments later with a man who looked like Santa Claus. Same white beard. Same white hair. Same belly. Doctor Henry Monroe looked exactly the same as he had when Sinclair was a kid.

"So," the doctor said, moving toward the bed, a small old-fashioned doctor's bag in his hand, "this is the patient?"

"Her name is Larkin," Chase responded.

"And she's how old? Ten? Eleven?"

"She turned twelve last month. She's just small for her age."

"She's your sister, son?" Dr. Monroe asked, pulling a wooden chair up beside the bed and taking a seat.

"Yes."

"Does she have any underlying medical conditions?" He pulled an ear thermometer from his bag and checked her temperature.

"She's always been healthy."

"She's got a pretty high temperature. 103. She been around anyone who's sick?"

"I don't think so."

"Hmm." The doctor flashed a light in Larkin's eyes. "You in there, honey?" he asked, and the girl moaned. "Feeling pretty miserable, huh? How about we look at that throat?"

The girl dutifully opened her mouth.

A good sign, Sinclair thought.

"Hmm," the doctor said. "Mm-hmm."

"What?" Chase moved in close, hovering over his sister and the doctor. "Is she going to be okay?"

"How long has she been sick, son?" the doctor asked.

"A few days," Chase responded, his cheeks flushing.

"She eat much during that time?"

"She said it hurt to swallow."

"That's what I thought. Looks like strep. I'll do a culture, but I'm going to give her a shot of penicillin. I'll need your parents' approval to treat her."

"I'm her legal guardian," Chase said without missing a beat.

"You have proof of that?"

"A letter my mother wrote before she passed away." He pulled a folded sheet from his pocket. "She had a will, but that's back in Houston."

Dr. Monroe read the letter, then eyed Chase. "That's where you're from?"

"Yes, sir."

"You're a long way from home."

"Yes."

"Seems to me that a kid your age might want a support system around him while he was raising his sister. Friends. Family. You got those in Houston?"

"I have friends. My church." Chase shrugged.

"Then how'd you end up here?"

"It's a long story, sir."

"Tell you what. How about Addie and Sinclair go downstairs, and you and I stay up here? I'll give your sister the shot, write up a prescription for an antibiotic, and you tell me how a kid your age ended up eighteen hundred miles from home with no family and no friends and a twelve-year-old sister to take care of."

"I'd rather you just give her the shot, sir," Chase responded, and Sinclair smiled. He liked Chase. There was something about him that reminded Sinclair of himself at the same age.

"Sometimes, son, we don't get what we want." Dr. Monroe tucked the thermometer back in his bag, pulled out a syringe. "You mind if I have a few minutes alone with this young man, folks?"

That was Sinclair's cue to leave, and he headed for the stairs, snagging Addie's wrist as he passed.

She followed, shuffling along slowly as if reluctant to let the doctor be alone with Chase and his sister.

"They'll be fine," he said as he led her downstairs.

"I hope so."

"What are you worried about?"

"Chase ending up in jail. A young girl going back to live with a monster. What isn't there to worry about?" She sighed, running her hand over wild waves of hair.

She wasn't going to tame it.

He could have told her that.

He could have also told her that she looked beautiful just the way she was. That she didn't need to smooth her curls or fix her makeup or do anything other than just be herself.

He thought about that moment in the churchyard, the way he'd felt when they were swaying to the music, the warmth of their bodies mingling.

And, God! He wanted so much more than that with her.

"He's not going to jail if what he's saying is true. If his mother named him legal guardian, and if his mother had sole custody of her children, then the father has no legal right to Larkin."

"That's too many ifs for my liking," Adeline said, walking into the kitchen and grabbing a kettle from the old-fashioned stove. She filled it with water, her back to Sinclair, her hips cupped by shiny orange fabric.

She looked better than any woman wearing a shiny gunnysack should look, her body curvy and muscular.

"You know we have to call the sheriff, right?"

"Do we?" She placed the kettle back on the stove, fired up the burner.

"Adeline, you're way too smart to pretend that you don't know the truth."

"Sometimes," she responded, turning so

that they were facing each other, "I don't want to know the truth. Sometimes I just want to live in my own little fantasy world where everything is happy and nice, and no one ever gets hurt."

"If that were reality, we'd all be worse off for it."

"That's an odd thing to say." She frowned, her freckles peeking out from beneath the layers of pancake makeup someone had applied to her face.

"It's the truth. We grow from our struggles. The things that hurt us the most, shape us the most."

"Not always for the better," she responded, grabbing mugs from a cupboard and tossing tea bags into them.

"I guess that depends on us," he said.

"And I guess you're right." She settled into a chair, kicking off her shoes and rubbing an ankle. "I'm not going to tell Brenna that, though. Not right now."

"Her fiancé dumped her?" He guessed, because he hadn't believed a word Janelle had said about a medical emergency.

"She dumped him. After she found out he was cheating on her."

"Bastard."

"Exactly."

"Is that what happened with Adam?" He

asked because he wanted to know, and because they were together in her kitchen, the kettle just beginning to steam. It felt comforting and comfortable, and all the things he'd been looking for when he'd hooked up with Kendra.

"Adam fell in love, but not with another woman. He wanted another lifestyle. Big city. Big career." She limped to the stove, poured hot water over the tea bags, and offered him a mug.

"That wasn't what you wanted?"

"Never. Not even for a second. He knew it, and he pretended that our dreams were the same. It was all a farce, I guess. All a lie."

"Or maybe he just grew out of Benevolence, Adeline," he said gently. "It happens."

"Is that why you left?"

"I left because I needed to be something other than *one of those Jeffersons.* If I'd stayed here, that's all I'd have ever been."

"And now you're the Jefferson who made it big? The most successful man in town?" There was no sharpness in her voice, no accusation, but he thought she was getting at something, pointing out some perceived flaw.

"I'm me, Adeline. That's either good enough for people in this town or it's not.

It's either good enough for you or it's not."

"What's that supposed to mean?" she asked as if she had no idea. The question pissed him off and the bad mood he'd struggled with all day returned. They'd danced in the churchyard together, they'd kissed as if they'd always had only each other, as if what they had was all that mattered, all that ever would matter, and now she wanted to act like there was a question about where they were heading?

Didn't work for him.

"If you have to ask, then I'm wasting my time." He headed to the back door, yanked it open. "Call the sheriff and let him know what's going on. If you don't, you're an accessory to any crime Chase committed."

He walked outside, closed the door sharply behind him.

She didn't follow.

He hadn't expected her to.

But it sure as hell would have been nice.

Because all the things he'd left Benevolence to find? They'd been there all along, and if he'd had a reason to stay, if he'd had someone to stay for, the town might be just the place he could finally call home.

CHAPTER FIFTEEN

Four days after the wedding, and Addie still hated making fudge. She also hated crying.

Somehow, she was doing both, scooping sugar into a bowl while tears ran down her face.

Thank God her sisters were at her place, saying good-bye to Byron. Both were leaving that morning, heading back to their busy lives. Even Brenna, cheated on and used by her ex, had a life that stretched beyond the confines of her apartment. She had friends who would rally around her. She had a career that people admired; she'd told Addie and Willow that the night before. They'd sat in Willow's old bedroom, sipping wine and eating cheese, and talking about what an asshole Dan was.

They'd bonded over that — the three of them a team in a way they hadn't been in more years than Addie could remember. Willow, the practical one, had made plans for Brenna, helping her organize what needed to be done to get Dan permanently out of her life. Not an easy task since Brenna and Dan had lived together for three years. They had a shared bank account, shared apartment, shared life. Not anymore, though. Brenna had been the tough one, making no bones about the fact that she was going for Dan's jugular. Whatever feelings she'd had for him, they seemed to be gone. And Adeline? She'd crunched numbers, figured out if Brenna could make it on the money she was bringing in from her clothing boutique. For the first time in way too long, they were the Lamont sisters, an unbreakable unit, the three of them against the world.

Adeline knew she wasn't the only one who'd felt it. Last night, the three of them had been just tipsy enough to do a bonding ritual, swearing over a white candle that they'd never again forget how close they were supposed to be.

God! She hoped it lasted, that those sweet feelings continued for years and years to come. She'd forgotten how much it meant to be part of their exclusive club, how wonderful it was to know that no matter who walked away from her, she always had her sisters. She'd hugged them both good-bye an hour ago, and they'd all sworn that they would never again go a week without talking.

She'd believed every word that she'd spoken, every word her sisters had uttered.

But believing couldn't make it true.

A hope and a prayer, that's what Byron would have said if she'd spoken to him about it.

She hadn't.

She'd had work to do, and she'd needed to get away from her little house that was suddenly filled to overflowing. Byron. Two kids. A giant dog who'd chewed up her sneaker in the middle of the night. She'd tripped over the remnants on the way to the shower.

She'd been reduced to wearing sandals. Not a terrible thing, if it hadn't been snowing. Which it was. Giant flakes falling from the dark gray sky. The weather fit her mood. Or maybe her mood fit the weather. Not that the snow and the sneakers and her sisters leaving were the reasons for her tears.

She was crying because the darn fudge refused to taste good, and because her life refused to look as perfect as she'd thought it was before she'd taken over the shop for Byron, before Sinclair had moved in.

Before he'd left town — just packed his

duffle and headed out. He'd been gone since Monday. That's what Gavin had said. Business to take care of. Things that needed doing. He'd flown a couple of guys in from Seattle to finish his grandfather's house.

He might or might not return.

And it wasn't any of Addie's business whether he did or not.

Hadn't she let him walk away?

Hadn't she pushed him out of her life?

What does that mean? she'd asked, as if she hadn't known what he was asking, as if she hadn't heard the question in his voice.

Am I good enough, Adeline? Can we make this work? Are you willing to try?

Those were the things he hadn't said, but she'd known exactly what he'd meant.

He could have asked her every one of those questions, he could have begged her for an answer, and she would have given him the same response — that same, stupid non-answer.

Because she was an idiot, and now she was crying into the damn fudge that was never going to taste right. No matter how hard she worked at it.

Her cell phone rang.

Byron. Of course.

He'd been calling at six every morning.

Just to make sure she was on schedule with things.

"What's up?" she asked, her voice shakier than she wanted it to be.

"You crying, doll?" Byron asked.

"Why would I be?"

"That's a good question, and you're the only one who can answer it."

"Did you need something, Granddad?" she asked, completely avoiding the question.

"Just to tell you that your sisters are on their way to the airport. It was good seeing them."

"It was."

"Also, the sheriff just stopped by."

"It's early for a visit," she said, her heart thudding painfully. This was what they'd been waiting for. Kane had been doing research, contacting lawyers, checking with an attorney in Houston who'd worked with Chase's mother.

"He had good news, and he didn't want to wait to share it."

"What news?"

"The kids' father has no legal right to the girl. When he took Larkin from Houston, he was breaking the law. Their mother filed an order of protection nine years ago, and he lost all parental rights. Only supervised visitations. Which he never asked for."

"And?"

"The will that Chase claimed she had left? It checked out. Chase is Larkin's legal guardian. If he can get a full-time job and a permanent address, CPS is willing to work with him."

"They can live with us," she said, mentally reconfiguring the attic. If they cleaned out the storage room, insulated it . . .

"That's what I told Kane. Also told him I was hiring the boy full time."

"Can you afford that?" She set the vanilla on the counter, eyeing her list. There was plenty that Chase could do to help. She had twenty favors to make for a baby shower. Another three dozen for a wedding shower, and sixteen online orders to fill.

"I can afford to do whatever the hell I want," Byron retorted. "Now that Kane has cleared things up, I'm sending Chase back to work. Tomorrow. Today, we're going over to the school to get Larkin enrolled."

"You aren't driving!?" She hurried to the list and scribbled *Enroll Larkin in school* at the end of it. She added *Buy a twin bed* beneath that.

"He's driving, and we can handle it, so you just cross that right off your list."

"How did you know I wrote it there?" she

asked, running her finger through the words.

"Because I know you. Now, how about you tell me why you were crying?"

"I didn't say I was crying."

"And you didn't say you weren't. So, what's wrong, kid? You missing the Jefferson boy?"

"He's not a boy."

"Ahh," he said. "It is Sinclair, then. What happened?"

"Nothing."

"You're lying, Adeline, and it surprises me."

"Nothing happened, Granddad. He lives in Seattle. I live here. He has his life. I have mine." She poured a bucketload of vanilla into the fudge mixture.

"And suddenly your life doesn't seem as exciting as it did?"

"My life —" She grunted as she lifted the bowl and poured the mixture into a huge sheet pan. It looked like crap, chunky and mud brown. Not a speck of sheen or shine in it. It probably tasted like crap too. She wasn't going to try it. If she never tasted fudge again it would be too soon. "— has never been exciting."

"Sure it was. When you had Adam and all those dreams people have. When you were thinking about making a life with someone, having kids, growing a family and growing old. That's exciting stuff for someone like you, Addie. Just like it was exciting for me."

"You make me sound like a boring old maid," she said, her throat burning with the need to cry again. She held back the tears because she didn't want Byron to worry.

"Only because that's the way you're feeling. So, how about you pick yourself up by your bootstraps like I taught you to do? How about you go after what you want, just the way I've always told you? You want those things you used to dream about? Stop being so afraid of not having them that you miss out on what's being offered. Stop being so afraid of losing that you never give yourself a chance to win."

"What is that supposed to —"

"Damn! Your mother is at the door. You think about what I said, doll."

He hung up, and she dropped the phone into her apron pocket, walked over to the list, and wrote *GET A LIFE* in big bold letters over everything else, because if her grandfather was lecturing her on going after what she wanted, she obviously did not have one.

"You are pitiful," she muttered, grabbing the pan of fudge and tossing the entire thing into the trash.

She stalked to the pantry, pulled more ingredients from the shelves.

Maybe she didn't have a life.

Maybe she was as pitiful as she felt.

But she'd be darned if she was going to let the fudge beat her.

She measured sugar into a giant pot, poured in cocoa nibs, evaporated milk, and half a bottle of vanilla, stirred it as if everything depended on that one batch of fudge turning out well.

Someone knocked on the back door.

She ignored it because she was sure it was Janelle, hurrying over from Byron's to complain about Addie adding two kids to her household. Permanently.

That was a big word.

It was a word that meant she was committed to making sure Chase and Larkin did okay. That they were successful. That they found the right paths to walk down.

That was a big responsibility. One Janelle probably didn't think Adeline was capable of taking on. Even though she had a successful accounting business, even though she'd been running Chocolate Haven, even though she'd taken over Byron's rehab, making sure he got to appointments, had rides when he needed them, took the pills the doctor had prescribed, in Janelle's mind,

Addie would always be just a little less capable than her sisters.

She slammed the spoon on the counter, splattering chocolate everywhere.

Whoever it was knocked again, and she yanked the door open.

"What do you . . ." The words died as she met Sinclair's eyes.

He looked tired, his eyes deeply shadowed, his jaw covered with a couple days' worth of stubble. He'd been running. Or it looked like he had, his black gym shorts falling to midthigh, his long-sleeved compression shirt clinging to his chest and biceps.

"I thought you were in Seattle," she said, her voice shaking because she wanted to pull him into her arms, ask him what was wrong.

But of course she couldn't. She wouldn't.

Because she was a coward. Too afraid to lose to ever win.

"Portland. Getting that project started."

"The old schoolhouse?" she asked as he moved past, the scent of snow and outdoors drifting into the kitchen.

"Yes."

"You won the bid?"

"I didn't come here to discuss business, Adeline," he said, his voice cold.

"Then why did you come?"

"I was out running. I saw the light." He shrugged.

"When did you get back?"

"An hour ago." He leaned against the counter, his arms crossed. There was a deep purple scar on his thigh. A couple of inches thick in some places, it snaked up from his knee and disappeared beneath the hem of his shorts.

He must have seen her looking. He touched the thickest area. "I'm lucky to still have the leg."

"I can see that."

"And my life."

"Is that what the demons are about?" she asked, and his face softened, all the hardness gone.

"They're more about having everything I've got when some of my buddies are gone. More about the memories, watching people I cared about breathing their last breaths, telling them they were going to be okay, even though I knew they weren't."

"Sinclair —"

"Maybe most of all," he continued, cutting her off, "they're about guilt. I was given a second chance. A lot of people weren't. I want to honor that. Make good on it. That can be a heavy burden."

"So you run? To get away from that?"

"And I play the guitar, and sometimes I visit people who may not want me around." He smiled ruefully, and her heart ached.

"I want you around," she said, and he shook his head.

"How about we don't overstate things, Adeline? How about we just talk about the facts. I was out. I saw the light. I wanted a distraction, because I kept thinking about all my buddies, the ones who had dreams that are never going to come true. Everything I do, every job I take, I have that in my mind — that I have to do my best, because I'm still here to do it and because they aren't."

"You've made good on that, Sinclair," she said, because it was true. He'd come back from what had nearly killed him, created a successful life, one that he could be proud of.

"Some days that's enough," he said with a sigh. "Some days it isn't." His gaze drifted from her to the trash can, the giant pan lying in it, and then to the whiteboard and her list, *GET A LIFE* written so boldly across it that he couldn't help seeing it.

"New list?" he said.

"I was . . . frustrated," she responded, turning away because she didn't want to see the sympathy in his eyes.

He'd been through way more than she ever had, and he'd done exactly what Byron had said Adeline should: pulled himself up by the bootstraps and gone on.

"The fudge?" He lifted the pan from the trash, scraped out the chocolate and set it in the sink.

"Yes."

"Want some help?"

She should have said no. It was the family recipe. Top secret and not to be shared. Ever. With anyone. But Sinclair was standing there, the scar purple and thick, his face tired and worn, and she thought maybe he needed to make the fudge as much as she did.

"Sure," she said, taking his hand, leading him to the pot that was sitting on the burner. "But we need to start again, because I poured enough vanilla in there to kill a canary."

He laughed and lifted the pot, dropping it into the sink with the pan.

"Now," she said as she pulled out a clean pot, "remember, this recipe is top secret. If Byron finds out I shared it, he'll disown me."

"He would never disown you."

"Probably not, but he might kick me out of the kitchen. For good."

"Isn't that what you want?"

"Maybe."

"You like running the shop more than you thought you would?"

No. Yes. Maybe.

She wasn't sure.

There was something nice about being in the shop every day. People she knew walked in all the time, buying treats or gifts, telling her stories about what they were doing, where they were headed.

She liked that.

She liked the familiarity of it, the constancy, every day rolling into the next.

"We're not here to talk business, Sinclair," she responded, because she wasn't going to lie and she really didn't know the truth. "We're here to make fudge."

He laughed again, moving in beside her, his arm pressed close as he helped her measure ingredients, stir the thick mixture, pour it into a waxed-paper-lined pan.

It felt so good to have him there, so wonderfully right, that when they finished, she pulled more ingredients and showed him how to make peanut butter swirl fudge.

When the back door opened, they were hip to hip, cutting squares of fudge from two different pans.

Janelle stepped in and stopped short when

403

she saw the two of them.

"Good God in heaven, Adeline! You have an assistant. You don't need to make Sinclair do the work for you."

"It would be very difficult to make me do anything I don't want to do," Sinclair said, setting his knife down and washing his hands. "Speaking of which, I've got to head over to my brother's house. The crew should be finishing up the floors. See you this afternoon, Janelle."

He walked outside without saying goodbye to Adeline.

She noticed.

A lot.

"What was that all about?" Janelle's gaze focused on the closed door. Maybe she thought Sinclair would walk back through it.

"He offered to help with the fudge. I let him."

"That's not what I'm talking about, and you know it." Janelle eyed the pans of fudge, the cut pieces, the pots abandoned in the sink. "You do know that Byron would have a coronary if he knew you'd let anyone in on the fudge recipe, right?"

"Did you stop by to criticize me, or did you actually need something?" The words slipped out and just kind of hung in the air between them.

Janelle blinked. Opened her mouth. Closed it again.

Finally, she cleared her throat, tugged her suit jacket closed. "Is that what you think?"

"About what?"

"Me. Do you think that all I do is criticize you?"

"Mom" — Adeline sighed — "you criticize everyone. Not just me."

"I'm . . . sorry. That's not the person I ever planned to be." She twirled her wedding ring. The one she'd moved from her left to her right hand a year after Brett died. "But after your father died . . . I just wanted to make sure all my girls would be happy. I just need to know that you have the things you want in life."

"Because you don't?" Adeline asked, all her frustration flying away.

"I do. Mostly." Janelle smiled, but there was a hint of sorrow in her eyes. It was enough to make Addie sorry that she'd snapped at Janelle, enough to make her wish she could take the words back.

"I'm sorry, Mom. I'm in a mood today. I shouldn't be taking it out on you."

"You didn't do anything to be sorry for. And you're not the first person to call me critical this week."

"No?"

"Noah said the same thing. Right after May's wedding." Her cheeks were red, and Adeline thought the memory wasn't a good one.

"Mom —"

"I just stopped by to make sure you were okay. Byron thought you were upset, but it looks like everything is under control."

"Everything is great."

"Good. Wonderful. I'll talk to you later, sweetie." She ran out the door, nearly slamming it behind her.

Adeline walked to her list, jotted a tiny note in one corner. *Make sure Mom is okay.*

And then she took the fudge out into the service area and put it in the display case.

The Jefferson house looked great.

Sinclair walked through every room, checking floors and window frames. The team had done a fantastic job, but then, that's why the men and women he'd hired were on his payroll.

"What do you think?" Angel Ramirez asked as Sinclair ran his hands along the handrail that led from the second floor to the attic area.

"It looks good."

"Good? That's all you have to say?" Angel

demanded, hands on her narrow hips, her dark eyes blazing. She'd joined the team two years ago and had made foreman within six months. She had a reputation for being the hardest taskmaster on the team, but she was also the best.

The fact that she wanted to get out of Seattle, start fresh somewhere else? That was a bonus, because he *was* buying May's building, and he was opening an office in Benevolence. He already had two jobs in town — Byron's and a church restoration. The old parsonage needed to be torn down or rebuilt. He'd learned about that while he was waiting for May's wedding to begin.

He'd contacted the pastor the next day. The job had been his within an hour. He had other prospects too: Three Victorians in Spokane that had been bought at auction and were sitting empty, waiting for the right person to restore them. A hotel in the next town over that had been a brothel eons ago, and the new owner wanted that part of its past wiped out, the glamorous gold-rush days restored.

"It's outstanding, Angel, and you know it, so stop fishing for compliments," he said.

"Just demanding what I've earned." Her smile lit up a face that was usually somber and a little hard.

"You still looking to get out of Seattle?" he asked as he walked into the attic, checked the new insulation.

"You know I am, Sinclair."

"How'd you like to move to small-town America?"

"You mean *this* small town?" She looked surprised but not horrified by the idea.

That was a good start.

"I'm buying some property in town. I figure this part of the state is untapped as far as restoration goes. I need a team here. Just a small one to start. I'd like you to head it up."

"Are you kidding?"

"I'll pay your moving expenses and give you a stipend for the first year. If things work out the way I think they will, we should have a pretty active business here within three or four years."

"And if they don't work out?" she asked, because she was that kind of person, always looking at the variables, figuring out cost versus risk versus potential profit.

"We'll cut our losses, close things down, and you'll get back your old position in Seattle."

"Sounds too good to be true."

"Only because you're cynical by nature."

"True." She ran a hand over her short-cropped hair. "Tell you what, Sinclair. I'll do it, but I want all of that in writing."

"I didn't expect anything less of you."

She smiled and headed for the attic stairs. "Give me the address of the first project. I want to go take a look. See what kind of rattrap you've picked this time."

"I'll text it to you. It's rough." He'd warned Byron that shoring up the Bradford place was going to take a lot of time and a lot of money. Byron hadn't blinked an eye at the numbers or the timeline.

"Aren't they all?" she responded, jogging down the stairs and shouting something to one of the crew as she went.

She was right.

All the properties Sinclair chose were rough. All the projects that he took on were difficult. He liked them that way. It kept his mind and hands busy, kept his thoughts from wandering to dark places.

Places like the one where he'd been earlier.

This was the anniversary of the explosion, and no matter how much he tried to forget the day, it always grabbed him by the throat and tried to choke the life out of him.

He'd left Seattle at two in the morning, sleepless and desperate to outrun the thing that was inside of him. The thing that demanded he grab a few beers, a few pills, step on the gas, and drive like hell through the snowy mountain passes.

Byron's apartment hadn't offered solace, but the run had done what it could, the adrenaline oozing out of him as the snow fell from the still-dark sky.

He'd run until he couldn't run anymore, and then he'd turned back, seen the light in Chocolate Haven.

Maybe he should have ignored it.

Adeline didn't seem brave enough or strong enough to go after what they both wanted, and he didn't have the time or patience to convince her.

He wanted someone more mature than that.

Someone who knew what she wanted and went after it 100 percent. He wanted what he'd thought Adeline was. Apparently, he'd been wrong.

Yeah. He should have gone up to the apartment and ignored the light, but he hadn't, and when he'd seen Adeline, he hadn't been able to make himself leave.

"Bro!" Gavin called from the bottom of the stairs. "You up there?"

"On my way down." He left the attic and walked through the hall that had once been filled with junk. It was clean now, the old wood floors gleaming, the walls painted creamy yellow. Gavin stood near the top of the stairs, his jeans tucked into work boots, his jacket hanging open.

"This place is hot!" he said as Sinclair approached. "I don't know how to thank you."

"Keep it looking this way. That'll be thanks enough."

"I will. I can promise you that. Lauren is going to love it here."

She would. Sinclair knew it, and that was enough to make all the time and money invested worth it. "She'll love it as long as it stays clean and neat and —"

"No need for a lecture, bro. I know what I need to do, and I plan to do it."

"I hope so," Sinclair muttered as he headed down the stairs.

Maybe Gavin would do what he needed to.

Maybe he wouldn't.

If he didn't, he'd have to dig himself out of whatever mess he created. Sinclair had done what he could. He'd made something beautiful out of all the bad memories and the piled-up junk.

He walked down the stairs, bypassing the display of antiques set on old shelves. His grandmother's things. Just a few. The rest were spread out around the house. According to his friend, some were worth nothing.

Others were worth thousands. The value didn't matter. What mattered was honoring the vision his grandmother had had.

Outside, the snow had stopped, leaving a layer of white on grass and pavement. It was pretty. Prettier than he'd remembered when he'd been thinking about returning. Prettier than he'd ever thought it was when he was a kid just trying to get by.

He waved good-bye to the crew, hopped in his truck, and headed back to town. He and Janelle were looking at a couple of properties. Most were big old farmhouses that had been left to crumble.

If he found one he liked, he'd buy it and restore it. If he ended up spending his life there, good. If not, he'd sell it for a profit. No harm. No foul.

He wanted to be excited about the venture, but he just felt tired.

CHAPTER SIXTEEN

Adeline had sold the first piece of fudge at ten that morning. By noon, a line had formed, dozens of people standing in the shop and outside of it, all of them waiting to get their hands on Lamont family fudge.

Because of the fudge Addie and Sinclair had made?

That's what it had tasted like: Lamont fudge. Not the poor facsimile that Adeline had been making. The stuff she'd sold that day had been the rich, beautiful confection that her family had been making money on for generations.

That had been a surprise.

As a matter of fact, Addie had been so sure that the fudge was going to suck, she'd almost thrown out both batches. She'd seen Millicent hightailing it toward Chocolate Haven's door about three minutes after the shop opened, and she'd known exactly what was going to happen: Millicent was going to come in. She was going to buy fudge. She was going to be disappointed. If Addie had had time, she would have yanked every piece of fudge from the display case and tossed them in the trash.

She hadn't, and Millicent had done exactly what Addie had expected. She'd ordered a pound of each type of fudge, biting into a piece of one before she'd even left the shop. Addie had braced herself for the complaints that she'd known were coming.

Only they hadn't come.

Millicent had walked out of the shop without a word, but an hour later, a group of church women had arrived. They'd heard that the Lamont family fudge was finally being served again. Every one of them ordered a pound. To a person, they'd bitten into a piece and offered rave reviews.

That had made Addie curious.

After they'd left, she'd taken a small piece of fudge and tasted it. She'd nearly died from joy as it melted in her mouth, because the fudge tasted *exactly* the way it was supposed to. Creamy, rich, silky, and smooth, with just a hint of family and love thrown in.

By one o'clock, she'd sold the last piece of fudge.

By five, the last piece of chocolate was gone.

The display case was empty, the shop silent.

She felt . . . good. Better than she had in a long time. Not just happy. She *was* that, but she also felt content and excited, interested in seeing what the next day would bring.

More fudge success maybe?

She wasn't counting on it, but she had a feeling she knew the secret to her sudden success. She could hear him walking above her, the floor joists creaking as he moved across the room.

Outside, the soft splash of rain pouring from the gutter downspout offered a quiet tribute to what had been an epic day. Record sales. Record for Addie, anyway. She really did think she had Sinclair to thank for that.

And she really did think she should thank him.

Only she wasn't sure she could face him again. Every time they were in a room together something happened. Every single time, she forgot that she didn't want to date anyone, that she didn't want to be in a relationship, that she didn't want or need a man to make her life complete.

She hung the CLOSED sign, wiped down the counters, thought about that fudge and the way it had changed from nothing special to something special because of Sinclair. She couldn't explain it, but she knew it was true, knew that having him there had added that elusive thing that the fudge had been missing.

Joy? Contentment?

She couldn't put her finger on it, but she'd felt it while she and Sinclair had worked together, and she'd known that something magical was happening.

Too bad she hadn't told *him* that.

Too bad she was too much of a chicken to do it now.

She walked out the back door, her toes curling as cold water splashed onto her feet.

She really needed to buy shoes.

And she really needed to go home, but Sinclair's truck was parked in the back lot, and she thought she heard the soft strains of a guitar drifting along on the quiet night air. Early morning snow had changed to rain, and it fell in soft, silent sheets, soaking her hair before she'd taken a step away from the door.

Her head told her to keep walking, to get in her car and go home. She had a whole list of things that needed doing. A bed to buy, grocery shopping to do, dinner to make. The house probably needed to be cleaned. It was amazing how messy the place got with two kids in it.

Yeah. Her head was telling her to leave. Her heart, though? It was saying something else. It was telling her to walk up the stairs, knock on Sinclair's door, see if the magic she'd felt earlier was something that just might last, because if it was, that was something special. She'd be an idiot to turn her back on it.

She walked to the bottom of the stairs, rain splattering on the pavement and on her hair. She could see Sinclair's door and the light that filtered out from beneath it. The guitar music sounded a little louder there, and she thought she recognized the tune. An old blues song that made her eyes sting with tears that she had no reason to shed.

She stood there, listening to the music and wondering if risking her heart was worth it, if she could actually go into a relationship with Sinclair, knowing that maybe it wouldn't last, that maybe in a year or two or three, it would be over.

The song ended, the soft splash of rain on pavement filling the silence. She swiped rain from her eyes, told herself to go up the stairs or to leave. She couldn't stay there all night.

She'd freeze to death. Or get carted away to the psychiatric hospital, because it really was crazy what she was doing, standing out in the rain wishing she had the courage to go after what she wanted.

The apartment door opened and Sinclair appeared, standing on the threshold, a guitar in one hand, a can of soda in the other.

"You going to stand there all night?" he asked, and she knew she had a choice to make, that this was it. If she walked away, she was walking away for good. If she stayed, she was staying forever.

"I've got a million things to do," she responded, because what she really wanted to say was *I want to spend time with you. I want to come up to the apartment and sit on Byron's couch while you play guitar, and I want to look into your eyes and I want to know that we're building something that's going to last.*

"Then why are you standing out in the rain?"

"Because I don't know where to start." *I don't know what to say. I don't know how to be braver than I am.*

"The beginning is always a good place. What's the first thing on your list?" he asked, setting the guitar in the apartment behind him.

"You," she said, but the rain seemed to carry the word away. Or maybe she just didn't say it loudly enough, fear making the sound catch in her throat.

He didn't move from the doorway, and she thought maybe she should just leave, but leaving meant giving up something wonderful. Someone wonderful.

"Adeline," he finally said. "You need to get out of the rain. You're going to freeze to death if you stand there much longer."

He didn't move toward her.

Things would have been so much easier if he had. Sinclair moving at the same time she did seemed so much less risky than her moving on her own, putting herself out there, being vulnerable again.

She grabbed the railing, icy metal stinging her palm, but Sinclair had turned and was heading back into the apartment.

"Sinclair," she called, her voice hot and scared and rusty from all the things she was feeling.

"What?" He turned back, his eyes hidden by shadows, his jaw hard.

"That fudge we made, it was the best the shop has ever sold."

"Yeah?" His expression didn't soften, and she thought he was going to go inside and close the door.

"Yeah. I wanted to let you know, and I wanted to thank you for helping me with it."

"No problem. I'm glad I could help out." He crossed the threshold, walked inside, and she knew she could turn around and go home, forget what she'd felt and what they might have had.

Or she could do what Byron had said and fight for what she wanted.

She walked up the stairs, the metal clanging beneath her feet.

He hadn't closed the door, and she stepped into the apartment, rain dripping on the floor and pooling around her nearly frozen feet.

He was there, just a few feet away, old jeans hugging his hips, a soft T-shirt clinging to his chest.

"Sandals," he said, his gaze dropping to her feet, "are probably not the best idea on a day like today."

"Tiny ate my sneaker."

He didn't even crack a smile, just watched her silently as she wiped moisture from her cheeks. "Maybe you need to replace them," he suggested.

"It's on my list."

"Is visiting me on your list too?"

"No." Her throat was so tight she could barely get the word out.

"What do you want, Adeline?" he said wearily. "Because I had a long night and a long day, and I'm too tired for games."

"I was hoping," she said, "that maybe you'd help me make some more."

"More?"

"Fudge. For tomorrow." Her mouth was so dry, she barely got the words out.

"That's why you were standing at the bottom of the stairs? Because you wanted me to help you make fudge so that you could cross an item off your damn list?" He walked into the kitchen, set the soda on the counter.

"No," she admitted.

"Then why?"

"Because I can't do it without you, Sinclair."

He laughed, the sound more bitter than amused. "You can run a shop and have your own business. You can take care of your grandfather and a couple of kids you barely know. I think you can make fudge."

"Not like the fudge we made together."

"What's your point? We could spend hours together in that kitchen, Adeline. None of it will matter to me if I go home alone when we're done."

"Sinclair —"

"You want to be safe, right? You want to keep from being hurt. You want to be careful and cautious and certain that things will work out before you ever risk your heart again, but that's not the way things work. It isn't possible to be in a relationship without taking risks. Not when you give someone everything you have. And that's all I want from you."

"I —"

"Like I said, Adeline. I'm tired. How about we talk about this another time?"

She could have left then, walked out the door and gone home, but she couldn't leave him. Not when he looked so tired. Not when he seemed so discouraged. Not when everything she'd been looking for and wishing for and secretly longing for was in his eyes.

"I have a better idea." Her heart pounded frantically in her chest.

"What's that?" His dark green eyes stared straight into hers, daring her, it seemed, to tell him exactly what she wanted.

Not help with the fudge.

They both knew that.

But it was hard to be vulnerable again, and even harder to believe in something that she'd given up on long ago.

"We can go down to the shop and make the fudge together," she responded. "I'll put on a CD, and we can listen to Bing croon while we do it."

"Bing, huh?" He smiled so gently and sweetly, her breath caught.

"I've always had a crush on him," she said. "If he were alive, I might just stalk his house and beg for autographs."

"And since he's not, I'm second choice?" he joked, but she didn't want to be funny. Not with so much riding on the moment.

"You're the only choice, Sinclair," she said, pulling him out the door and into the rain.

They went down the stairs side by side, hand in hand, and she didn't think anything could be more perfect than the rain and the darkness and the man walking beside her.

They walked into the dark shop, and she turned on the light, the clean counters and quiet kitchen comfortingly familiar. She hadn't wanted to take over the shop for Byron. She'd done it out of obligation and concern. She'd grown to love it though, and she thought it would be strange to wake up one morning and not go to work, odd to not have the scent of chocolate clinging to her hair and clothes at the end of the day.

"You're sad," Sinclair said, taking a dish

towel out of a drawer and using it to dry her hair. His hands were gentle, his warmth seeping through her soaked clothes as he worked.

"Not really."

"Then why do you look like your best friend just died?"

"I was thinking about how strange it's going to be when Byron comes back to work."

"And you go back to your life?"

"Yes." She took the towel from his hand, stood on her tiptoes to run it over his hair.

God! He smelled good. Like rain and sunshine and cold winter mornings.

"Isn't that what you want, Adeline?" he asked, his voice husky and deep. "To go back to the way things were? To have your life back the way it was?"

"No." She looked into his eyes, seeing the softness there, the quietness of his spirit. He was the toughest man she'd ever met, and the gentlest, and she couldn't believe he hadn't always been in her life. Couldn't fathom him ever not being in it again.

"Then what do you want? A fudge-making partner? A friend? Someone to play the guitar for you while you work?"

"I want you, Sinclair. That's it. Just you."

He smiled and bent to kiss her, his lips cool from the rain, his hands warm on her back. She lost herself in that kiss, lost herself to everything but him. His hands. His lips.

A dog barked, the sound barely registering through the haze of longing that seemed to be consuming her. She wanted more. Not just of his kisses, of his hands sliding along her spine, finding their way to her waist, not just of his fingers trailing across her skin. She wanted more of him. More minutes and hours and days. More time to enjoy his smile, his humor, and even his moods.

Sinclair broke away, panting, his eyes blazing.

"I've been waiting a lifetime for you, Adeline. You know that?"

She thought she did, because she felt the same.

She touched his cheek, her palm resting on warm, rough skin. "I feel like I've been waiting even longer for you."

"Then I guess it's good we found each other." His lips grazed the side of her neck as the dog barked again.

Seconds later, something slammed against the back door with enough force to make it shake in its frame.

The dog howled, the mournful cry reminiscent of a wolf calling to his pack.

"Tiny?" Sinclair asked, cupping her face with his hands and kissing her one more time. A quick kiss. A gentle one. But she felt a lifetime of promises in it.

"I should check," she murmured, reluctant to leave the warmth of his arms.

"You should," he agreed, but his hands stayed where they were, and neither of them moved.

The dog howled again and again.

"Someone is going to complain," Sinclair said, his hands dropping away.

"Or call animal control."

"Does Benevolence have animal control?"

"No, but if Tiny keeps howling like that, we're bound to get it." She crossed the room, opened the door.

Sure enough, Tiny was there, his tail thumping wildly.

If dogs could smile, Tiny was, his tongue lolling out of the side of his mouth, eyes sparkling with happiness.

He'd found his people.

Which was a whole lot better than him finding the neighbor's trash or Mrs. Grizzle's old tomcat. Yesterday, Tiny had chased Sebastian from one end of Mrs. Grizzle's yard to the other. If Chase hadn't been home and heard the elderly woman screaming, Sebastian probably would have gotten sick of the puppy's unrequited love and scratched his eyes out.

"What are you doing out there?" she asked, and Tiny barked in reply.

"The better question might be, how did he manage to get out of the house? There are three people there now, right?"

"Maybe. Or maybe Byron took the kids out to dinner. Larkin tried her hand at cooking last night. It didn't go well."

"What did she make?" Sinclair asked as he snagged an apron from a hook and attached one end of the tie to Tiny's collar.

"That's a good question. I think it was supposed to be meatloaf, but none of us were sure."

"You didn't ask?"

"And crush her spirit?"

"I think she probably could have handled it."

"She's been through a lot, Sinclair. She doesn't need to be hurt any more than she already has been."

"And now she's here," he pointed out. "With you and Byron and her brother. She has people who care and are going to make sure that all the stuff she's been through becomes a memory of something that made her stronger."

"I hope you're right."

"I usually am."

She laughed at that, and he kissed her,

Tiny whining at their feet and nosing in between them.

"He's jealous," Adeline said, scratching the puppy behind his ears.

"He should be, because I've never been very good at sharing."

"I'll keep that in mind when there's one piece of fudge left and we both want it."

"I don't want fudge, Adeline. I want you." He took her hand and pulled her out into the rain. "Let's bring the mutt home and listen to some of that music you love. We can dance in the moonlight together while it plays."

"There's no moonlight tonight," she said with a laugh, her heart tripping and dancing with happiness.

"We'll dance in your living room, then."

"And have Byron and the kids making faces at us?"

"Why not?"

And she knew he was right. Why not dance in front of everyone? Why not bring the joy they'd found into her little house and share it with cranky Byron and two kids who were still trying to find their way?

Why not?

Because Addie had found what she hadn't known she'd been looking for. She'd been given a gift that she hadn't asked for. All the things she'd stopped dreaming about when Adam had broken things off? They were a possibility again.

But that wasn't the reason why she didn't care if Byron saw her dancing in the living room with Sinclair, and it wasn't the reason why she'd smile if Chase and Larkin laughed while she waltzed through the house with the man she'd fallen hard for.

She didn't care about all the dreams she'd had.

She didn't care about revisiting what she'd lost.

She only cared about being with Sinclair, making what they had work the best way it could, sharing what they'd found with the people she cared about most.

"Hold on," she said when he started to close the shop door. "I forgot something."

"A coat?" he asked, standing on the threshold with Tiny while she ran back inside.

"A coat would be helpful," she responded, but that wasn't what she'd gone back for.

It was that list. That damn list with all the things she should do and needed to do and wanted to do. That list with *GET A LIFE* scribbled across it and *Make sure Mom is okay* written in tiny letters in the corner.

She eyed it for a moment, looking at all

the things that had filled her time, all the stuff she'd made important because she'd been afraid to face what she'd lost.

Only, really?

She hadn't lost anything.

Her life had always been exactly what she'd wanted. The town had always been exactly the place she wanted to be.

And Sinclair?

She glanced his way.

He was the icing on the cake, the cherry on the sundae, the best part of the things she'd found because she'd stayed in Benevolence.

She ran her palm across the list, smudging all the letters together until there was nothing left but a mess of black and red and green.

"Wow!" Sinclair said as she wiped marker off her hand. "You finished it all?"

She shook her head, taking his hand and walking outside. "No, but I've decided I don't need to."

"Because it's too much for one person?" He urged Tiny into the back of the truck's cab.

"Because I'd rather dance in the moonlight with you."

He was laughing when he lifted her into the truck, laughing when she pulled his head down for a kiss.

The rain stopped as he drove her home, the lights from houses and businesses reflecting on the pavement, sparkling on the wet grass and the glossy leaves of the trees.

It was beautiful, this town she loved, and she didn't want to be anywhere else, with anyone else. Ever.

She would have told Sinclair that, but the silence was too lovely, his hand resting on her thigh too nice.

They had time to talk, time to dance. They had all the time in the world to figure out where they were headed and what they were going to do. And they had each other.

That, she thought as Sinclair pulled into her driveway, his headlights flashing over Chase, who stood in the yard, yelling for Tiny, *is all that matters.*

The employees of Thorndike Press hope you have enjoyed this Large Print book. All our Thorndike, Wheeler, and Kennebec Large Print titles are designed for easy reading, and all our books are made to last. Other Thorndike Press Large Print books are available at your library, through selected bookstores, or directly from us.

For information about titles, please call:
  (800) 223-1244

or visit our Web site at:
  http://gale.cengage.com/thorndike

To share your comments, please write:
  Publisher
  Thorndike Press
  10 Water St., Suite 310
  Waterville, ME 04901